SAM CRESCENT

EVERNIGHT PUBLISHING ®

www.evernightpublishing.com

Copyright© 2018

Sam Crescent

Editor: Karyn White

Cover Artist: Jay Aheer

ISBN: 978-1-77339-777-1

SAM CRESCENT

DEDICATION

I want to say a big thank you to all of my amazing readers. Your support means the world to me as I head into this new venture of my writing. I love hearing from you guys and I hope you love Axton and Taylor as much as I do.

Love Sam. X

SAM CRESCENT

AXTON

Four Kings Empire, 1

Sam Crescent

Copyright © 2018

Chapter One

"Carla, come on, pick up your damn phone." Taylor Keane glared down at her cell phone, hoping that her best friend would pick up. When it went straight to voicemail, she clicked "end call." The lake was completely crowded, a bonfire blazing to keep them warm. The cold winter's night was not enough to stop her fellow peers from fighting.

She avoided high school parties.

The truth was, she avoided every single damn party. There was no point coming here as most people just wanted to get drunk, have sex, and talk about who was screwing whom.

As she glanced around the bonfire, the music was so loud that she couldn't even hear herself think. Each crowd was so clichéd that it wasn't even funny. The jocks, the nerds, the druggies, the musicians. She glanced across to the left, and there were also "the four kings." That was what they were known as. The four guys that came from the richest, most powerful families in King's

Ridge, hence their name, the four kings. Axton Farris. Romeo Delacorte. Karson Cross. Easton Long.

If anyone messed with them in any way, shit happened.

It was the way of life at her school.

Avoiding them was the only way to survive.

She'd seen what happened to anyone who came up against them and lost. They ended up having to leave King's Ridge for good. Those four families owned the town, the school, everything.

They knew it as well.

They did what they wanted. None of the teachers possessed any real control.

That in itself was the illusion.

Carla had been fascinated by them all of their lives, watching them from afar. Taylor had never seen anything interesting about them. Carla had wanted to be part of their crowd. She came from a family that was not wealthy, and Taylor had heard Carla's parents many times arguing about money. At times, she didn't think it was about being in the popular crowd. It was about the money, the wealth, the income, that life that was out of her reach. Whereas Taylor, she didn't see the benefit of it.

The four kings used their popularity to get what they wanted and their names to keep everyone off their back. Rumors were always rife around them.

Their treatment of women and girls annoyed her as well.

They treated them like meat, something to use and throw away once they grew bored.

The deadliest one, the cruelest one, was Axton. He'd humiliated one of the cheerleaders to the point she had to leave school. He'd posted a video of her begging to suck his cock, which went viral.

Even Taylor had gotten a link, which she'd been too curious to not open up, especially as she'd been surprised to see Axton's number already in her cell phone.

Again, she didn't know how it happened, only that it did. Rumors were always a nasty, vicious thing, and she, for one, hated them.

Taylor quickly glanced away, taking a deep breath to calm her nerves. If they were at the party then things were going to go bad. Fights, sex, whatever took their fancy. Even car races, which she had no interest in attending.

Carla had been very specific about this party and how much she wanted to attend and had even told Taylor that there was a surprise about something. Carla had been acting strange lately. Every single time Taylor would ask her about it, Carla would close off and brush it aside as if it was nothing.

Taylor hated parties, but Carla had been so different over the past couple of weeks. Her best friend wasn't the same person, and she didn't know why. She'd begged Carla to tell her what was going on, but nothing.

Tonight was supposed to be a big reveal, to finally know what was going on with her friend, and so far, said friend was a no-show.

Tapping her phone on her lip, Taylor decided to give her one final call. She listened to the ringtone, and once again, Carla didn't answer.

"Look, Carla, I'm getting ready to call it a night. You said to meet you here, and well, I'm still here, and you're not. What's going on? I wish I knew what was happening." She moved toward the edge of the lake, glancing down to see the ice covering the surface. In the heat of the summer the lake was always full of kids partying and having fun. Right now, no one would even bother jumping through the ice.

As she closed her cell phone, something bright in the grass caught her attention. Stepping to the edge of the lake, she picked up the cell phone, noticing it was Carla's. She ran her thumb across the screen, seeing her missed calls and messages.

"What?"

She looked back toward the party, and she couldn't make out anything out. She stared at the phone, and then turned her attention to the lake. Something floated across the surface.

The lake was no longer still. Even with the moon shining down, Taylor saw something on the surface, bobbing around. It was several feet away, and the moment she realized what it was, she screamed.

Without thinking, she dropped Carla's cell phone and broke through the thin sheet of ice, rushing toward the body. She didn't know who it was, but there was no mistaking what she'd just seen with the sliver of moon casting light down.

Breaking into a swim, Taylor felt the cold deep in her skin as she moved toward the body. It didn't matter though. She needed to see what was floating in the water. The moment she got close, she saw who it was, and she cried out.

"No, Carla, no, no, no. What the fuck?" She lifted her friend's face, but she was so cold, so still.

The music had stopped, and as she headed toward the bank where she came from, she saw several people waiting for her, watching. Someone had a flashlight and was shining it onto her.

"Someone, get an ambulance." She yelled the words, struggling to speak past the cold. As she got to the surface, someone helped pull Carla out. She didn't know who helped her, but she was out of their arms and kneeling over her friend.

A flashlight shone down on Carla's pale face. Her lips were already blue.

"Carla, what did you do? Come on, Carla." Taylor felt her tears welling up, and she pressed two fingers to her friend's neck, finding no pulse.

Releasing a sob, she held her hands together and began to do CPR, pressing down five times before breathing in her mouth. No one was helping her, and everything felt numb. Carla was *not* dead.

She wouldn't accept that.

Breathing into her friend's mouth, Taylor worked her chest, refusing to let this be over.

Time passed, and suddenly the ambulance was there. She was pulled aside. Someone held her arms, keeping her at bay. She watched as the men worked over Carla. She answered their question as best she could. What the hell was happening?

For a couple of minutes, the two paramedics worked over Carla without success, and when she saw them shake their heads, she screamed at them. Pulling away from whoever held her, she knelt down beside Carla.

"Come on, Carla, you're fine. You're perfectly fine. Nothing is wrong. You can't give up."

"Who are you?" one of the men asked.

She didn't answer them as she pulled her best friend into her arms. She kissed Carla's head, holding her close, trying to get her warm.

"You're not dead. You're not dead. It's okay. It's okay."

She rocked with Carla in her arms, humming, trying to calm her own nerves. Wiping the tears from her eyes, she ignored the cold and whatever was going on around her. The music had stopped, and everyone had walked away.

Her best friend couldn't be dead.

This wasn't supposed to happen.

"What's her name?" She heard someone speaking in the background, and she closed her eyes, not interested in whatever anyone had to say.

"Taylor," someone said.

"Taylor, you're going to have to let her go."

Through blurry eyes, she looked up to see one of the paramedics staring at her. Next to him was a cop.

"You need to let her go."

She shook her head.

"I can't. She promised she'd be here. She shouldn't be dead. No, she can't be dead." She held her friend tightly to her. There was no way Carla could die. It just … she was so young. They were eighteen. Their whole lives were ahead of them, and it just wasn't possible for her to be dead. Taylor couldn't handle this. Not right now. Not with so much for them both to do. They had a list they wanted to do, to accomplish together, and there was no way it could be all over now. Not now.

She's dead.

You've got to let her go.

Even as she tried to fight the paramedics, she knew they would have to use force, and she couldn't handle that.

Nodding her head, she lowered Carla's still body to the ground and stood back, watching as they covered her body. Someone placed a blanket over Taylor, and she didn't even realize she was shivering or shaking.

She was so cold.

How did her friend end up in the lake?

What had happened?

There were so many questions that were

unanswered.

"We're going to go to Italy, and you're so going to find a guy to make all of your kinky fantasies come true."

Italy.

Seeing the Grand Canyon.

Bungee jumping.

Seeing the United Kingdom.

College.

Drinking.

They were all plans that they'd made together, and yet, they weren't going to get the chance to do them together because there was no time.

Carla was dead.

Gone.

She watched the ambulance pull away, and then her parents were there.

"Oh, honey, we came as soon as we heard."

Taylor didn't know why they were there, and she didn't question it. Wrapping her arms around her mother, she felt them both try to comfort her.

This was senior year.

Death wasn't supposed to happen, not to Carla.

She didn't know what happened next. Her parents took over, and rather than fight them, she let them do what they did best, take care of her. This lake would never be the same again, not to her.

School.

She'd have to go to school.

Would they call her weird names because she'd held her dead friend? That she didn't want to let go?

Staring out of the car window, she didn't really see anything. Feeling someone's gaze on her, she found Axton, one of the four kings, staring at her. He was standing with the other three of his boys. She couldn't look away from his dark gaze, watching her. There were times when she looked at him that she had to wonder if he was real or not. Was he as evil as people said he was?

As he was the self-proclaimed leader of the four kings, the other three boys were gathered around him, waiting.

What were they waiting for?

Her mind was a mess right now. She'd held Carla's dead body in her arms. Her best friend.

Dead.

Never coming back.

Looking away, Taylor stared down at her lap, the blanket held tightly in her fist. She was so cold.

Shivering, she closed her eyes, resting her head against the window.

"It's going to be okay, honey. We're taking you home."

Her mother reached out, touching her knee. She glanced down at the touch and felt nothing. There was nothing.

She took a deep breath before releasing it.

"I'll tell you tonight. It's going to be fun. You're not going to believe it."

"Come on, Carla, I hate surprises."

"You'll love this one."

"She wasn't supposed to be dead," Taylor said. Carla was happy. She'd been laughing, smiling. People who were happy didn't die like that.

She'd seen Carla's wrists. They'd been cut, slashed up, bleeding out.

No one who was happy did that.

Was Carla happy?

She knew her friend.

They'd been together since playschool.

There's no way that Carla would have taken her

own life.

No way.

Something pushed her over the edge.

What the hell was the big reveal tonight?

Wiping her face from the tears that didn't seem to stop, Taylor couldn't help but think something else was going on here. She had to find out why Carla did what she did. Nothing made any sense to her.

Her parents pulled away from the party and from everything that was going on. She didn't recognize anything as they drove home. She was numb. Completely broken. What the hell just happened?

She couldn't stop replaying that moment in her head of when she looked out at the lake. Of the body floating on the surface.

No one spoke in the car, and that alone terrified her. They weren't speaking.

Silence.

She hated that more than anything.

It was why Carla had been such a great friend. She knew how to fill up the silences. Her laughter, constant jokes. Just the way she was, and it always made her laugh. Right now, though, there wasn't any laughter.

Far from it.

Tapping her fingers on her leg, she tried to think of something, anything, but just turned up blank.

Arriving home, she felt nothing.

Everything was so completely numb.

Like her body.

A frozen pit of nothing.

She didn't know what to do or what to say. Everything was just still within her. She couldn't process what had happened. She'd pulled her dead friend out of a freezing lake, and now nothing made sense.

Carla was gone.

She had to keep saying it over and over in her head to make sure everything was fine. There was no way this was happening. She pinched her thigh, and still she didn't wake up from this dream.

"I spoke to her parents. They're going to arrange the funeral as quickly as they can," her mother said.

Taylor wiped away the tears. This was the last thing she wanted to hear.

Climbing out of the car, she didn't say anything or respond as her parents called her name. She ran upstairs, going straight to her room. Her reflection caught her eye, and she saw her clothes. They were dry now, but she'd been in the lake.

Rushing to the bathroom, she leaned over the toilet and threw up. Gripping the edge of the bowl, she threw up everything she'd eaten that day, and she was sure even some of the lake water.

Resting her head against the edge of the seat, her stomach empty, her mind filled with stupid ramblings, all the same. All about Carla.

This couldn't be happening.

Not now.

They had so much to do.

Standing up, she removed her clothes and stepped in front of the sink. In the distance she heard her parents knock, but neither of them entered.

They didn't know what to do or what to say.

Staring at her naked reflection, Taylor grabbed a toothbrush and began to scrub at her teeth, to rid her mind of the memory of what happened today.

Up and down, left and right, backward, forward. Any way she could clean, she did. They had to be clean.

They felt dirty.

She hated this feeling.

Clean teeth were so important.

Good hygiene.

Why are you thinking good hygiene right now?

It seemed so pointless.

Turning on the shower, she stepped beneath the water.

Carla won't brush her teeth again.

Carla won't take a shower.

There are a lot of things that Carla will never do again.

Turning the heat up, Taylor stayed beneath the spray. Her body went red from the heat, but she didn't move. Her skin got warm, but she felt nothing.

Her body, her feelings, it was like she didn't have any.

Where was the pain?

The sadness?

The anger.

The pit inside her was empty.

No fire.

No nothing.

Carla had taken a part of her away with her.

****

Axton Farris told the cops everything he knew while his friends did the same, speaking about the party, why there was alcohol on the premises. He gave the cop a pointed look. He was a young cop, couldn't be older than twenty-five, and yet it was Axton that held all the power here, not the law.

They all took payment to look the other way.

He held no respect for them.

If there was a guy at his feet right now, bloody from his fists, and he told them the guy had walked into a wall repeatedly, they'd make a note and walk away. They were nothing. He was the power in this town. The four kings, and everyone knew it.

It's why he could do the shit he did.

Watching the cop note down everything he said, he waited for his friends to be done. Their parents didn't come to pick them up, not like other kids.

A dead kid in a lake wasn't noteworthy to their power-hungry parents. Especially as Carla Smith was nothing. She didn't have any prospects other than her high grades. Her parents worked at a local diner. Her house was small, more like an apartment.

So, to everyone he knew, she didn't matter.

Climbing into his car, he didn't need to tell his friends where they were going. King's Ridge only had one place for them to go, and that was their hangout at the fighters' ring. They organized all the fights, all the parties, and they had the run of the place.

Pulling his Ferrari 599 GTO onto the main road, heading out of King's Ridge, he saw his friends doing the same.

Smirking, Axton overtook a small campervan and followed the road. He loved his car, especially as it had been a present for his seventeenth birthday. His dad offered to get him a replacement for his eighteenth, but there was something about this car. He didn't know what it was, only that nothing else would ever compare to the feel of this beauty. To him, it was *his* car, and he knew how to drive it. He knew his braking distance, the speed he could go, and he trusted this machine more than anything else in his world right now.

Following the road, he navigated the traffic, slowing down when necessary, pushing his foot to the gas during a long strip of road, loving the rush that came to him at the prospect that anything could happen within a single second. Like tonight. The party that had turned to shit. Romeo had been trying to get Julia to come and party with them. Not that anything would be done, nope.

Several of the chicks at King's Ridge High School knew the score and loved that they'd been fucked by the four kings.

The security gate to the compound where they dealt with all their fights was open, which wasn't unusual. Everyone knew to say away from their shit, and not only that, there was security everywhere inside.

Parking, he didn't wait for the other three to arrive. Climbing out of his car, he headed toward the court that was marked with paint. There was probably blood, piss, and semen on the ground as things always got a little rowdy on these nights. Mix drugs and alcohol with teenage need, and crazy stuff happened.

"What the fuck just happened?" Romeo asked, the first to join him.

"Wait for the others."

"They were too busy jerking off to overtake the camper van. They were a couple minutes back."

"Then we wait." He folded his arms as Romeo lit up a cigarette. Smoking was something that didn't appeal to Axton in the slightest.

"You're not a little bit spooked by what just fucking happened?"

"Do I look like it?" He stared at his friend, waiting for a response.

Romeo just shook his head. "I don't know what's with you, man."

Axton was saved from answering as Karson and Easton finally turned up. He stared at all three of them. Romeo and Easton were a lot alike, tending to be the two that chased the chicks and did their pranks. He and Karson had stared death in the face and knew the world wasn't all sunshine and roses.

All four of them had families that weren't exactly good. They thrived on being the best by making sure people feared them and were willing to do anything to keep their power. His father had taught him from a young age to make others fear him, to be willing to do everything that kept them alive. Lie, cheat, fucking, anything that kept them all on top. So many secrets, so many lies, blackmail all of it. He knew, and he intended to keep this power because if it fell in the wrong hands, people would die.

"What the fuck, man?" Easton said. "You saw that. You saw what just happened."

"Keep your shit together," Axton said.

"She pulled her out of the fucking water! Carla. You saw her. We all saw it, Axton. There was no getting away from that."

"She slit her wrists," Karson said. "Carla killed herself."

"No, she didn't. She wouldn't fucking do that. Carla was strong. There's no fucking way she'd take her own life like that."

Easton was losing it.

"Nothing happened tonight."

"You really think I'm going to believe that, Axton? Shit, you knew what was happening. What I was waiting for. I told you."

"And now you don't tell anyone," Axton said. "She killed herself."

"She didn't fucking kill herself, Axton. You all know that. You know she was pregnant with my fucking baby!" Easton stormed up to him, swearing, cursing, pissed off. Axton expected it. "My baby. My kid, and now she's gone. Fucking gone. You made me stand back and watch as Taylor tried to help her. You saw her. She jumped into that frozen fucking lake, and you made me watch."

"As far as anyone knows, she killed herself, and

you can't change that."

Easton threw the first punch. "Fuck you. Who made you the fucking boss?"

Axton smirked. He'd been expecting that all night. The pain meant nothing to him. He'd dealt with far harder fighters than Easton. Sure, his friend could hold his own, but out of the four of them, Easton wasn't the fighter.

Reaching out, Axton wrapped his fingers around Easton's throat. Karson and Romeo knew to keep out of this. He wouldn't hurt his friend.

They were the only people he trusted in the world, even before his own parents. They all had a pact to stay together, to fight together, and it would be like that for the rest of their lives. Nothing came between them. Not money, or drugs, or pussy. It was as simple as that.

"You want to hurt me, that's fine. Fucking hurt me, Easton. I get it. You hate me. You want to fucking kill me. That feeling is not going to go away. Carla Smith killed herself, and you better hope nothing falls back on you. You think someone is going to let this slide? You're one of the biggest names in town, and all it takes is for the wrong person to get ahold of the facts, and you're someone's bitch in jail. You want that?"

"No," Easton said, gripping his arm. "Did you kill her?"

Axton squeezed just a little tighter.

"Like you said, she was a fucking useless whore. That I shouldn't be spending the time with her. I liked her, Axton. Liked her a whole hell of a lot."

"And that liking got her killed, Easton. Think about that. Remember that."

"Like you remember that?" Easton asked.

He released his friend, stepping aside.

"What do you need us to do?" Karson asked.

"You know they're going to try to figure out why she killed herself."

"And they'll discover a miserable teenager. Nothing more."

Easton spat on the ground.

"You going to say something more? You want it to be known that hours before she killed herself, she saw you?" Axton asked.

"Fuck you. Fuck all of you and fuck our fathers. They don't have control over me."

"That's where you're wrong," Axton said.

Easton wasn't listening. He'd already walked away, and Axton watched him go.

"I guess that's my cue to go and make sure he doesn't throw himself off a cliff," Romeo said, taking off.

"What went wrong?" Karson asked.

"I don't know."

"You didn't kill her, did you?"

Axton didn't answer. "Make sure her locker is decorated. The usual shit when something bad happens."

"What about Taylor?"

"What about her?" Axton asked.

"You think she's just going to let this go? She's not going to ask questions?"

"If she knows what's good for her, she'll stay well away." He walked away, heading back to his car. Climbing inside, he didn't look back. Karson would close up.

There was shit he wanted to do all the time, but right now, he couldn't just drive away. Responsibility was a pain in the fucking ass. The drive helped him to clear his head. To think about everything that had gone on tonight. Drinking beer, watching chicks dance or be on their cell phones. Hearing Taylor's sudden scream. The ensuing chaos as she dragged her own friend out of the lake. It would stay with him for a long time. Carla shouldn't have been at the lake. Easton and his fucking infatuations with cheap bitches were starting to make life fucking hard. No matter what Easton tried to do, Carla would never be one of them. Pregnant or not.

He shouldn't have chased after the bitch, and yet he had. Now his mess had to be cleaned up.

Axton pushed those thoughts to the back of his mind. If life was different then Carla would still be alive, but life wasn't different. It was very fucking evil, and it was filled with monsters.

He knew because he was one. Rather than hide it though, he wore it like a suit of armor. No one dared to challenge him.

He was a king, and he made sure everyone knew it. There wasn't any room for weakness in his world.

Arriving home, he noticed Easton's father's car parked in the driveway. This wasn't unusual, but after the night he'd experienced, he'd had a feeling this would happen.

Climbing out of his car, Axton made his way inside, and went straight to his father's office. The door was closed, and he opened it up.

While other kids had parents come to collect them, he had a call from his father ordering him to deal with it. By dealing with it, he meant talking to the cops, containing Easton, and then making sure nothing came back on them.

Leaning against the office door, he watched as his father screwed the maid that had started a week ago. She was a small thing, kind of dainty, but with a world of knowledge behind her gaze. Within two hours of her working for them, she'd let him know exactly how available she was. He didn't have any interest in the women in his father fucked. Axton was sure his mother wasn't too far away, probably spending money while drinking the most expensive wine. Benjamin Farris could have his little whores, so long as he knew how to pay his way. This was the life he'd been born into.

It didn't even surprise him to see Nial Long, Easton's father, standing in front of the woman, screwing her mouth.

At a young age, Axton had been ordered to fuck several whores, which included the maids. His father didn't want a pussy for a son, so he made sure to present him with all the women money could offer. Axton played his part well, and soon he wouldn't have to play this game.

The four kings had a plan, which had already been set in motion by all of their trust funds. None of them wanted to be under their fathers' control for much longer, so Axton had set the wheels in motion that would guarantee the Four Kings' Empire fell to them.

The moment his father saw him, the fucking stopped.

He didn't say anything to the maid as she passed, holding her clothes to her body.

"What you had to say couldn't wait?" Benjamin asked.

"I have stuff to do as well." Axton folded his arms. "Easton should be home." He glared at the other man, not wanting him here. Out of all of their parents, Nial was the one he didn't like. He was a piece of shit, hiding behind security and the four kings' name. Axton had seen firsthand what that man was capable of, the damage he'd caused to many families by being the asshole that he was.

"I'll be going," Nial said.

Axton didn't say a word as he waited for the room to clear. The moment it was, he looked at his father, who had already sat down, lighting a cigar. "You talked to the cops."

"They've put it down as a suicide."

"And that is exactly what it is, Axton. I told you there would be things you'd have to do. Sacrifices that needed to be made and it is all for the greater good."

He chuckled. "This is no greater good. This is just power."

"Cannot have the kings divided. I told you that."

"There are a lot of things you tell us. Don't always listen to them."

"One day you'll know what it means, Axton. You'll feel that power in your hands, hold it in your palm, like a piece of fruit, and only when you're ready will you squash it."

Staring at the arousal in his father's gaze sickened him, but he didn't show it. He'd witnessed that power play many times in this very office. Some of the women his father liked to fuck, and they'd end up pregnant, he'd hold their lives in his very grip, and little by little, he'd make them beg for their lives.

He had learned from the best.

Knew all the tricks.

"Are we done?" Axton asked.

"She had to go, son. You know that. She made the collective weak."

Axton didn't say anything in response, simply walked away. What more was there to say? An innocent girl died tonight, and there was no rewriting that.

Chapter Two

Two weeks later

Taylor knocked on Carla's parents' door. It had been two weeks since Carla had taken her own life, and it was still so surreal to still be coming around.

She'd been told to take it one day at a time.

So easy to say.

One day at a time.

Fourteen days had gone already, and nothing felt right.

So many questions were still there and no way of anyone answering. The cops had questioned her about Carla's cell phone, which had gone missing, and about what she'd seen, how she'd gotten her out. How she'd been at school? That cell phone had been in Taylor's hands, and now it was gone. No one had seen it.

According to the cops, Carla had been seeing a counselor, who had mentioned severe depression and anxiety.

None of it made any sense.

Carla never went to the damn counselor. She didn't go to any school activity. Taylor and Carla had always hung out together after school, either going shopping, or doing their homework.

She'd not been sick or sad.

They'd been like any other teenage girls.

Apart from the last weeks that Carla was alive. She'd been different but not suicidal. Wouldn't she know that? Wouldn't she have seen?

The door opened, and she was pulled out of her thoughts to see Carla's mother.

"Hey, Trudy," she said.

"Taylor, it's good to see you."

She hugged the other woman, who'd been like a second mother to her.

"I'm so sorry for stopping by."

"It's fine. It's fine. Shouldn't you be in school?"

"I can't go back there. My parents are setting everything up for me to stay home for a little while. There's too many memories, you know." She bit her lip because she stood in the doorway of Carla's home.

"I understand, completely. It just seems … surreal she's not here."

"I know this is rude, but … I think I left something upstairs in her room. I understand if you don't want me to go in there."

"No, no, it's fine. You can go to Carla's room. I know you won't ruin anything. I … I can't bring myself to change anything, you know. It still smells like her. Would you like a drink?"

"Yes, I'd love one."

"Go on, sweetie. I'll get us a drink."

She made her way upstairs, taking her time. Scared of what she'd feel. Standing outside Carla's room, she reached up, touching Carla's name. This room had been her friend's all of her life. The mini-chalkboard outside had stayed the same with Carla writing her name as she grew up. There was a heart at the end of her name.

"Don't you think that's a little childish?" Taylor asked.

"Nah, come on. Okay, it's a little childish, but I love it. I can see how good my writing is. Look." She finished her name with the final curve of a heart. "See, perfect."

Pulling out of the memory, Taylor found this happening more and more at odd times. She'd been standing with her parents at the supermarket just last night when she'd gotten a carton of ice cream and recalled their argument when they were twelve about the best flavors in the world.

They were just that, memories.

Times they'd shared together that she'd taken for granted.

So many plans and nothing they'd done about it.

When she opened the door, tears flooded her eyes at the sweet scent that so reminded her of Carla. Stepping inside the room, she closed the door and took a deep breath.

The room was small, with a tiny closet.

"One day I'm going to have a huge walk-in, one where I can have shoes, and everything be color-coordinated."

It was like Carla stood with her in the room. Wrapping her arms around her waist, Taylor took a deep breath and stepped inside.

Nothing made sense to her.

Carla wouldn't hurt herself. She just wouldn't.

"What happened to you?" she asked. Pushing some of her black hair off her face, she wiped the tears from her eyes and stepped up to her friend's bag. Lifting it off the floor, she rested the bag on the bed, ignoring the small brown stuffed bear named Snuffles that lay against the sheets. Pulling out her school books, she looked through them, seeing the notes taken for each of their classes.

Once she'd gone through the bag, she placed everything back and glanced behind her.

Carla's desk stood opposite. Taylor ignored her own reflection, already knowing she looked a mess from lack of sleep. Each night she went to sleep, she'd wake up screaming. The dream was always the same—Carla in the lake, begging for help, and no matter what she did, she couldn't move. She couldn't save her.

Opening several drawers, she saw tampons, makeup, notepads, pens, nothing out of the ordinary. Then, remembering Carla's secret, she turned back to the closet.

"Mom is so worried about everything to do with having a teenager, she goes through everything. My desk, my bed, everything. Nothing is sacred."

"How do you keep things private then?"

"This."

Moving toward the closet, she opened it up, and pushed the clothing out of the way. Running her hand over the wall, she pressed in until one of the pieces of wood gave way, and there was the book, hidden away.

Carla's secret.

The diary that contained the mystery of her friend. She stepped back, tucking some hair behind her ear, and opened up the book. The last date that had any writing was the day she died.

May 30th 2008

He knows.

And he's happy.

I didn't think he'd be happy about it. He said he didn't want kids. That he couldn't have them. How we have to keep things secret. Everything has to be kept a secret. He doesn't want anything to happen to me and he said bad things happen to people that are near them.

They're dangerous.

I know. I can't tell Taylor about us when I really want to. I've told her everything. I don't keep anything from her, and yet, I can't. He begged me not to, so I can't, can I? I don't know why he does what he does, or why he's always warning me. He constantly tells me it's better this way. Where no one knows who we are together.

I know Taylor would be angry. I think. She'll hate

me for keeping this a secret. We tell each other everything. How can I tell her though that not only have I fallen in love with one of the four kings but I also carry his child?

Who?

What?

When?

Why?

Taylor knew how dangerous the four kings were. This was just insane. There was no way it could be possible.

Even as I write this I know he'll be angry, but there are four kings. No one needs to know which one, not here anyway. Tonight though, I've already promised him I'm going to tell her something.

A baby isn't easy to hide.

Not for long at least.

He'll tell his father, and everything will be okay.

I had hoped that first test had been wrong. Now, after taking six tests, I know without a doubt that I'm pregnant.

I have hope. Even if Taylor is a little pissed at me, I know she'll come around. Auntie Taylor. She'd make one hell of a mom one day. She doesn't make bad choices, ever. She's all about being reliable, predictable, and just herself. I love that about her. She's not desperate to fit in. I am.

I want to fit in so bad. I pretend not to care, but I love this attention. I love it when I'm around him, and I want everyone to know that he belongs to me. That I'm going to have his child, and sometime soon, we're going to get married.

I can't wait.

Baby?

Closing the book, she slid it inside the pocket of

her jacket before making her way into the kitchen. Trudy stood swirling the teabag within the cup.

"You know, she really liked tea. Said it was better for her than coffee," Trudy said.

"When did she start saying that?" Carla was a coffee addict. She was always drinking the stuff and laughing at anyone who thought decaf was a good substitute.

"A few weeks ago. She even came home with this lemon variety. I don't know." Trudy handed her over the tea, and looking at it, for Taylor, something wasn't right.

"I know this is going to sound weird, but did anyone at the hospital say anything? Comment about Carla's condition?"

"Carla's condition? You mean the depression and anxiety?" Trudy asked.

Taylor wanted to ask more, but Trudy couldn't handle it. She started to cry, handing her over the cup.

"I'm so sorry. I just feel like the worst parent in the world. I didn't even notice what was going on, you know. I should have seen it, right? I should have noticed that something was wrong with my daughter? That she wasn't happy."

Taylor wanted to argue with her. Carla wasn't sad.

She was happy.

They'd been making plans for graduation.

This was wrong. So fucking wrong.

"I didn't notice either," Taylor said, playing along. "I thought she was happy. That she and I still had a lot of plans." She gritted her teeth and sipped at her drink.

"Oh, honey, it's not your fault. It is never your fault." Trudy cupped her cheek. "You're a good person, Taylor, and a wonderful friend. Carla was lucky to have someone like you in her life."

She didn't say anything more, sipping her tea before leaving Carla's home.

She walked to her car, and without even thinking about it, she went straight to Paul. There were too many questions, and she needed answers. Paul was a computer nerd and proud of it. She and Carla hung out with him a lot when he wasn't busy on his computer as they all had chemistry together. He showed them once how easy it was to hack into the school's system and to find out any information he wanted. No one was safe.

Paul also happened to be rich, almost as rich as the four kings. The only difference was, he didn't take the power that was given to him. He didn't fit in with the crowd. Also, he'd had the biggest crush on Carla.

Something wasn't right, not to Taylor. They were hiding Carla's pregnancy, and she needed to know why. It wasn't like a teenage pregnancy was unheard of. There had been a couple of girls throughout high school that had gotten pregnant and they'd not been seniors either.

Parking up in his driveway, she saw there was only one car there. She climbed out of the car and walked up the long driveway. Money never excited or impressed her. She understood from the start that money was needed to make the world go around, but that was about it.

Her parents weren't rich, but they were well off. She didn't have to worry about getting a job to support herself through high school or college. College applications were sorted, and she already had a dorm ready for when she arrived. Everything was going smoothly, until Carla.

All of her plans were centered around her best friend, and with Carla gone, she didn't know what to do.

Paul opened the door. He was dressed in sweats,

his hair completely unkempt and in serious need of a cut.

"You're here."

"I'm here."

"What do you want?"

"I know I've not stopped by," she said. Seeing his tears, she remembered exactly why she'd decided against coming to see him.

Paul not only had a crush on Carla, he'd loved her more than anything. He'd admitted the truth to Taylor months ago and begged her not to say anything. She hadn't. This crush wasn't hers to tell, not now, not ever.

"I'm pleased you did. I … you're all I've got of her right now." He sniffled.

"I need you to do something," she asked.

"What?"

"Can I come in?"

"Sure."

After she stepped over the threshold, he closed the door behind her. "What do you need me to do?"

Opening up her jacket, she withdrew the diary.

"What the hell are you doing with that?" he asked.

"Read the last entry." She trusted Paul with Carla's diary. She'd often read them out excerpts of her life and feelings.

He took the book, clearly uncomfortable with reading it. She wasn't.

He flicked through the pages and came to the last entry. She watched and waited.

When he finished, he looked up. "She was pregnant?"

"Yeah, but here's the thing, Paul, her mother doesn't know."

"Wait, they'd have done a thorough investigation, wouldn't they? Assessed her body. She died in the lake. I don't understand."

"The four kings. I need you to go online, do your thing, and find out what is in those reports or something. I don't know. Something is missing." She paused, trying to think of anything else that could be important, putting all of her movie watching skills to use. "I also want you to see if there have been any interesting transactions to any of the doctors." That was what people did, use money to bribe others to get what they want.

"Taylor, she's gone. I get that—"

"She was my best friend, Paul. Now she's gone, and I want to make sure no one is covering this shit up. Do you understand me? She didn't have fucking depression or anxiety. I knew her. She was happy. We were all fucking happy. Something isn't right here, and I need to know what the hell is going on. Don't you get that?"

"I get it, but what good will it do? Knowing the truth doesn't change what happened. It doesn't bring her back."

"I'll know. We'll both know the truth."

Paul sighed. "This is fucked up. I can only find what they document with a computer, and even records like that can be erased."

"Whatever you can find. Please. I know it's a lot to ask."

"It is, but it's for Carla so … I'll get to it."

She followed him as he walked upstairs to his bedroom. His parents wouldn't mind. One day when she and Carla stopped by his father had been there, and even said it was good to see his son taking anything beside his keyboard up to his room.

His bedroom was a mess. Empty cans of soda, snacks, and clothing littered the floor. She perched on the edge of his bed and waited as he started to do his thing.

"You shouldn't have her diary."

"Don't tell me what I should and shouldn't do. You're starting to sound like a parent, and that sucks. I'd hate to have to put you in the naughty corner," she said.

He chuckled.

There was a pause. Carla would often speak about the naughty corner.

"I miss her."

"Me too. I just need to know that I'm wrong, Paul. Really. If she did have depression or anything, please let me know so I can stop thinking about her being fine and that everyone else is wrong. She never went to a counselor, Paul. You know this. She was always with us in high school. None of this makes any sense. She was never alone for long."

"I get it." He reached out, giving her hand a squeeze. "I'll find it."

She released his hand, and he got to work, typing away. His fingers moved so fast that they were like a blur to her. Time passed as he started to break through certain firewalls, building them back up so it didn't show anyone trying to hack their system. She didn't have a clue what he was doing. Computers were never really her thing.

She could type and work a spreadsheet and surf Google. That was all she needed them for.

"I have her cause of death," he said. He scrolled through. "It says suicide. No signs of a pregnancy."

"You're kidding?"

"No. Look, cause of death, suicide. There's not even a note on pregnancy. Maybe she got it wrong?"

"No." Carla wouldn't have documented it if she for even a second thought it was wrong. She knew Carla and there's no way she would have written about it and been wrong, right? The coffee change, the way she'd been acting, it all pointed to Carla being pregnant. Taylor knew there was a relationship going on, just not with whom.

She climbed off the bed, reading through the file. "Find out if there's been a payment to any of those signatures."

"Okay. This isn't a crime show, Taylor. You could be wrong, and people do hide their depression."

"I know. I just … I need to know."

He did his thing, and after a few minutes, he brought it up.

"Yeah, from an offshore account. Wired five million to him." He pointed at the screen.

"Can you find out where that offshore account came from?"

"Taylor?"

"Please, for me. Don't pretend you can't do this. I know you can. It's why you're going to have one of the best technology firms in the country and be rich beyond your wildest dreams."

"I'd have given Carla a good life as well. If she'd only looked at me."

Taylor placed a hand on his shoulder, hoping to comfort him. They were both grieving.

He got to typing again, and she waited, feeling sick to her stomach, knowing what it would come back to.

"Taylor?"

"Let me guess, someone within the Four Kings' Empire?"

"I don't like this."

She fucking hated it, but now everything was becoming clear.

"I don't like that look on your face. You don't know this for sure. This could be anyone. It could have been anyone."

Taylor paced the length of his bedroom.

Someone from the four kings had gotten her pregnant. She'd intended to tell her that night. Carla was scared about it. There was no notice of the pregnancy, and money had been wired to the doctor in charge of her autopsy.

"I'm not going to let them get away with this," Taylor said. "They've been in charge too long!"

"You're a teenage kid. Look at us. There's no way we can take this to the cops. What I did was fucking illegal, Taylor."

"They own the cops, so they'd make it go away."

"Yeah, they do. We can't do anything. We've got to find a way to move on. Let them win."

"Not right now we can't do anything," Taylor said. "But in time we can. When we can't be pushed aside. When we won't be laughed at."

"What are you going to do?"

"Simple. I'm going to take the kings down, one by one. Carla didn't kill herself. What they are trying to say about her is a lie. I won't have them lying about my friend. They messed with the wrong girl, and now, I'm going to mess with them."

****

The flowers and cards around Carla's locker had been removed. Axton watched as the janitor opened it up and began to place her books and belongings within the bag. He noticed her pictures on the inside of the locker. Most of them were of her and Taylor.

The girl in question stood a few feet away, watching. Her own locker stood open, and she was filling it up.

He saw the tears in her eyes as she watched.

Carla's parents stood together.

He couldn't believe they'd done this as a

spectacle for them all to see. He was many fucking things that were despicable, but he even saw how heartless this was.

Easton, Karson, and Romeo stood with him, watching. They all watched and waited.

Paul came to stand behind Taylor.

Axton watched as he placed his hands on her shoulders, and whatever daydream she'd been having, he'd pulled her out of.

She handed Paul her bag, and Axton watched as she walked over, hugging Carla's mom. Next, she hugged her dad, and then took over from the janitor, clearly sensing the coldness in the man. She reached into the locker and carefully removed every single book.

He watched, fascinated by her face as she took the pictures off the locker, placing them inside the bag.

When it was all over, she hugged the parents again and turned back to Paul. She stopped though, and glanced over at Axton. For the first time that he could recall she actually looked at him, and there was something about the way she did that didn't sit well with him. Her gaze didn't linger on him. She passed over to Karson, to Easton, to Romeo. The look she gave them was assessing, curious, questioning.

Why?

Watching her, he waited to see what would come of it. Why she kept looking at them until she finally walked away.

He didn't leave the corridor even as other students started to filter out.

"Hi, so, Axton, I was wondering—" A perky little blonde started to speak, but he wasn't interested.

"Fuck off."

"But—"

He turned and finally gave her his full attention.

"Get gone now."

She stepped back and quickly rushed away. Paul was whispering something into Taylor's ear, and Axton wanted to know what it was. Why the little shit kept looking over at them and still whispering.

"We need to go," Karson said.

Walking away from the corridor, he ignored the stares that all four of them got. Anyone who stood in their way quickly moved out of it. They were not known for budging for anyone.

Once outside to the football bleachers, Easton was the one who started to lose it.

"Did you see the way she looked at us?" Easton asked. "She knows. She knows about Carla."

"Didn't I tell you to keep your damn mouth shut?"

"You can't hide from this, Axton, don't you get that?"

"Taylor knows nothing otherwise we'd know something, wouldn't we?"

"You think your father would make you go after Carla's friend after what happened?" Karson asked.

"In case you haven't noticed, my dad makes sure nothing falls back on him or us. It's that simple. She knows nothing."

"Paul's a computer genius," Romeo said. "Nothing will get past him. Not if he's smart enough."

"He's not smart enough. Dad covers his tracks. That's all you need to know," Axton said. "What we can't have is you losing your cool right now." He looked directly at Easton. "You want to draw attention, keep acting like a spoiled little brat that lost his favorite toy. Remember how this started with Carla. You wanted to see what it was like on the trash side."

Easton stepped right up to him, and Axton raised

his brow.

"You think you got what it takes to overthrow me on this?" Axton said.

"I didn't toy with her."

"Come on, Easton, we all knew you were screwing with Carla to get back at your dad."

"I love her. I loved her. People change. Feelings change."

"Then you should look in the mirror and realize that *you're* the one that got her killed," Axton said.

He felt nothing. No remorse. No pain. Nothing. Even as Easton was clearly struggling with everything that happened.

Axton saw everything and felt nothing.

"You're a fucking asshole."

"I'm the asshole who is going to make sure you live a long and happy life."

"Come on, Easton, you can't be pissed at him for knowing the truth. We've even got it all on camera of you bragging about taking one from the other side, remember."

Easton paled and looked at Axton. "What?"

"You were drunk and it was funny, but I knew what you were doing held risks. So I made sure I got some collateral if it ever came to a point that I'd need it. You want it to be released now, Easton? You want to answer a few more questions other than why you were there last night?"

The tension in the group rose, and he felt that. He saw the anger, the rage, every little piece of emotion that flittered across Easton's face. He'd been the weakest of the group. Always searching for Daddy's approval.

The difference between him and Easton was Axton didn't give a fuck about anyone or anything. Even if he did, he'd do everything in his power to take them.

Easton flirted with everything, never fully committing to anything other than the four kings' brotherhood. Easton couldn't hack life without the money and power that came to them. Even though he kept trying to deny who he really was, there wasn't any getting away for them, not really. They were who they were, but rather than embrace it, Easton would have his little rebellions until he was put firmly in place.

It would be easier to cut him out, but they were not the three kings, they were four. Besides, when Easton was on his good behavior, he made this all work.

Carla was simply a little glitch that needed mending, nothing more.

"I suggest you step back, Easton," Karson said. "You know the way it has to be."

"No, it doesn't have to be this way."

Axton sighed. "Okay, you want a reality check? Here is one. Say it gets out that you and she were hooking up. No one knows about it. Not even us three." Easton frowned. "Of course, until someone releases a potential video, with amazing editing that shows exactly what you thought about Carla."

"That was in the fucking beginning—"

"I'm not finished. Shut the fuck up. So now they know not only did you have a reason to be at the bonfire that night, besides hanging out and partying, you suddenly have something to cover up. Purely because they'd just released the little detail that so far has been missing." Axton gasped. "That's right. She's pregnant. Little goody-two-shoes has a bit of a thing for Easton Long and is expecting his baby. You're rich. You've got everything to lose while she has the most to gain. So, what do you do? An argument gone bad because, kind officer, he was only gone for a minute or so, I swear. The press will lap that shit up. A small-town girl. Struggling, desperate to get out of King's Ridge, and oh, look what happened, one of the town's richest people suddenly has a motive. Your life will become a shit show before you even realize it. That what you want?" He paused, giving Easton time to answer. Silence rang out. He waited, smirking. "That's what I thought. I'm getting out of here."

"You're wrong, you know," Easton said after he'd taken a couple of steps.

He glanced back at his friend.

"I loved her, a lot. We were going to make a life together. I wanted to get out of this. To start over. She … was everything that I'd been missing, and now she's gone."

"Get over it," Axton said. "There's nothing you can do, and this shit you're pulling, having your little dramas, it's not good. It'll never be good for you. Remember that."

He left his friends by the bleachers.

On his way to his car, he passed a couple of teachers, but they knew better than to stop him. He walked to his car and stopped when he felt someone's eyes on him. Turning left, he saw her.

Taylor Keane once again was watching him, waiting.

Instead of ignoring her, he walked right over to her car and knocked on the window. He saw her jaw clench. She clearly did not want to talk to him.

She reached out and pressed the button for the window to start winding down. Leaning against it, he smiled.

"Shouldn't you be at school?"

"I am at school."

"In class?"

Taylor hadn't looked at him, but she finally

turned those startling blue eyes on him. "Shouldn't you?"

"I do what I want, Taylor. You should know that by now." He saw the shock on her face and laughed. "Yeah, I know your name. I'm curious, do you know mine?"

"Everyone knows your name."

"Then say it."

"Why?"

"Because I'm curious." He didn't recall ever hearing her say his name before.

"I'm not going to say your name."

"I'm sorry about your friend," he said.

He saw her hands clench into fists on her thighs. *Interesting.*

"What do you want?"

"Nothing. Just curious as to why you're watching me and not in class watching the lesson."

"That's none of your damn business. I'm heading home."

He saw the bag she'd been filling at her locker. "Where are you going?"

"My family has decided a clean break is what's needed for me to move on." She looked up at him. "That's why I'm not in class. I'm leaving."

He didn't say anything.

She turned to look at the school. "You know, I always imagined graduating here. Moving to college, spending so much time but I can't. Not anymore."

"Why not?"

"Too many memories are here. Walking down the corridor, I see her and I feel her."

He saw the tears glisten in her eyes, and he gritted his teeth.

"I can't stay here. Not anymore. You know, I think this is the most we've ever talked. Let go of my car. I've got to go."

He didn't move away when she asked. Staring at her, he waited, but nothing happened.

She stared at him, and for a few seconds he could get lost in her eyes. The blue was so striking, reminding him of the ocean in the summer. Right now, they were filled with pain.

Finally, when *he* was ready, he moved away from the car.

He watched her wind up her window before pulling out of the parking lot.

Whatever had happened between them had come to an end. A few seconds of seeing that pain in her eyes, of talking to her, and he'd remember this moment for a long time to come.

So much had changed in a matter of weeks, and now it was time to move on. Graduation was a couple of months away, and soon he would be out of this town for good, only to come back when needed.

They all had plans, big plans, and not any of them took place here.

Moving to his car, he looked up at the large school. This had been his kingdom for a long time now. The place that he could say he ruled. People were afraid of him. They feared what he and his family could do.

That feeling had become like a drug to his system, and no matter what, he wanted that but now on a bigger scale.

His father's company wasn't enough. Nor was Karson's, Easton's, or Romeo's. He wanted more. The empire he intended to have was just the beginning. No one was going to mess with his plans, no one.

Taking a deep breath, he climbed into his car, and took off out of the high school. The town of King's Ridge would forever look at him as something more. He intended to surpass his father's reputation, to become a king in his own right. He had no intention of just being another Farris in a long line of them.

He had big plans.

None of them included Carla, or a baby, or Taylor, or any chick from this town.

Power and money made the world go 'round.

They made sure people stayed down where they needed to be.

The first part of his plan had already been put in motion. The board would have no choice but to vote, and when they did, they'd come for him. His father's incompetence should be dealt with by none other than his son.

Arriving at home, he found his father lounging by the pool. His mother was nowhere in sight.

"You're supposed to be in school."

"I got bored," Axton said.

"I've got a meeting with the board tomorrow. Be in school, or else."

Axton smiled. "I will, Dad, don't worry, I will."

Chapter Three

Ten years later

"Oh, fuck yeah, your pussy is so fucking tight." Easton moaned as he pounded away inside the little slut, and it was also his birthday and they didn't even have to pay extra money for another woman.

Axton watched the show as the woman in question kept sucking Romeo and Karson. Pulling out his cell phone, he walked around the woman, making sure to get a perfect view of Easton in her pussy and a finger in her ass, then the way she was sucking their dicks like a fucking pro.

Sitting back down, he kept his camera on her face, watching the rapture as she came close to orgasm. She was begging, screaming at them to make her come. None of them did though, and he smirked. Little Catherine Riley. She didn't for a second believe they wanted to screw her nasty pussy for fun, did she? Easton was getting off, but this was also a job.

Oh, well, she'd go in the list of many other women and men before her who thought they could come after the four kings and get away with it. That shit didn't happen, not on his watch. As Easton pulled out of her, he got a clear shot as with one quick thrust, he embedded himself into her anus.

The moan was captured, the begging was taken, and victory was all theirs. Axton enjoyed his scotch, watched the show, and made sure every single second was captured. Once it was all over and his friends had come either in her mouth or on her face, and Easton completed in her ass, Axton put his cell phone away, job well done.

He wouldn't spill shit tonight, but when she came

calling for money and using blackmail tactics, he would be ready.

Ten years he'd been dealing with this kind of stuff.

Ten years of companies thinking he was just a regular punk-ass kid.

He was Axton Farris, not a kid. Never a kid. From the time he could learn to read, he'd been forced to grow up.

There was no childhood for him or his friends. It's why they were all so ruthless. There was no love involved in power and wealth.

Contracts.

Business.

Winning.

That's what he knew.

It was in his blood, and when the time finally came for him to have a child, that kid would have the same upbringing, none of this bullshit that kids seemed to relish nowadays.

As far as he was concerned, keeping it real was the only fucking way to roll.

"Now that was a damn fine way to spend a birthday," Easton said, slapping Catherine on the ass. "Well done you for being a good sport."

He stepped away, sliding his condom off before wrapping it up and placing it in his jacket pocket. With their wealth, they had to deal with their fair share of gold-diggers, and attempted bribery. Also, Axton knew for a fact that Easton had left a condom lying around and when he'd entered the bathroom after getting dressed, had found the woman trying to use the semen inside to impregnate herself.

That shit was just nasty, but some people would do anything for money.

"Now that's what it's like to be banged by the four kings," Catherine said, wiping her face clean.

She had a big smile on her face as if she was the cat that ate the cream. It sickened him just to watch.

"Three, babe," Karson said, slapping her ass.

"Yeah, that's right. I didn't even give you a piece of me," she said, coming toward him.

Axton lifted his bare foot and placed it on her stomach.

"Don't come any closer."

She pouted. "But I can make it so much better."

"If I wanted your nasty cunt, I'd be in it, Catherine. I don't want you. I never did. You were merely a present for my friend."

"And now I'm done with her. Had my fun and she's all used up. Get her out of here," Easton said.

"You heard the man. Get dressed before I call security and have you expelled from the club."

"You can't be serious," she said, looking around the room.

Karson laughed. "You really think we want a second round? I'd give you a two for effort, but really, if I wanted a real woman, I'd go and pick out from the number of them out at the bar willing to take my cock. You're nothing but a nasty whore."

She wasn't offended.

They all knew about Catherine.

How she used her body and her little secrets to try to stay on top. She thought she could come between the four kings, to make them her bitch, and to do her bidding. She couldn't have been more wrong.

None of them bowed to a woman.

None.

Women bowed to them and were grateful for whatever little speck of attention they granted.

"Now, where is the real fun?" Easton asked.

Ten years ago, Easton wasn't all that much fun, but it seemed the threat of living life on the streets really affected him. After that day in school when he'd lost his cool and they'd told him straight what would happen, he'd been a different man.

No woman ever lasted on his arm.

The world was full of willing women, and Easton seemed determined to be the kind of guy to taste them all.

They all had a part to play in their empire. The four of them made up a complete unit. Nothing and no one could come between them.

They had their pact, and even if they didn't always see eye to eye, their friendship remained firmly in place.

Catherine dressed quickly, shooting them glares. If her looks alone could kill, they'd all be dead.

Glancing down at his watch, Axton grabbed his cell phone and made sure she heard as he dialed security. Just as he was about to call, she huffed out of the room, promising them they'd regret it.

Once the door closed, they all burst out laughing. The idea alone of her taking them on was so fucking funny.

She'd messed with the wrong men, and now he had a long video that he could unleash at any time.

"You know, I think her pussy has been well-used already," Easton said. "It's why I had to take her ass too. She just couldn't handle me, and her ass wasn't too bad. Not as tight as I'd like."

His friends were not dressed, and Axton poured himself another shot of whiskey. This would be his last for the night. Drinking would always be in moderation. There was no way he'd ever allow himself to be out of control.

Control meant power.

There was no way in the world he'd give someone the same kind of ammunition against him. He'd already sat through three of Romeo's indiscretions that had cost them all millions.

"Let's get down to the real business right now. Holly left. She found a job elsewhere that guaranteed less stress and was something she enjoyed a lot more," Axton said.

"For fuck's sake. For one night can't we just have a little fun? It's my birthday." Easton glared at him.

"You've just had a fuck of the lifetime. You took her ass and pussy. Move on. I've got business to deal with. Holly's gone, and that means we're advertising for someone to fill that position."

"Then interview them," Karson said.

"I don't see what the big fucking deal is. There are more than enough chicks to fill the gap. Just get it done," Romeo said.

"It doesn't matter who we employ. You'll only fire them and hire who you want to in the first place." Easton shrugged. "This is not our decision but yours."

That's because he hired competent women.

Women that were not likely to file a lawsuit.

They didn't want another man around them. Too much testosterone right now that another male wouldn't work for any of them.

"This is supposed to be our decision," Axton said.

They all burst out laughing, but he didn't find it the least amusing.

"You're paranoid, Axton. God, anyone would think you've got something to hide."

He glared at Romeo. They all had something to hide.

"You know what, my job here is done. You don't want to take this seriously, then I'm out of here."

"Oh, come on, stop being such a party pooper," Easton said. "There's chicks all over this place that want a bit of your cock. It's been so fucking long since you got it wet. No wonder you're a giant pain in the ass. All work and no play makes Axton a very dull, boring boy."

He ignored them all and made his way out of their VIP room.

Pulling his cell phone out of his pocket, he called to his driver, Eric, to bring the car around. He was done partying for the night.

"Is everything okay?" Michelle asked.

She was the woman they'd picked to manage the club.

"More than fine."

"You know, you could stay," Michelle said, reaching out to run a hand down his shirt. "I wouldn't mind taking you for a little ride myself."

He caught her wrist, holding it tight to the point he saw her wince. "Not going to happen. I don't fuck where I work."

She thrust out her lip. "Come on. You're the only one that hasn't tasted me. Ask your friends. They know I'm good to party." She moved in close, and he gave her a shove.

"Then take your nasty mouth and pussy somewhere else." He didn't linger to make it better. "And you're fired. Enjoy the benefits of tonight while you can."

Not only did he have to interview for a new PA but now a new manager of the club as well.

His night was going from shit to worse.

Fortunately, Eric was parked right outside waiting for him, with the door open and a smile on his face. He and Eric had been together for some time now. He'd given him the job the moment he took over from his father with the Four Kings' Empire.

Other than Romeo, Easton, and Karson, Eric was the only other person he trusted. Holly had been in that position once as well.

He'd thrown out all of his father's close employees and replaced them with people of his own choosing. Holly had been a struggling single mother. She'd been desperate for the job, and every single test of loyalty he'd thrown her way, she'd passed. From leaked footage onto her desk, to a hacked email, to anything that he thought she'd try to take, she'd come to him to report, earning her place as a valued employee.

The people that were loyal to him, his friends, and the company were always treated like family and fully compensated. Those that went against him, well, they longed for death as he made their lives a living hell, and he took great pleasure in seeing their lives unfold, just like the sick fucker that he was.

Axton had known from a young age that he wasn't like most people. He rarely understood or cared for love. He'd come to see love as a weakness, a tool that could be used against someone at any point in their life.

He thrived on seeing others suffer, from taking what didn't belong to him and building an empire that rivaled his enemies. This wasn't so different from when he was a kid, seeing others fail, loving their pain, basking in it. He'd watched his father do it for so long that he'd wanted that kind of pleasure. Only as he got older he realized his father cheated. That he never won by playing fairly. In the beginning of learning all about his place within the four kings, Axton hadn't cared about the means his father used. A win was a win. Getting older, it started to mean something to him. He needed more than just the win. He needed it to fucking count.

Anyone could win via cheating.

That didn't make a person great. No, that made a person weak, and he wasn't weak. Every victory he made was because he played by the rules and made sure he stayed on top. All of their fathers' pasts were part of who they were. All the lies and cheating had helped to keep the Four Kings' Empire alive.

Axton didn't want that as his legacy.

From the time he took over, he'd made sure to forge a new path, but he was still very much aware of the danger that surrounded them all. If anyone tried to look deeply within the company, they will see the poison that even now he was trying to push out. This empire was his whole life.

There was no room for weakness.

He would fight to the bitter end to save this place. He'd taken it from his weak-ass father and made it into something great.

No matter what, though, he did have a weakness, and he fought like fucking hell to keep that private. There was no way he could ever let the truth get out. It was bad enough that his friends knew. He wouldn't let anyone ever know what his secrets were, and he was damn good at keeping them. Even if his father liked to try to blackmail him with the truth of the company, at least his father didn't know about one tiny detail.

Pushing those thoughts and memories aside, he climbed into the backseat and released a sigh.

"Would you like some privacy, sir?" Eric asked.

"Yes, I would."

He stared at his email on his cell phone, reading through Holly's resignation letter. As per her contract, which she asked for the change, when she wished to move on, she wouldn't be forced to serve her notice. It was rather unconventional, but that's why she'd worked well.

Still, he didn't mind having a change.

It was an inconvenience, but he'd rather have a change than someone doing a shitty job simply because they didn't want to work with him.

Closing her resignation letter, he went to the emails marked with the PA position. The moment it opened up, there had been close to fifty applicants. Sitting in the back of the car, he read through each one.

"Sir, we're home," Eric said.

"I'm not ready to go home. Keep on driving please."

Once again, they were back on the road. He liked working in the motion of the car. It seemed to calm and relax him in ways that a blowjob never did, nor a woman. The moment he was done with a woman, getting her out of his space was a top priority to him.

Just going through the applications once, he was able to reduce the number of interviews by half. Some of the people who'd applied had done so with a journalism degree. That shit wasn't going to happen on his watch where they thought they could investigate him or get the next juicy story. His life wasn't for public pleasure and never would be.

He reduced the interviews to only ten after another hour, but as he was about to put his cell phone away, another beep alerted him to a new email.

Checking through, he saw it was another application for the job as PA, but he wasn't even interested in it. Everything always looked good on paper, but he needed to get a sense for them in person. He'd been about to place it straight into the trash bin when the name caught his attention.

Surely, it wasn't her.

Clicking on the email, it opened up, and there was an introduction about her and her work, reasons why she wished to work for him, and also her views on privacy. This was why a few applicants were dismissed immediately. They didn't have a cover letter telling him in detail why they wanted the job.

Taylor Keane.

A name he'd not heard in a very long fucking time.

So long in fact that just seeing her name brought an immediate smile to his lips, recalling the way she'd held that damn steering wheel ten years ago.

Wow, ten years.

It had been ten years since he last saw her in person.

He wondered what she looked like.

Closing down his email, he immediately typed her name into social media, and nothing. She had no account and wasn't attached to anyone either.

His curiosity was piqued.

Searching through her resume, he saw she'd been working with several small companies as either a secretary or a PA. She'd gotten a degree in business but hadn't taken it anywhere.

He'd heard of people doing a business degree then gaining their knowledge through work, taking on expertise like that.

What did she look like?

Why had she applied to his company?

Was he just being paranoid?

"Sir, we're here again," Eric said. "Would you like me to keep on driving?"

"Eric, if someone from your past got back in touch again, what would you think?" he asked.

Glancing up, he saw his driver was indeed

shocked. He never asked anyone for advice before, and right now he was regretting asking.

"It depends, sir. Are there reasons for you to doubt their intentions?"

The night of Carla's death flashed through his mind.

"I'm not sure."

"Sometimes we do things we're not always proud of. It doesn't mean that others feel the same way, sir."

"I'll stay in for the night. Thank you."

He had a long day week ahead of him, but he was suddenly looking forward to Monday.

****

Monday lunchtime

Standing in the elevator making her way up to the top floor of the Four Kings' Empire building, Taylor stared at her reflection. She was the only person within the four walls. Her heart thumped inside her chest.

Ten years since she last saw these four boys.

They were never boys.

Men, now.

Men who she intended to bring down.

"Look, it's not the body shape they're attracted to," David said.

"It's not?"

"No, it's the woman's mind. You walk in there trying to cover your body, it's going to turn them off. You stand with your back straight, your head held high, and rocking those curves. They'll want a piece of you. It's all about the perception you give. You don't want to do the surgery, get rid of all your weight, then you've got to work with what you've got, and, baby, you've got a lot to work with."

And her body was all on display right now. Not with flesh hanging out. But rather than wear larger clothes to cover her curves, she wore a figure-hugging pencil skirt that ended at the knee but curved up over her thighs, going in at her waist. The blouse she wore, white and crisp, was tucked in at the waist, giving her the perfect hourglass figure.

She wanted to bring justice to Carla, but there had been limits along the way in the last ten years. The first limit was not educating herself. She'd refused to not go and get her college education. Besides, if she once again worked her way into the kings' lives, she wanted to do so with something about herself. So, she'd gone to college, and she'd worked her ass off in business. A boring degree but she'd done it.

Then of course, she had to wait. Her plan would never work without careful planning. She didn't want to scream at them and throw insults. The kings had been in charge for too long in town, and now in the city. She wanted to bring them down from the inside, and make sure they had no way of crawling out of the dirt she put them in.

With that, timing was everything.

Now at twenty-eight, she was ready.

In the last ten years, she'd made a lot of changes. Staring at her reflection, she saw them. Her long, raven hair wasn't tied up on top of her head, but she'd let it grow out, and worked it into curls that cascaded around her body.

Like David said, the escort she'd paid to help her, and of course Paul was still on her side. His love of Carla had never waned. Taylor and Paul didn't spend every moment with each other, but he'd been there for her when she needed him. Her grandparents had left her a small inheritance that had helped to fund all of her plans until she got a job that paid her well.

David had taught her how to dress. He'd taken

her to the gym with his own personal trainer, where she'd been given a strict diet and a set routine. Her curves were not gone, and they never would be.

The trainer had told her unless she starved herself, her body was naturally curvy, and he could work with that. So she was primed and toned, and ready for anything.

Next, David had worked on her confidence.

She smiled, just thinking of the lesson in applying makeup. Her eyes looked smoky with the dark eyeshadow she'd applied. Her lashes looked dark with the mascara, and her lips plump. She wasn't biting her lips to try to hide them. Their fullness was on display.

"Lips like these make a man want to sink his dick inside them. You've got to be prepared to be the ultimate fantasy, Taylor. Men like the kings can pay for ten of you. You've got to learn to stand out."

Which was why she hadn't approached them in a bar and why she had no intention of acting like a whore to achieve her goal.

She may be different in a lot of regards, but she wouldn't change herself to them, not the woman she was.

What she was doing was unspeakable. Even now she had her doubts about bringing the four men down, but all she had to do was remember Carla and she didn't doubt for much longer. There were nights she woke up slick with sweat, screaming because Carla died right in front of her.

The elevator dinged.

Showtime.

Pushing a curl off her face, she stepped off the elevator, leaving her nerves behind her. Walking with a sway of her hips to the reception desk at the top floor, she placed a smile on her lips. The blonde woman gave her one scathing look, and immediately phoned down to the front desk.

She knew from her sources that the kings had a receptionist stationed on each level of their building so no one could get past if they didn't want to. This woman, whoever she was, called down to the main desk to double-check.

Stepping up to the counter, Taylor placed a hand on her hip and waited.

The woman kept looking her up and down, as if that look would make her think badly of herself. She'd met women like this in the gym, in life, and in work. They wanted to make her feel small because of the way she looked. The truth was, the receptionist must have felt her position was challenged here.

Taylor wondered which man was fucking who.

"How can I help you?" the woman asked, her voice meaning the complete opposite as it snapped the words out.

"I'm interviewing for the PA position. I had Mr. Farris email me a time and date." She checked her watch. "And I'm twenty minutes early."

There was some clicking on the computer, and she waited.

"Yes, you're signed in. Please, go and take a seat with the others. It has been a busy day today."

"I'm sure it has been." She flashed the woman a smile, turning on her heel.

Bitch.

Taylor held in her giggle, thinking about David once again. He'd warned her that some women would feel challenged by her and the way she was dressed. She couldn't believe how apt he'd actually been.

Entering a waiting area, she saw five other people waiting. Taking a seat, she placed her bag beside her and pulled out her resume.

Opening the file, she checked through her details. None of them were lies.

Her life for the past ten years was laid out for her to see.

Ten years of careful planning to this very moment.

She couldn't even believe that it was really happening right now.

Someone walked past, and she recognized Easton. He was a lot bigger than she remembered; harder too. He stood in the center of the waiting area, and he cursed on the phone, spinning around as he did.

She stared right back at him as he looked at her.

Raising a brow, she waited.

"I've got to go." He snapped the phone shut. "I know you."

"You do?"

"Yeah, I know you."

She folded her arms, staring at him.

"You're not going to tell me who you are?" Easton asked.

"I'd like you to guess." She wanted to hurt these men. That was her initial thought on looking at Easton. One of these or all of them were responsible for Carla's pregnancy and death. Of her taking her life, of keeping her baby a secret. She was going to find out who it was and then why. For ten years she'd waited. Letting everything stew around inside her, waiting for the perfect opportunity to strike. Now was that time. She was ready now, even if Paul wasn't so happy with the plan, not that he'd ever been happy with it.

Before he got a chance to say anything, her name was called.

"Taylor Keane."

Grabbing her bag, she stood, the six-inch heels

giving her some height.

"Taylor?" Easton asked.

"I've got to go."

"Wait, Taylor from King's Ridge?"

"Very good," she said.

"Wow, it's been fucking…"

"Ten years," she said, tilting her head to the side. "I better go and see—"

"Wait, you're here for the position of PA?"

"That I am."

"Wait until Axton sees you. He's going to lose his shit. I know it." Easton gave her the once-over.

"When a guy checks you out, don't sneer. Don't ruin the illusion that he wants you."

Keeping a straight face, she kept on smiling, pretending to be completely oblivious to his gaze.

"I better go." She walked away, feeling Easton's gaze on her.

She met a brunette. "Hi, just go through there," the woman said.

Axton Farris stated a sign on the door, which was closed. This was it. Ten years of hard work had brought her to this moment.

She couldn't fail, not now.

Knocking on the door, she released a breath, especially when he called for her to come on in.

Taking hold of the handle, she clicked it open and stepped through the door.

Axton sat behind his desk. He was typing away at his computer while on the phone.

One look up, and she saw she'd surprised him.

Staying by the door, she waited for that moment of shock to pass. Once it had, he hung up his call and stopped typing.

"Taylor Keane, in my office."

"I have my resume." She was so fucking pleased her hand wasn't shaking. Stepping up to his desk, she gently placed the file down and took a seat opposite him, putting the bag beside her.

Axton had always been a good-looking guy. He'd been the guy that every single girl in high school wanted. They all wanted to be the one girl that tamed him, that controlled him. Taylor didn't want to do that.

In high school, she'd recognized that he was hot, but that was about as far as her attention went.

Now though, he was all man. He'd filled out, if that was at all possible. He was now a lethal mix of hot and deadly.

She waited.

He stared.

The way Axton looked though was having a nervous effect on her body. She liked his gaze, felt her nipples tighten, and wanted him to keep on looking. His once-over felt more like a caress as he went down then up.

She licked her suddenly dry lips.

"Water?" he asked.

"Yes, please."

He got up, and she wished she'd declined the water. Damn, sitting behind a desk he was a handsome force of steel. Standing up, he was large, muscular man, confident, sure of himself. The suit he wore fit him like a second skin.

Keep your cool.

He stood beside her chair with some water in a plastic cup. She took it and thanked him. Sipping the cold liquid, she waited for him to take a seat.

"I hope you don't mind me asking, why did you come to us?" Axton said. "You could take a job anywhere."

"As I'm sure you're aware, the Four Kings' Empire has a reputation for being the best. Since finishing my business degree, I've worked in smaller places, building myself up. I've made sure I understand the way business works. It's okay to study it from books, but something comes from experience. At my last job, I found the daily routine boring. I want a challenge. What greater challenge than to try and get a job here?" She smiled. "I guess I want to challenge myself. Have a change of scenery, learn more. I think I could learn and be a valuable asset here. I'm loyal. I'm hard-working, and I have no other commitments outside of work that will keep me from doing the best job possible."

"No children? No boyfriend?"

"None. I found that they only seem to demand time that I find is better suited elsewhere. I, of course, have some friends, but they understand my career comes first."

"Interesting."

"Don't show your nerves. Stay your humble self but own your shit."

David's words kept repeating around her head. They should do, she'd heard them enough times to recite them.

Crossing her leg over the other, she rested her hands in her lap, still holding the cup, taking a sip every now and again.

He fired questions at her, relating to certain business practices and how she'd deal with circumstances. If an employee, for instance, came to her with a problem of possible sexual harassment, she explained she'd consult with HR, but if she felt the situation wasn't being handled, she'd bring it to him.

She'd also done her research.

The Four Kings' Empire took their business

practices seriously. She didn't know yet if they actually did or just bought people off, throwing money at everything as if it was a magical Band-Aid to cure everything.

There was no magical cure for losing someone though.

"Well, it has been a pleasure hearing from you," Axton said. "I will certainly give you some consideration."

"I hope you do. Please let me know by the end of the week."

"The end of the week?"

"Yes, I understand that your time is precious. I would really love this job, but if I don't have it, then I need to continue looking."

"You've got a second placement?" Axton asked.

"Yes. This morning I had a call from Hammer Industries. They saw my resume and heard I was looking for a new job. They want me to confirm an interview." Hammer Industries was the Four Kings' Empire's biggest rival.

Seeing the way Axton's nostrils flared, she knew she'd piqued his interest just a little more.

"I will call you as soon as I'm able."

"Certainly, sir."

He held onto her resume, and she knew this was it. This was her one and only chance. She stood up, bag on her shoulder. Walking up to the desk, she held her hand out. "It was a pleasure to see you again, Mr. Farris."

He shook her hand. She smiled, and then turned on her heel. She paused for a second. At the door, on display, was a very expensive-looking vase. It wasn't the vase that caught her attention but the red roses that were inside it.

Getting her wits together, she walked toward the

door and out of the building. Out of the corner of her eye, she saw Easton standing on the edge of the waiting area, with two other men. Karson and Romeo.

Glancing behind her, she saw Axton in the doorway.

If this was a game of chess, she'd just moved her pawn and declared the game. They were all staring at her.

"Never wave. Never give them a hint that you've seen them looking. Keep moving as if you don't have a care in the world."

Stepping onto the elevator, she pulled her cell phone out of her bag, and as the doors closed, she finally looked up.

Chapter Four

Eleven years ago

"I mean come on, Tay. You can't be serious right about now," Carla said.

Taylor laughed as her friend continued to beg.

"Come on, Paul has a pool. We could totally hang out, like, all summer."

"All summer?"

"Yes, all fucking summer, Tay. You got to understand that. All summer. Like, lots of fun. The pool. Relaxing."

"You do know he'll be on his computer the entire time and he'll want us to play video games," Taylor said, stopping at her locker. She leaned against it and laughed at Carla's shocked gasp.

"I will do anything. Come on, there's a pool. How can you say no to a pool? That's not even, like, legal or something."

"Legal?" Taylor loved to string Carla along like this. Her best friend thought she didn't want to hang out at the pool of their friend Paul's place. Of course she wanted to hang out there.

Summer was going to be a nightmare at the local pool, and she didn't want to spend her time being laughed at for wearing a costume.

Paul had already come to her anyway and asked her thoughts on what Carla would think if he suggested the pool and hanging out. She'd told him straight, Carla would love it. What she couldn't guarantee was Carla going on a date with him, which was what they both wanted.

"Please, please, please," Carla said. "I will do your laundry all summer. I'll wash your car."

"I like washing my car, and I can do my own laundry."

"Please, please, please. I'll clean up your dog's shit when we take him on walks. In the baggie things."

"Promise?" Taylor asked.

"Promise. Like, with a cross over my heart and everything."

"Fine, count me in."

"Seriously?"

"I was going to go for free, but seeing as I now have a poop cleaner, I'm all good." She winked at her friend.

"Oh, you're nasty," Carla said, laughing. "I can't believe you."

"A deal's a deal. You will clean my dog poop."

"You're such a goody two-shoes. Say shit."

"I don't need to swear or curse. I'm a lady."

"Yeah, yeah."

Carla paused, and Taylor saw her gaze move elsewhere.

Glancing behind her, she saw the cause. Axton, Karson, Romeo, and Easton. The four guys that ruled the school were heading down the long corridor.

"They really are something," Carla said. She sounded all dreamy.

"They're not all that, and please stop drooling."

"Come on, you have to admit they're hot." Carla gave her a pointed look.

"So, they're hot. I think Brad Pitt is hot, but that doesn't mean if he came asking for a date I'd actually go with him."

She worked the combination of her locker and opened it up.

"See, I don't know why I'm friends with you right now. You sound weird to me."

"It must be my dazzling personality." Taylor rapidly blinked her eyes.

The four kings of King's Ridge high school passed by, and she looked into her locker. She frowned.

On the shelf right in front of her was a single red rose. She loved roses so much. Any shape or color. There were times she found herself stopping by a florist just to stare at the array of colors. She didn't even mind that there were thorns along the stem. To her, they were a thing of beauty.

"What is it?" Carla asked.

Picking up the rose, she looked at her friend.

"You're giving yourself roses now."

"It wasn't me," she said.

She picked up the piece of paper to see some fancy writing on it. She didn't recognize the writing. Flicking the letter open, she read the words. *"This rose doesn't even compare to your beauty. You have no idea how truly beautiful you are, and that you are admired from afar."*

"A little love letter. That is so sweet," Carla said, reading the letter.

The rose was beautiful for sure. Taylor loved it. Bringing the flower to her nose, she breathed it in, smelling the floral scents.

"Do you know who it is?"

"I don't have a clue." She didn't care though. The flower and note were sweet, and she didn't need anything else. Not even confirmation of who it was from.

****

Present day

"Holy shit, did you see her?" Easton said. "I mean that ass. The things I could do to it."

Axton watched as Easton held his hands out and pretended to kiss air. Since Taylor had left, his friends had descended on his office. Karson was reading through her resume.

This was the first time someone from their past had even come to their workplace. No one from their high school came looking for a job here. Most of them were back in King's Ridge.

The only other person he'd seen from that life was Paul Motts. He was as successful as they were, but he'd designed some technology that had put his father's company on the bigger map. Mott Enterprises had grown in the last ten years. They didn't compete in the market as their businesses were vastly different. Technology wasn't something the Four Kings were about. Their resume went from industry through to media, and across a much broader scope. They had many pies, and it was what made them the four kings.

"This all seems legit to me," Karson said, closing the file.

"I didn't say it wasn't."

"You don't look happy."

He glared at Easton. "Anyone would think he's a fucking boy, not a full-grown man."

"Oh, come on, man. I'm the one that has learned to have some fun in my old age. Maybe you should start to have some fun. Live a little and stop being a stick in the mud like our parents." Easton dropped down onto the sofa. "It's all work for you."

"We're responsible for thousands of people's jobs, Easton. That doesn't give us the chance to have a break."

"Please, we're the best there is. No one is going to try and take us on because we all know they'd lose. Like, really fucking lose. You're panicking over the wrong shit, Ax. Give yourself a break. Fuck someone for a change. Hey, fuck Taylor. With a body like that, I bet she's got all kinds of tricks up her sleeve. Did she always have a body like that?"

"As I recall, you were only interested in her friend," Axton said.

He was being a dick, bringing up Carla. Even after ten years though, it was always the key to bringing Easton under control.

It was like a switch went off inside Easton's head, and he stopped being a dick, and went back in time when he was not only happy but also determined.

"Now that you're listening. We're on top because we keep it that way. Have your fun, I don't care, but the company comes first. It will always come first. That will never, ever change."

They all nodded in agreement.

"What do you want to do, Axton?" Romeo asked, speaking up.

Out of all of them, Romeo was the one who rarely spoke up until absolutely necessary. Strange considering most of the ladies loved him because he turned on the charm and showed them a side of himself that he rarely let out to play.

"She's the most qualified," Karson said.

Axton turned to Karson, who held his hands up.

"So sue me for speaking the truth. This is the truth, and you fucking know it. She's qualified to handle this. More so than any other candidate."

"What's the problem then?" Easton asked.

He stared at his friend long and hard.

Easton rolled his eyes. "Fine. Fine."

Axton picked up the file and flicked through it.

"If you don't trust her, put her through all of your tests, Axton. You know you want to," Easton said, smirking.

"The inner workings of our empire must remain

between us until she has passed her tests. You understand. She cannot know how we got here, and she certainly can never get ahold of the information from the past." They all agreed. There were no traces of it within the office, and Axton himself had removed all backup files. They were now located in safe places just in case someone wanted to try to take revenge. That evidence kept potential enemies in line. Looking toward Karson, he nodded. "I want the investigator on her. I want to know everything. Who she's friends with. What she does. Where she lives, and who she hangs out with."

"On it," Karson said.

"Anything else or are you going to continue being paranoid?" Easton said. "She'll be a PA to all of us. It's what Holly did."

He'd gotten an email from her, letting him know that she'd found work in a field that she loved, that her new job provided her with regular hours and allowed her to write code. She thanked him for all the time and experience he'd provided her and also that she'd loved working for him. He completely understood and knew she had a passion for technology and code writing. The demands of her job didn't allow her all the time possible with her child, and she'd been with them long enough.

Axton accepted that. He'd noticed she'd been having that long-lost look whenever one of his employees had a baby and brought them in while on maternity leave, and she was clearly missing her kid. They worked long hours, and that had to take its toll on normal parents. He didn't know. He didn't have a normal childhood, nor did he have a child of his own.

"Where are you going?" Easton asked as Axton grabbed his jacket and started pushing them out of his office.

"I'm going to have some lunch."

He also knew where to find Paul. They all moved in the same circles, and he'd seen Paul several times at the one restaurant where he liked their steak.

As he closed his door, his three friends moved to their offices. The other candidates had already been sent home. After seeing Taylor, he'd not been interested in interviewing anyone else.

He'd already sent a message to Eric to be there to pick him up.

Stepping into the elevator, he was sure he smelled Taylor's vanilla scent. She'd always worn vanilla, even in high school. He'd been passing her one day when she sprayed it on herself. Carla had made some weird choking noise, and the two had laughed about her smelling like a cupcake.

Ignoring the memory, he stepped out into the underground parking, climbing in the back of the car.

Eric took off, and he gave him the restaurant where to take him.

Today had been … different.

He didn't recall a time he'd ever been more surprised than when he saw Taylor entering his office. She'd changed so much and yet one look in her eyes, and it was like the ten years hadn't passed at all. He was back in high school.

Leaning his head back against is seat, he closed his eyes.

"Are you okay, sir?" Eric asked.

"It has been a long day."

His driver chuckled. "You start at five. I imagine a lot of things in life are long."

He smiled and enjoyed once again the motion of the car. When he'd relaxed enough he stared out the window at the passing city. He loved the chaos of city life. People rushing around, the constant movement and activity. Nothing stopped here, and he liked that. He always had something to do. He hated it when there was nothing to do and life seemed to come to a standstill.

It's why the Four Kings' Empire rivaled every other business out there. They never stopped, not once.

He liked the challenge of staying ahead. Of keeping their secrets locked up tight so no one could access them. There was no secret code for success, no point in trying to take them on as all would fail. They'd had some bids come through, companies wanting to take them over, and they'd all failed.

No one would ever take his company from him, no one.

Eric pulled in front of the restaurant.

"I'll be an hour," he said, climbing out.

He didn't want to hear from his driver. Entering the restaurant, he buttoned up his jacket and went straight to the main desk.

"How may I help you, sir?"

"I'm here to see Paul Motts."

"What's your name?"

He glanced past her shoulder and saw Paul sitting by himself like normal, looking over the paper.

"That's fine. I see him now."

"Excuse me, sir. I will call security."

He stopped. The woman was clearly new.

"My name is Axton Farris of the Four Kings' Empire. You want to get security that's more than fine. I'll have your job from you and make sure no one will employ you. I'm more than happy to do that."

She went visibly pale. "I'm so sorry, sir. Yes, I see your name is here. I apologize."

He was already walking away. Dropping down into the seat opposite, he waited as Paul glanced up over his paper.

"You know I didn't invite you here. I like to eat my lunch in peace and quiet."

"It's the quiet life we're always after, but I'm curious though, Paul. You see, I had a very interesting visit from an old high school friend."

Paul laughed. "Friend? If I recall you and Taylor never spoke."

"So, you knew she was coming to me for an interview?"

"I know most things. Tay and I have stayed in touch, off and on. Why?"

"Why is she coming to me?"

"You got a problem with her wanting a job from you?" Paul asked. "Is she not qualified enough for the role?"

"It's not about having those qualifications. You and I know that."

"Then what's the problem?" He folded up the newspaper, placing it to one side. "If you're going to interrupt my lunch then you may as well give it all to me. What is it you want to know?"

"Why didn't she take a job with you?"

"Wow, and here I thought you'd have something of interest for me. If you want to know why she won't come for a job with me, why don't you just ask?"

"I'm asking you."

Paul tilted his head to one side. "Multiple reasons."

"Which are?"

"You seriously talk to everyone this way?"

"You're just special to me."

"Oh, yay," Paul said. "Fine. First, she has no interest in technology at all. She'd be bored, and I don't want anyone giving me substandard work."

"And the second?"

"She wouldn't be able to work for me."

"How come?"

"She's not got what it takes to work in the technology field. The last time we got together, I bored her to sleep with what I did. Our lives don't cross paths much. She wanted a challenge. Your company is top of the list. Taylor's never been one to shy away from hard work. Ask her."

"You two stayed in touch this whole time?"

"Well, we did, and we didn't. We'd talk and then life would get in the way, and then we'd reconnect. When she left town, she distanced herself a lot. Then we had college. In the past few months we've reconnected again. I don't know how long it'll last, but I do try to look out for her when I can. Taylor's her own person."

He stared at him, watching.

"Is that all?"

"She's changed a lot over the years."

This time Paul threw his head back and laughed. "Taylor's grown up. That's all that's happened, Axton. I take it you like what you saw?"

"You're not claiming that?"

"First of all, Taylor would hate to be referred to as a 'that.' Secondly, she and I don't have that attraction. Never have. Never will."

He was happy with that. "So, what's new in your world then?"

"We're not going to do this now. You and I are not friends. We'll never be friends. We're not even good enough to be enemies. Just tell me what you want and leave."

"Now I'm hurt."

"Cut the bullshit. We're not in high school anymore. I'm not afraid of you."

Tilting his head to the side, he had great respect

for Paul. He could squash the other man like a bug, but he rather liked seeing him succeed. He was a good man, and of course he had his uses.

"She's not attached to anyone?"

"Nope."

"She ever been with anyone at all?" he asked.

"It's like I've turned into her fucking father." Paul leaned forward. "Taylor's never been with anyone long. There's no boyfriend or stalker. She's ... focused on her career right now. She doesn't even go googly-eyed over newborn babies. She has one objective, and that is work."

"You've met some of her past boyfriends?"

"If you call them that. I don't think she's ever had a steady boyfriend. Some of the men I've met were passing interests."

Sitting back, he signaled to the waiter. "I'll have a coffee, black please, and a bagel."

"They don't do bagels here," Paul said.

"They do for me."

"Unbelievable. Now I've got to sit through lunch with you now as well."

"You don't have to sound like that. Some people consider me rather excellent company."

"I'm not most people."

"I know, which is why I have no problems eating with you."

Silence fell between the two.

Something was going on. Axton didn't know what, but he sensed something. A change in the air maybe. He couldn't be sure exactly what it was, but he didn't know if he wanted to hire Taylor or not.

"Are you going to give her a chance?" Paul checked the time, looking bored.

"I'm not sure."

"Well, it's your loss. I've heard what people have been saying about her, and it's a lot of good stuff."

"How close are you two exactly?" he asked.

"Close enough to be having drinks with her later and for her to tell me all about her interview." Paul watched him. "You've got that look that says you don't believe me."

"I don't know. I just think it's strange that Taylor wants to work for me. Don't you find that curious?"

"Why would I find that curious? Last I heard neither of you really knew each other. It's your company she's interested in, and the knowledge you can give her. Nothing more."

The waiter brought over his coffee and bagel. Cream cheese and ham, exactly how he liked it.

What Paul said was very true. He and Taylor didn't have anything in common. They'd rarely spoken in high school. A few of their classes were the same, but that was about it. They were from different backgrounds, different circles, and nothing he could think of would give him cause to believe Taylor was after anything different.

The only problem was he remembered Carla.

He knew his involvement, along with that of his friends.

Keeping her far away from the Four Kings' Empire was important, but now he couldn't let her go, not until he knew for sure if she was innocent or not.

His curiosity was piqued.

****

"Will you chill out?" Taylor asked.

"Chill out? I was having fucking lunch and then he was right there in front of me, Tay. Forgive me for not being okay with that. And you're not twelve anymore. 'Chill out' is so outdated."

She rolled her eyes and watched her friend pace the length of her apartment. It was a nice place, not as big as his, but then they weren't all rich billionaires. She'd made enough money to afford a few luxuries in life, not that it mattered. Her goal had all been the same.

She was one step closer to achieving it. All she needed was that phone call to let her know she had the job, and she'd be another step closer.

Justice was so close she could almost taste it. Patience.

For the last ten years she'd shown great patience. She was still showing it.

"I think you're overreacting. You've said many times before that he comes to that restaurant. You're the one that visits the same place over and over again. He knew you'd be there."

"He's curious about you," Paul said.

"This is what she needs," David said, finally speaking up.

David was an escort she'd found many years ago. He was one of the few people she trusted.

It had taken some time, but she'd finally been able to think of Carla without bursting into tears. That had been an achievement for her. Time really did help heal, even if she still had the nightmares.

Still, it took a lot to get over dragging your dead friend out of a lake.

"Needs? Do you have any idea how powerful those men are?" Paul asked. "If they find out, they could kill her."

"They won't find out," Taylor said.

"How do you know this? You can't stop them from discovering everything about you. He's curious."

"Axton?"

"Yes. And believe me out of all of them, he's the

one you *don't* want to be curious about you. He's the deadliest son of a bitch, and everyone knows it. You're putting your life in danger here."

"He'll never know. Not until it's too late," Taylor said. "You think I'm going to do everything I've done, all that I've trained for, to stop now. I don't care if he finds out the truth because I'm going to be the one to do the same. He can come after me. What will he find? My friendship with you? Newsflash, Paul. We've always been friends. You think he's going to find out about David. Why not? Hey, a girl has needs, and he's an escort. What's the big deal? Women use them all the time. As far as my life is concerned, I'm a healthy, single, free, career-driven woman. I've got nothing to hide." She'd made sure of it as well.

She'd not entered into this plan to fail.

She didn't believe in failure. She wasn't going to start now.

"Taylor's right," David said. "She's been careful. There's no paper trail. It's just us talking. The only way they'll ever know what she's doing is if one of us talks about it. I'm keeping my mouth shut."

"What about you, Paul? You want to go and tell him?" she asked, staring at her friend. Folding her arms beneath her breasts, she waited.

"She wouldn't want you to do this," he said, his voice a whisper.

"Carla."

He flinched.

"I'm doing this to find out the truth."

"We know the truth. She killed herself."

"No, that's the lies. You saw the evidence."

"We didn't really see anything. Her diary is not evidence."

"One of the four kings knocked her up. She then

magically killed herself and the guy who handles cause of death had a lovely lump sum, which was handled by the Four Kings' Empire."

"They didn't run it then," Paul said.

"Their parents did, but I know Carla. She wouldn't have gone sleeping with one of their dads. She was talking about one of them in high school. I know it. I know the parents got overthrown. I don't care if you want me to back down, Paul. I get it. It's dangerous, but there have been times over the past ten years that only the plan and finding out the truth has kept me going. That's what has helped me every single day. You think I don't find it hard? You think even now I don't wonder about her? Remember what it was like when we had a sleepover and she'd be there, smiling. Something happened to her, Paul. I don't care what you think, but I'm going to find out the truth and you're not going to fucking stop me, no matter what."

"I don't want you to get hurt," he said. "Carla wouldn't want anything to happen to you, and neither do I."

She was sure his love for Carla was still as strong as ever. "I'm going to be careful. I won't do anything stupid."

She walked up to him, and he held her close.

"I just can't even begin to think about anything happening to you."

"I'm going to be okay. You know that, right?"

"I know. I know that nothing I say is going to stop you either." He kissed her head. "I better go."

She walked him to her front door and saw him out. Closing it behind her, she leaned against it, blowing out a breath.

"He could be a problem."

"He won't be," she said.

"Be careful with this, Taylor. He's a weak link."

"Not you, too." She moved past him, heading straight to the kitchen. Opening the fridge, she pulled out the bottle of wine she'd started the night before. "You want one?"

"Can I share your bed?"

"You can, but not to fuck."

"And here I thought we were making progress," he said.

"I know that we're never going to be anything more than friends, David. You know I appreciate everything you've ever done for me."

He'd taught her everything she knew.

"You do realize that you're still at risk here? No matter what you say to Paul."

She poured them both a large glass of wine. Handing one to him, she took a sip of her own.

"I know. Paul will worry if I don't try and make it better. You know. He's always been like that. He's not liked what I've got to do for some time."

"And you said he loved Carla?"

"With the way he talks about her and the fact he won't move on, he still does," she said.

"You've done a lot to get to where you are now."

"I know. It has been a long road." Staring down into her glass, she recalled their first lesson.

David had entered her life because she needed someone to teach her everything from seduction to sex. He'd been her teacher in everything, from how to use her body to being confident in herself, and they'd had sex many times.

She still felt uncomfortable about that last part.

He'd taught her everything, showed her it all, and she'd done it time and time again.

"There is a risk as well that you could fall in

love," David said.

This did make her smile. "Okay."

"I'm being serious here."

"I remember the lesson clearly, David. You told me straight men and women are wired differently. How some of the women who work for you struggle to see that they're being used, even after all the years of knowing the lines and stuff. I get it. You still haven't fallen in love?"

"No, I haven't."

She touched her heart. "Ouch."

David had told her to not fall for him. That he wouldn't love her. He loved his company, and that was how it would always be.

Taylor wasn't even brokenhearted about that. They were friends and would always be. They weren't even attracted to each other.

All they had done was get each other off, and David had showed her the moves she'd need in order to accomplish her plan.

She had to get one of the men, if not all of them, on her team.

Up until today, she'd never even experienced physical attraction. Watching Axton, seeing him behind his desk, and knowing what he was capable of, she'd been shocked by her body's response to him.

"What's wrong?" he asked.

"Nothing."

"Going and seeing four men you intend to bring down is not nothing."

She pushed some hair out of her face. "I … I think I was attracted to him."

"To Axton?"

She nodded.

"Makes sense. I've seen pictures. He's a damn

good-looking man."

"I don't want to be."

"Honey, be thankful that you are," David said. "You can stop now though. No one is holding this to you. You don't have to continue."

Carla's dead face flashed before her. "I can't *not* do this. She died alone, David. I've done so much." She closed her eyes, feeling the tears starting to form.

I'm not going to cry.

I'm not going to cry.

"After everything that I've done so far to get us here, I'm not … I can't stop. Not now. Not until I know I've done everything I can."

"This is going to be tough," he said. "You know that. When you start this, you're going to have to handle that attraction I've spoken about. The risks that this will push you in deep. You've got to be ready for that." He reached out, stroking a finger down her hand. "You need to be ready to accept his touch, his attention." David got up and moved behind her. His hands were on her hips as he pressed himself against her. He wasn't hard right now. He'd done this many times though, with arousal. She still found it hard to deal with. "You're going to need to see it through because if you don't, he'll know. With me, you tell me to stop, I back off. You've got to learn to be all in."

She took a deep breath. "I'm ready."

Her cell phone rang, and she frowned. She walked toward her bag and saw a blank number. Accepting the call, she placed it against her ear.

"Hello," she said.

"Miss Keane, I hope you don't mind me calling this late."

"Mr. Farris," she said. "Of course not."

"That him?" David mouthed the words without

making a sound. She nodded her head.

"I've been thinking long and hard, and yes, you've got the job. You start on Monday."

She smiled, rather happy with herself. "That is fantastic news. I'll be there on Monday."

"Let's be clear here, you'll be working for all four of us, me, Easton, Romeo, and Karson. The work is intense, and we demand excellence at every point. Do I make myself clear?"

"Perfectly."

"Then, we're more than happy to have you with us. I look forward to working with you."

Snapping the phone closed, she smiled at David, who looked worried.

"What's wrong?"

"Be careful there, honey, be careful."

Chapter Five

Monday morning

Axton sat at his desk, going through his latest mails, waiting, hoping that he'd have everything in order by the time Taylor arrived. She'd been down in HR, getting her details together, and he tried to pretend that he didn't care. The truth was he cared a hell of a lot. Easton, Karson, and Romeo were all curious about her.

He didn't like it.

Finishing up his last email of the day, he walked toward the doorway of his office just as the elevator doors opened up. Taylor stepped out. Once again, she wore a figure-hugging skirt, crisp white shirt, and a black suit shirt. She looked fantastic. The shoes with the thin straps set off her look to perfection.

His cock twitched inside his pants.

Ignoring his own desires, he walked over to her. "Have you done everything?" he asked.

"Yes. I'm now an employee of Four Kings' Empire. How amazing is that?" She showed him her badge, complete with a picture along with her name and details.

All of his employees had them.

Identification was something he took seriously. Without it, no one was getting into his building. Simple as that.

His father had gotten sloppy with it.

He wouldn't.

"You're happy."

"Of course I'm happy. What's there to be sad about? I can't wait to delve right in. To learn."

He waited to see if something slipped. Her smile was as bright as he remembered it, even with the dimples in her cheeks.

"Would you care for a tour?"

"I'd love one. Louise, the HR woman, she said she'd gladly give me a tour. I know your time is precious. Making money, keeping people in jobs."

"I don't have a problem. It has been a long time since we've seen each other."

She tilted her head to the side. Some of her hair had fallen over her cheek. "So it has. Not that we were ever the kind of people to talk and get to know each other, Mr. Farris."

"Axton."

"You're the boss."

"I am, Taylor."

"Long time no see," Romeo said, walking up to them. "Taylor Keane."

He took her hand, pressing a kiss to the knuckles.

Axton didn't like the urge to beat the shit out of him for touching her. Taylor wasn't his to touch.

"Romeo Delacorte, the charmer," she said.

He used the charm to get what he wanted. Most women fell for it. It had also been a game among the four of them to see how long a woman would last without falling for him. Axton didn't like this.

"I'm taking her on a tour."

"Wow, getting the boss himself to leave his desk."

"From what I heard you're all the bosses. The Four Kings' Empire. You turned this place into a fortress."

"Not us, Axton did. He's got a keen eye on everything. Be warned."

Her gaze moved back to his. "Don't worry, I am armed and ready."

"We better go. We've still got a lot of work to get

through," he said.

"Nice to see you again, Romeo," she said.

Axton took hold of her arm and led her back toward the elevator. She didn't pull away from his touch. Pressing her against the back of the elevator, he clicked the button to take them down to the ground floor.

"I've just come from the ground floor, Axton."

"Yeah, well to succeed in life, you start from the ground and work your way up."

"Did you start at the bottom when your dad ran the company?"

He watched her in the reflection of the metal doors. Her head was once against tilted to the side, and she was watching him.

Old memories flashed quickly in his mind of other times. Ignoring them all, he focused on the challenge at hand. He'd agreed for her to work for him, under him, and that was how it would stay.

"Yes."

"Really?"

"I delivered the mail for all of his workers." He'd been ten years old, and his father had made sure that everyone knew not to give him an easy time. All of his life nothing had ever been easy. He didn't resent his father for that.

He fucking thanked him.

The hard lessons he got as a child were why he was so successful now.

Coming to a stop, he kept on staring at her, not wanting to look away. Ten years it had been since he talked to her in her car.

So much had happened between then and now.

It seemed almost surreal to him to be talking to her now. He wanted to know everything that she'd been through. To understand why she'd not found a man, settled down. She'd always struck him as the kind of woman that would love a family, to be a wife, to love her kids. The kind of mother he used to see in those programs growing up as a kid, baking cookies.

"Are we getting off here?" she said.

Her words made him think of something else.

Instead, he grabbed her arm, leading her out into the mail room.

"You know I can follow. I don't need to constantly be led everywhere," she said.

He looked at where he held her. He liked touching her.

Releasing her, he waited.

"Wow, you do listen."

"You have reason to believe I don't?"

"I remember what I heard in school," she said. "You were all take, and no one told you any differently."

"Not much has changed."

"You still take."

"Always."

"Good to know. So, this is the mail room that you grew up in."

"Yes."

She stepped away from him. "It's huge. I would have loved it down here."

"Why?"

"You know, being alone. I mean, people will probably think it sucks. No windows and it has that dusty smell, but there's not a lot of people here."

"They arrive in an hour."

"They're not here before you?"

"I need my workers to get on with business that is important to them. That's the stuff right in front of them, right now, nothing else."

"Interesting," she said.

"What?"

"I figured you'd be the kind of boss that would demand their employees do everything at once."

"I'm not a bad boss."

"How does one take a company from near ruin and make it what it is today?" she asked.

His paranoia came back tenfold. "How do you know about that?"

"Not long after I left King's Ridge, I heard about the scandal that hit your dad's company. It was a big deal, right? Investments went down the drain. People wanted to pull out. Stocks plummeted."

"You've done your homework?"

"It's business, and of course it's juicy gossip."

"You like gossip?"

"Sometimes. Depends on who it's about. Remember, I've heard some of the bad stuff that's been talked about."

Not long after Carla's suicide, the school had been rife with rumors. Some had even suggested Taylor and Carla had a pact to end their lives together.

It was the kind of shit people said to make themselves more important. He'd nipped all the rumors he heard in the bud. There was no time for shit like that, not on his watch.

"This is pretty awesome." She lifted up some envelopes before placing them down.

"I take loyalty very seriously."

"Okay. As I'm sure most companies do."

"I will not tolerate you going to the competition or trying to sell company secrets or anything."

She held her hands up. "Wow, I really don't know where that came from right now. I have no intention of doing anything like that."

"You'd be surprised what people are willing to do

for money."

Her mouth formed into a perfect O. He couldn't help but imagine his cock sliding deep into her mouth, hearing her moan.

His cock tightened even more. The scent of vanilla was heavy in the air, and he wanted her so much.

"You know what, I'd rather have Louise take me for a tour."

Any lust he felt instantly died. "Wait, what?"

"I will continue to work for you, but there is no way I'm going to be subjected to that. I don't know what kind of women you've been around, but I won't do stuff like that for money. I'm a damn good worker, and you have my references. Is this how you treat all of the people that work here, or is this just personal to me because we grew up in the same town? Wow, I mean, what happened to you? Have you always been this way and I never saw it?" She shook her head. "You know what, forget it. I have never been so insulted in my life. I'm your employee, Mr. Farris. This is not what I signed up for."

He'd pushed her, and now he'd fucked up.

"Taylor." He went to grab her, but she pulled away.

"No. You don't know me. I've been here a matter of hours, and what you knew about me back in high school doesn't count. What you said, that was wrong. I can't even believe you'd think that kind of stuff."

"I'm your boss, Taylor."

"Then start acting like it. I know my place. I don't want to talk to you right now. I just want to get back to Louise and let her handle everything."

He was tempted to stop her, but he watched her as the elevator took her away. He hated watching her walk away. She was right though. He didn't react like this with

Holly after she'd signed her employee agreement. It was all pretty standard stuff. The agreement was signed and understood. With Taylor though, the lines blurred. He wasn't just a boss with her. The past was getting to him, making him react stupidly.

"Well, that was interesting to listen to," Karson said, surprising him.

"What are you doing down here?"

"The best way to learn about someone is to know what they're getting in the mail." Karson shoved his hands into his pockets. "What's the deal with Taylor?"

"I don't know what you mean."

"Your bullshit may work on everyone else, but it doesn't with me. I remember in high school. I knew what you wanted."

"Fuck off, Karson, this is not your concern."

"This is my company as well. My neck is on the line. You don't think I know about what happened ten years ago? What we all know. What we all could have been part of."

He stared at his friend. Between him and Karson, they'd been the ones to make the toughest decisions yet.

"What's the deal with Taylor?" Karson asked again.

"I don't know."

"You clearly have your doubts about why she's working here. So why don't you tell me from the start? You think she's working for the opposition? Our enemies? What?"

"I don't know," he said.

Karson snorted. "She's clearly got a bad temper. Out of all of the candidates, Taylor is the best one, except for that. She knows us, and she's more than qualified. All of her references check out. If you want to fire her, be my guest, but that decision is yours to make."

"You know as well as I that there are a lot of people that would love to see us fail. I'm not going to make any mistakes."

Karson stepped forward. "I forgot how good the scent of vanilla was." He closed his eyes and breathed in deep. "You know this bullshit you've got going on where you make sacrifices, it doesn't make you a better person. Maybe I'll let Taylor know what's she's been missing all these years."

He wrapped his fingers around Karson's neck and pressed him against the wall. "You'll stay away from her."

"Come on, Axton. Don't you want to know how good that pussy will feel wrapped around our dicks? You can take her ass, and I'll fuck her tight little snatch."

He slammed his fist in Karson's face, pushing away.

His friend was laughing at him.

"You see, Axton, when someone makes you want to hit them over saying shit they don't really mean, you've got to acknowledge you have a problem."

"Leave her alone."

"You have to admit, she's turned into a really nice piece of ass."

"Fuck off, Karson."

"Maybe I will fuck her. Tape it and let you see. Romeo, Easton, and I are looking for a bit of action. It would only make sense to fuck her. To give her the real Four Kings treatment."

Axton grabbed Karson and drew his knee up, winding his friend in the process.

Karson didn't fight back, just kept on laughing.

He didn't get his friend's sense of humor. He was pissed off, and he wanted the asshole's blood so badly.

Axton pulled away.

"She must really mean a lot if you're willing to go for blood, Axton."

"Fuck you."

"Nah, I think you'd like that a little too much." Karson winked. "Damn, it has been a long time since you hit like that. This woman has an effect on you."

He watched as his friend got up from where he'd pushed him on the floor. Karson pulled out a handkerchief from his pocket and wiped the blood from his lip.

"Stay away from her."

"You don't think she'll put it all together while she works here? Who you are? What you did?" Karson asked.

Axton had his back on Karson, but now he turned around, looking at his friend.

Karson shrugged. "You've got to understand that you put yourself at risk with this."

"She'll never know anything."

"Why don't you just tell her? Why do you have to keep everything a secret?"

"Because it's for her own safety."

"Our parents stayed together."

Axton smiled. "All of our parents were power-hungry whores, Karson. That's the difference. They all knew what they were getting themselves into at the start. I'm not going to do that. Don't keep lurking in the mailroom. It looks creepy."

"I'll stop working in the mailroom when you admit your feelings and stop sounding like a complete asshole. Are you going to fire her?"

"No."

"Then let's try and stop pretending we're back in high school. Taylor gets to you. She always has, I get it. You got your suspicions, I'll follow your lead. I will always do that. Just keep your head on straight."

"Got it." Axton saluted his friend and stepped onto the elevator. He needed to get back to work.

It was rather interesting.

Over the years he'd pulled together little tests that helped him to determine their true intentions.

He was rather surprised that she'd not passed the test. He didn't expect such a reaction from her, but clearly, she was passionate about it. Not what he remembered from high school.

Before they hired Holly, he'd gone through a lot of women, seeing past the façade they liked to show. When he asked them clearly, they'd tried to seduce him or they would have different reactions. He wasn't interested in hiring a woman that was highly emotional or prone to screwing to get what they wanted. What he tried to find out was how they would react to certain questions. Sometimes he was sure some women truly believed he'd give up his empire's secrets for a bit of pussy. The empire was everything to him.

Just because she'd been insulted with his honesty didn't mean that he was going to let her off the hook easily. Taylor wanted to work for the Four Kings' Empire, then he was more than happy to show her how fucking hard she had to work.

They didn't take laziness here, or work that wasn't up to standard.

Stepping off the elevator at his floor, he saw that her desk was clear. Her bag, which she kept on her at all times, sat by her chair.

Louise would keep her busy for the next hour.

Without an ounce of guilt, he picked up her bag and made his way into his office. Closing the door, he walked toward his desk and opened it up.

A bag was supposed to be sacred for women, at

least that was what propriety told him. Pulling out her purse, he found a small bag, a bottle of water, her lunch, and other few items. He checked through the bag, looking for a camera. To get into the building she had to pass security, but even now, people found ways of getting cameras inside, trying to get into his building to locate shit that he didn't want anyone to know.

Checking through the whole bag, he saw it was just an innocent label knockoff, which was fine. Next, he placed her lunch back inside, followed by her makeup after checking through them.

Opening up her purse, he saw her bank cards, and he pulled them out, seeing there were no credit cards. A picture of her from high school with Carla and Paul caught his attention. All three of them seemed to be in a field of some kind and were smiling up at the camera.

He didn't recognize it, but he didn't like that anger he felt either.

Closing her purse, he put that inside the bag then her cell phone.

She didn't have it password protected.

Turning it on, he checked through her last calls, seeing nothing of any value.

Her messages were next. He saw only two contacts. David and Paul.

Clicking on them, he quickly read through. It seemed she'd deleted her messages prior to this day.

David: **Good luck. Have a lot of fun. Remember, be sexy.** ☺

Paul: **You know what you're doing.**

Tapping his fingers on the desk, he was curious about both messages but saw that his time was running out. With everything back in her bag, he left his office, and placed it back by her chair just as he heard the elevator open up.

Without waiting to see her, he left and found Romeo in his office as he entered.

"You know, rummaging about in a woman's bag is kind of creepy."

"It's necessary. What do you want?"

"Are you going to do this to her every single time she enters the building? Just because you have suspicions?"

"What do you want?" Axton asked. He never liked to repeat himself.

Romeo sighed. "You know, you could actually be causing this shit."

"How do you figure that out?"

"Quite simple, you're not keeping it in the past. What happened back then should stay there. Taylor's been nowhere near us between then and now. You got to learn to let shit go."

Axton laughed. "You remember that last day in school when the parents cleaned out the locker?"

"Vaguely."

"Taylor was doing the same with hers. She stopped what she was doing and walked over to Carla's locker and finished doing what the janitor clearly didn't want to do."

"Your point being?"

"The way she looked at all of us as she walked back to her own locker. That's my point. She knew something or suspected something."

"Maybe Carla told her all about her relationship with Easton."

"And maybe she knew about the baby. Paul can find shit out. It doesn't take a genius to figure out the Four Kings' Empire paid off the guy. There's always a paper trail. Even on internet transactions. Someone will always find out your business."

"For fuck's sake, Axton. You need to go and see someone. You're fucking paranoid. No one can touch us. No one but you. Think about that. We all know you've got files on each and every single one of us. You're the one that holds all the power here, and we're okay with that. So long as that fucking power stays with one person, got it."

There was a knock at the door.

Looking over Romeo's shoulder, he saw Taylor waiting.

"I'm here for the morning debrief. Louise said that to get started, Holly always got her orders from you first."

"We'll talk later."

"Come in," he said. "Close the door."

Taylor closed the door. He saw her hands clasped in front of her, and she bit her lip.

"I'm sorry," she said.

This was not what he expected. "About what?"

"Down in the mailroom. This is your company, and you have a right to protect this place as you see fit. I was … shocked and a little put out by the way you asked, and I shouldn't have flown off the handle like that. I accept if you wish to fire me. It's what you *should* do. I shouldn't have acted that way. We're not in high school anymore, and I do apologize. I accept all responsibility."

He tilted his head, watching her, seeing if there were any signs of false sincerity.

There was none.

To him it appeared she meant every single word.

"I'm not going to fire you, but you're on a warning."

"Thank you," she said.

"Good, let's get to work."

****

For the next week, Taylor didn't even have time to think about what she'd heard or what she'd learned so far. All four men kept her occupied. Between writing letters, setting up meetings, handling clients, getting coffee, fetching lunch, and then going through everything again, from sitting in on telephone conferences and being an actual living computer, making notes on everything. It was all crazy.

Axton was the worst.

No matter how perfect her letter was that she'd typed out, he'd have a red pen at the ready, reading through it and marking through it.

His anger knew no bounds.

He'd even called her stupid and demanded to know where she got her business degree if she couldn't write a simple letter from them. She'd written the letter, but he found fault with it, changing it, marking it. Making her feel like a child, but that was fine. This was his company. He could act like he wanted to.

There was one letter at the start of the week. He'd made her type it out six different times before he finally came out, sat at her desk, and did it himself. Once he was done, he glared at her and told her that was why he ran a company, and she just worked for him.

She'd wanted to fucking slug him.

She'd rather feel this way though, than when she nearly screwed everything up on her first day. Reacting the way she did, she'd expected to get fired, so when he didn't, she was so damn relieved. Ten years of her life down the drain. That wasn't happening. She wasn't going to make *that* mistake again.

When she got home, Paul had been waiting for his regular update, but she'd needed a drink before she could even bring herself to speak.

She was going to turn her into an alcoholic before her mission was complete. She fucking hated Axton. Despised him.

So much so she'd found herself wondering how women were even attracted to him.

Sure, he had all this money, but that didn't make the man, far from it.

Not only that, he was a complete and total fucking asshole!

No amount of money would ever make her ride his fucking dick.

She'd been tempted on many occasions in one week alone to quit. No amount of justice deserved this kind of treatment.

Not only that, she was sick over the fact she'd been attracted to him. No matter what he said, whenever he entered a room, she found herself getting wet, wanting him.

All of her life she'd never wanted anyone.

Sex was just something that happened, not something she particularly wanted.

Karson, Easton, and Romeo were easier to deal with.

The only difference was they made her go out shopping for women they wanted to fuck or had fucked and needed someone to buy a special gift as a parting present. Their asshole ways knew no bounds.

Each night she'd climb into bed and read the last page of Carla's diary before she slept. It helped her to remember why she'd done what she'd done. All the years of hard work, of the training, of the teaching. It had come to this moment, and there was no way she was backing down.

She'd heard the argument between Romeo and Axton.

He had all the files that kept them all in place.

Taylor didn't understand why the men worked for such a fucking prick. There was no reason for it.

Standing at the copying machine, she placed the sheet on top of the glass plate and put the lid down. Typing in what she needed, she waited.

"You're here early," Easton said.

She turned to see him leaning against the door. It was seven in the morning, and in order to actually get much work done, she always arrived early. If Axton's car was in the parking lot when she did, she was always tempted to turn around and not come back.

"I've got lots to do, so I figured I'd get started early."

"Axton would say that you're not getting paid overtime. That you have more hours in the day to complete your tasks."

"What would you say?"

"That you can do whatever the hell you like."

"Awesome," she said, the sarcasm dripping from her voice. Keeping her back to him, she finished her copying and gathered the papers up.

"You're doing well."

"Why do you guys put up with him?" she asked. "I'm curious. You guys are supposed to be friends, but half the time you look like you want to murder him."

"We *are* friends. Make no mistake about that. We've all got … problems. Axton more than many. Being the boss, his father before him, there has to be a leader, otherwise you'd have chaos, and a business doesn't thrive in that environment."

"So you all bow down to him." She saw the flare in his eyes.

"We don't bow down to him."

"It's okay. We all know what it's like to have a

friend that seems to take something with them," Taylor said. "For me it was Carla."

She knew she'd have to talk about Carla to be able to do what she set out. Speaking her name in front of him though, she watched him wince, and that made her curious.

"I am sorry about what happened all those years ago. It would be fucking awful if I had to do something like that. I never saw Axton move so fast."

This made her frown. "Move so fast?"

What were they talking about?

"We all heard your scream. I don't know what was going on, but then you were in the water. Didn't you hear your name being shouted?"

"I can't remember."

"Axton was at the lake, walking in, coming to get you on your way back. You were struggling with her … body. You were freaking out. He was the one that got you and her out of the water. Don't you remember?"

"I … don't." The night was still hazy to her. "I … you were all standing waiting to talk to the police. I don't remember much else."

"He's the one that pulled you off," Easton said. "That stopped you from trying to revive her."

She recalled strong arms holding her back, maybe even lips at the back of her head. She didn't remember the whole of it, but those moments she did. "I had no idea."

"My point is, at times he may not seem like a good friend, but he's always got our backs, no matter what." Easton touched her arm, clearly trying to offer comfort. Right now, she wasn't feeling anything. "Hang in there. You're doing well."

She watched him walk away, more curious now than ever about Axton's deal.

Why had Easton flinched?

What did Axton have?

Would there be information back at home in his old house?

Where were all of their fathers?

They'd overthrown them when the scandal had broken out and had been proven to be incompetent.

People like that didn't back down without a fight.

There was more to this.

She had to know more.

Pulling out her cell phone, she sent a quick message to Paul.

Taylor: **Find the original four fathers.**

The moment it was sent, she deleted her message.

She wouldn't put it past Axton to search her bag again. It had been taken, she'd known it had. The bag had been by her chair, closed.

When she came back to her desk, her bag was by her chair, wide open.

Taylor didn't know if he'd done that on purpose so she could start throwing accusations around or not.

Paul had told her to tread carefully.

They first needed Holly to step out of the way. It just so happened that the Four Kings' Empire's previous PA had a knack for writing code. Paul had picked it up and offered a huge amount of money that meant Holly didn't need to work outside the home anymore and could stay home with her child. On paper, no one could be suspicious. It was pure luck for Taylor that with Holly's ability, it helped to open up the job she needed. She didn't have any personal contact with Holly, and to anyone who looked closely it was pure coincidence. Paul had been trying to convince Taylor to stop all of this nonsense and move on. She couldn't do it.

Placing her cell phone in her pocket, she walked

to Axton's office and knocked. There was no answer.

Taking a deep breath, heart pounding, she opened up his door and stepped inside. The morning sun filtered through the windows on the far wall of his office. The artwork he kept was boring, something that had clearly been picked out by a designer that had no relevance to the man who worked here.

Along one wall was a bunch of old business books. That side of the room looked more like a lawyer's office than a businessman's. In the past week, she'd come to see that Axton wasn't like most men.

He didn't have any personal tokens here, no achievements, no pictures, nothing. It was like the office was void of who he really was.

Stepping up to his desk, she saw it was neatly set out.

Three pens on one side of the desk, his laptop closed, waiting to be opened. The Four Kings' Empire letterhead notepad on his desk, waiting for whatever he wanted.

Sitting behind his desk, she glanced up at the door.

He could come in at any minute, catch her.

Placing the letters down on the desk, she tried the top drawer, and found it locked. The second was also locked on either side. The third, however, wasn't.

Sliding it open, she saw a stack of files. She picked up the one on top and found her name. There were pictures inside. Ones of her with Paul and David. Others of her shopping. Even some of her at her apartment room window, closing her curtains.

What made her go cold was the night of the interview.

There was one that showed Paul. He looked furious.

Axton was following her, or someone was. She didn't imagine for a second that he would follow her.

Snapping the file closed, she saw easily a dozen more.

She'd put her file inside when she heard the click of his door. Dropping the files, she slid the drawers closed and sat back in his chair. She'd discovered that none of the four kings had cameras inside their offices. She'd overheard Axton talking with one of the guys from security. They'd been advised to install cameras within the offices but Axton had said no. The building had been previously run by their parents. They had security cameras everywhere else but not in their offices, which made her wonder what exactly went down.

The moment he entered the room, she saw his anger.

The rage.

She was sitting in his chair.

"What the fuck do you think you're doing?" he asked.

"I was at the copying machine." She placed her hands on the desk, hoping he didn't see her nerves.

The bastard had gotten someone to follow her. Now she was going to have to try to act naturally so he didn't suspect anything.

"What you're doing is dangerous."

Yeah, she was starting to get Paul's warning.

No matter how dangerous, she wasn't stopping. She'd come this far, and if she didn't find what she was looking for and bring these men down for good, everything she'd done had been for nothing.

Her life wasn't going to be one long waste.

She intended to get justice, no matter what.

"Tell me what you're doing in my office, sitting behind my desk."

"A little over a week ago, you told me that everyone had a price. Since then you've worked me hard, and I accept that. You're not the best at what you do without a little hard work. Anyway, as I was at the copy machine." She held up his letters. "Which are here, I decided to leave them on your desk."

"You're going to tell me what changed your mind between then and now, and why you're sitting on my property." He stepped inside the room, and she watched him flick the lock in place.

That shouldn't arouse her.

Seeing him glaring at her, like he wanted to kill her, shouldn't turn her on. He could snap her in half, and he had enough wealth and power at his disposal to make sure no one could find her.

Still, as he walked to the desk, slowly, with purpose, she felt her tits harden. Moisture flooded between her thighs, and in that moment, she wanted him more than anything else.

"I suggest you give me a good reason before I call security and have you tossed out of here faster than you came."

He stood at the desk, and she gasped as he reached out. His hands grabbed the side of her, his thumb resting beneath her chin.

He pulled, and she stood out of his chair. He leaned against his desk, his legs wide open, and he held her close. They weren't touching, apart from the hand holding her hair and neck. His touch was rough. He could easily strangle the life out of her.

Easton's words kept running through her mind.

Axton had been the one to pull her out of the water.

That night, he'd been the one to help her.

Someone had, she just hadn't known who.

"You're an asshole," she said. "A big, giant asshole, and I've hated every second of working for you this week. After the copy machine, I sat behind your desk, and I realized you have to be. You have to be this way because there are people out there who'd take this from you. This is your entire life. Your hard work. You don't want to see it fail. Sitting in your chair, I appreciated everything you do because you're teaching me. You're showing me how to be a hard worker. How to be better. That's why I was sitting in your chair."

Her heart pounded.

For several seconds, maybe even minutes, he didn't say a thing.

Not a word. There were no sounds in his office.

She wondered if he heard the thumping of her heart against her breast.

His gaze moved from her eyes, down to her lips, then her neck. His thumb stroked over her pulse. His grip seemed to tighten for a split second, and he pulled her in so that his breath fanned across her face. Still not touching.

He was the one in control, not her.

"Be careful whose chair you sit in. You may not like what you find out."

He released her so gently, she wasn't even sure he'd been rough in the first place.

Axton picked up the files, flicking through them. "This everything I need?" he asked.

"Yes."

"Good. You may leave."

She stepped away, her legs like jelly.

Biting her lip, she closed her eyes and stopped the action.

Turning back to face him, she waited. "You've been checking through them with that red pen. I'm waiting for you to do it again."

"You want me to mark your work? I've been an asshole all this time. I wondered how far you could go."

She smiled. "I guess I don't have a lot of limits."

Now it sounded sexual.

From the look on Axton's face, he recognized it too.

"I'd be careful who you tell that. There are a lot of bastards out there who'd be willing to take a chance and show you how good it is to not have limits."

"I like to live dangerously. No one is going to save me. I've learned to bite back." He continued to watch her. "I better get back to work."

She didn't wait this time.

Unlocking his door, she stepped out.

She went to her desk and paused. There on her desk was a single white box. Sitting down at her desk, she looked over the box, not really sure who would leave her a gift.

Seeing a card slid beneath the ribbon, she turned it over.

Every lady should have designer.

Opening the ribbon, she lifted the lid, and inside was a designer bag. An exact one like the tan one she'd bought at the market the other month. The instant she saw it, she'd wanted it. Hadn't cared about labels or designer. She'd made a comfortable life for herself. Designer labels weren't part of it.

A nice apartment, food, bills paid, and a good, working car was what she spent her money on. Bags were something that she needed, not necessarily wanted.

Still, it was nice.

Looking up, she saw Axton at the door, watching her. His dark brown gaze was on her once again.

He didn't say anything, but he left the door open

this time.

You're getting in way above your head.

It had only been a week, but she was learning all kinds of things. Stuff that she didn't think was possible. Most of them had to do with the fact the Four Kings' Empire was indeed a force to be reckoned with. From what she'd seen, they worked within an ethic. Their takeover bids were legal and above board. There were no signs of manipulation or blackmail. She actually enjoyed working for them. The work was hard and never-ending. Axton was a force all on his own. She couldn't help but admire his tenacity for his company.

Licking her dry lips, she put the lid back on the box and slid it inside her drawer. She'd take it home and use it tomorrow.

Taylor had never been one to turn down a gift, and she wasn't about to start now.

Seeing several letters in her tray, she picked them up.

Starting up her machine, as it had fallen asleep, she quickly read through the files, seeing nothing of any importance. One from Romeo, one from Easton, the other from Karson.

Business letters.

Contracts.

Deals.

Even rejection letters.

Women actually asked them for dates via email.

It was all just crazy.

This world she was part of was crazy.

Pushing some hair off her face, she quickly escaped to the bathroom, needing to cool down.

Those few moments spent with Axton had fired her up inside.

Stepping up to the sink, she ran the cold water

over her hands, fingers, wrists, before pressing them to her neck. Taking a deep breath, she closed her eyes.

Flashes of the past came to her mind.

She couldn't stop it.

This was her life.

Opening her eyes, she stared at her reflection in the mirror.

Releasing a breath, she felt her eyes well up. In her mind she saw two people. The reflection of what she'd become and the girl ten years ago who had stood looking at herself. Her bag hiked up over her shoulder, hair in a ponytail, no makeup, happy. This woman, she looked … scared.

This is what you needed to do.
Don't forget why you're here.
You have to bring justice for her.

She chanted her mission in her head, refusing to speak the words aloud. No one could know. David and Paul were the only ones that knew.

No one else was allowed to know why she was here.

No matter that Axton pulled her out of the lake.

Or held her when the paramedics arrived.

Nor the fact he'd been there when she'd been about to drive away.

What she wanted hadn't changed.

She was going to bring them down once and for all.

Chapter Six

Ten years ago
"No! Carla! No!"

Axton heard the sound of Taylor's scream. He'd heard her voice enough times to know exactly what she sounded like.

He turned toward where he last saw her, near the lake, looking through her cell phone. He guessed she'd been waiting for her friend. Carla was set to arrive, and he knew for a fact that Easton was nervous. Carla wanted to tell Taylor the truth.

The last thing he wanted was for her to know what Easton was going to do. How he'd been fucking her for a bit of fun. To piss his father off, and to show him what a bad boy he was. His friend was fucked-up in the head. Where Axton went after the power, Easton liked getting his small victories. Easton didn't see the bigger picture.

Axton did.

"What the fuck is that?" Karson asked.

Taylor broke through the thin sheet of ice. The water must be fucking freezing cold. She didn't stop though, and he watched as she grabbed whatever was floating in the water. She kept screaming Carla's name, and he ran to the edge of the lake as she started to swim to the shore.

Breaking through the water, he felt how cold it was, going into his jeans and soaking his skin.

Taylor struggled, and he reached out, pulling her against him, helping them both. Carla was dead.

He knew that instantly. Her body was so heavy and so cold.

There was no way she'd survive that.

Taylor didn't even stop as he helped her out of the water. She knelt over Carla's still body and started CPR.

She wasn't stopping.

Calling Carla's name.

Telling her it would be okay.

Looking up, Axton saw Easton.

His friend was pale white.

This resolved his problem.

One dead baby momma and Easton's reputation would remain intact.

What he saw in Easton's eyes shocked him.

He was in pain.

Easton was in a lot of pain.

He'd not wanted Carla to die.

What did he think would happen?

The paramedics arrived, and still Taylor wouldn't move. She kept trying to revive her.

Removing his jacket, he wrapped it around her, and pulled her off, giving them room to do what needed to be done.

They knew what had happened.

That she wasn't going to make it.

Carla was dead before she'd even hit the water.

Whoever had left her had clearly been in a hurry to dump her.

Taylor was sobbing in his arms.

He held her, hoping that he could take the pain away.

Nothing would ever be the same, and in that moment, he knew, if Taylor ever found out the truth, she'd be his worst enemy.

****

Present day

Axton was typing away at his latest email when

his door slammed open.

"You piece of shit," Catherine Riley said.

It had taken her a week to realize that her tactics wouldn't work on them.

"I'm so sorry. She wouldn't stop," Taylor said. "I got a call from reception. She tried to stop her, but—"

"I will not be stopped. You think I don't know what you do, Axton. You think I don't get how women are lured into your trap. To be part of the four kings and that's how you bring them down."

Easton, Romeo, and Karson arrived.

Taylor stood in his office, and he watched her nibble her lip. She'd done that so often in high school that for a split second he was drawn to the action. So unsure, so nervous, so worried. Was she concerned for him? For herself? Why would she be worried about herself?

She had yet to pass another test.

"You thought you could blackmail us into giving you what you wanted. You wished to have one of us fall for you so that you could sell our secrets to the highest bidder. The contract we have with Skye Adams doesn't include you, and we've invested in her modeling company, and she doesn't wish to work with you or be associated with you. She warned us about what you planned, Catherine, and that is not going to happen."

Skye Adams owned the agency that kept models on their books. She'd been working for a long time to get their investment. Part of the companies were in beauty products. It was a no-brainer to negotiate a contract for models to advertise their products. The Four Kings' Empire had many different companies and crossed into a variety of organizations. The strength of their company was what made them unstoppable. So when the contracts had been close to being signed, Skye made him aware of

Catherine's ulterior motive, as she'd discovered the truth herself and was firing her.

"You think I don't know how your business got this far, Farris? I know. I know that you build this shit up on blackmail. Dangling little bones in front of people, waiting for them to take it like the loyal little dogs they are."

Axton raised a brow.

"You cost me my job. Do you know that?"

"Your boss didn't want to have a slut working for her. A slut that was willing to sell her body at any cost." He typed a few words into his laptop and brought up the footage. There in all of her glory. The night at the club. Easton deep inside her ass, her being butt-fucked and loving every second of it.

Catherine's grunts and begs filled the room.

Her face went livid. "I will fucking end you for this. How dare you mess with me."

"If you think for a second of coming after me, go ahead. You never know whose hands this might fall into, Riley. You decided to come after me. Thought you could blackmail me. I will always win. Do you understand that?" Security was just behind her. "Take her and the next time she gets past you, you'll both be out of a job."

"No, you cannot do this." She turned and glared at Taylor. "You think working for him is the answer. He'll find shit on you. Hold it over your head. It's what he does. He takes lives. Fucks them, screws them up. We're all just pawns in his game. Whatever secrets you're hiding, he'll find them."

Taylor stopped biting her lip, and before his eyes, he saw the confident woman in her place. The old Taylor was gone.

Catherine kept screaming profanity about how he used people. How he had dirty secrets on everyone. He listened as she fell apart, all the while keeping an eye on Taylor. He'd seen the worry in her eyes when Catherine started to rant. Taylor was hiding something, but what? He'd find out what it was.

He didn't have much of a choice.

"Well, that was pretty intense," Easton said.

"An interesting way to finish up that dealing, I tell you," Karson said.

"I'm so sorry. She just barged past the desk, and I couldn't stop her," Taylor said. "She clearly had something to say."

"That she did," Romeo said. "Now that the excitement is gone, so am I."

One by one, they left, leaving just him and Taylor.

"Are you okay?" she asked, once they were alone.

"Yeah. She's not the first woman to spew her hatred, and I doubt she'll be the last."

"You don't trust anyone."

He shrugged, placing his laptop down on the table. "Not a lot of people to trust in this world. They're all after what they can get."

"Not all people are like that."

"I've yet to meet anyone who can change my mind."

She held her hands up in surrender. "I better get back to work."

He didn't stop her as she left. Instead, he stood and watched the sway of her ass. The skirt hugged her hips and butt like a second skin. He wanted to run his hands all over it to feel her beneath him, to drive his cock so deep inside her that she couldn't even remember her own name.

With a raging hard-on, he went back to work.

The rest of the day went by without much event. There were repercussions from Catherine's outburst. He was contacted by three different papers about the stories she wanted to sell. He pushed some money their way and let them know exactly how dangerous the woman was. Catherine wouldn't be able to come after them.

By the end of the day, he was ready to head home, but he also had one more stop to make. King's Ridge.

There was a knock at the door, and he looked up to see Karson there.

"What's up?"

"We're heading to the club. Easton's in the mood to party."

"Whenever we've had business like Catherine he always wants to party."

Karson glanced behind him and stepped into the office, closing the door. "I think this has to do with Taylor."

"What about her?"

"Seeing her, he's remembering Carla."

He clenched his teeth together. "Do you think we've got a problem here?"

"I don't know, but if he doesn't lose that tension, he tends to do something stupid."

"I don't have time for stupid. None of us do."

"Why don't you come along? It'll be good for all of us. You included."

"I have no desire to lose myself in some wasted pussy."

"Is that because the one you want is right outside this door?"

Axton glared at him.

Karson held his hands up. "I'm just speaking the truth. You can't keep bottling this shit up. It'll cause you more trouble."

"Why don't you let me worry about the running of this company and bottling shit up while you handle Easton?"

"He doesn't need to be handled."

"I don't need him spilling shit. Not now. We cannot afford a scandal, do you understand me?"

"What happened to you, man?"

"What do you mean?"

"You cut us off. All of us. We used to be a team, and lately you're acting like you're the only one that gets to make these decisions."

"Someone has to take the lead."

"We're all in this together. You can keep being the asshole or not. One way or another, we're not going to split. You'll always have us."

He watched Karson leave. The door remained open, and he caught sight of Taylor. She was shutting down her computer, her jacket and bag already on. She leaned over the desk to move something. Her shirt and jacket fell open, revealing her cleavage. His cock hardened once again.

Whatever happened, he'd need to find a woman soon otherwise he was going to fucking lose it. Just watching Taylor bend over, or twist this way, just staring at her seemed to turn him on.

He wasn't some punk-ass boy.

He was a full-grown man.

He shouldn't be losing it at the sight of a woman.

She looked up as Easton, Romeo, and Karson passed. He saw her say goodbye to them before looking back at the computer.

The next test had already been sent to her. When she got home this evening, it should be waiting for her.

His friends thought he was insane for doing these

tests, but they weren't designed for playing around. He needed to know the loyalty of the men and women around him, especially those that were close.

Leaving his office, he closed and locked the door.

Even though she had a reasonable explanation and he'd loved every second of holding her, of seeing her eyes dilate, and her nipples tighten, he still didn't trust her.

"You're leaving early," she said.

"I've got shit to do." He stopped at her desk. She'd plugged some earphones into her phone, and he saw a song playing but didn't catch the title or artist. "Your work has improved."

She chuckled. "I thought you'd go at me with your red markers again. You know, crossing everything out. Like a teacher."

"I expect excellence."

"I accept that," she said.

"I was being a dick."

"That's what you said, not me. Besides, there were errors to be found. It's perfectly acceptable for you to pull me up on it."

"Come on, I was being a dick, you know I was."

She groaned. "I've been in this job a couple of weeks now. Please, don't try and tempt me to put my foot in it. I rather like working here."

"It's a great place to be."

"You've really made this something. I can see why you're the best at what you do. You're also looking into apprenticeships as well, right?"

"I am," he said. It was common knowledge. He'd been approached by several schools who'd asked if he was interested in funding students who not only showed the most promise but also willing to extend into allowing them to work from the ground up.

After a long talk and debate with his partners, they'd all agreed to do it.

"I think that's pretty good."

"Did you have an apprenticeship?" he asked.

"I'm sure you're not interested in learning about me."

"I am."

"Oh, well, yes, I did. It helped me a lot. I've worked for companies that were a lot smaller but still competitive and rather cutthroat. It has been a lot to learn."

"Did you always want to be in business?"

She shook her head. "Am I being interrogated?"

"Sorry. I just … we don't really know each other. I feel we should."

"There's not much to know about me," she said.

He gazed down her body. "I think there's plenty."

She took a deep breath, letting out a little laugh. "Well, I better get going."

"You're not going to tell me anything? Something new?"

She blew out a breath, and he saw her thinking. "I don't like peas."

"I meant something I didn't know."

"You knew I don't like peas?"

"I knew."

"How?"

"I have my ways."

"And that is not creepy at all. Goodnight, Axton."

He watched her go.

Pulling out his cell phone, he brought up the security feed within the building and stared at her in the elevator. What was it that made him doubt her?

Was he just being paranoid?

Other than sitting behind his desk that day—and

he was sure she'd gone through his files as well—he didn't have anything.

Nothing on her.

He just suspected everything.

She left the elevator as it got to the ground floor. He waited in his spot as she climbed behind the wheel and took off out of the building. Nothing happened that would give him cause to doubt, and yet, here he stood, doubting, once again.

She knows something.

He'd find out.

No doubt about it.

People always made a mistake, and he was a master at finding out what their secrets are.

Pocketing his cell phone, he made his way to his own car. He drove the same car now as he did when he'd been eighteen years old. He could afford something new, a better model, but he was a little old-fashioned. He didn't wish to part with this car. It was his baby and had gotten him through a great deal.

Driving out of the city, he kept to the main road, heading toward King's Ridge. The drive was a long one, but he didn't mind it. He certainly wouldn't call ahead to alert the old fucker to what was going on.

Putting on the radio, he listened to the music and the incessant chatter of people going back and forth. All boring bullshit. All of it life that he had no desire to know about.

He took a quick stop for a piss and a cup of coffee, heading on the road for the last couple of hours.

Arriving in King's Ridge, passing the parking lot that headed out to the lake, he stopped, did a quick turn, and pulled back up.

He stopped his car, climbed out, and walked the short distance toward where the campfires used to take place.

The last he heard the town didn't allow any of the student bonfires anymore. They'd been deemed too dangerous and so had been stopped. The town had to be seen for helping their children.

The fire had nothing to do with Carla.

"Carla, what did you do? Come on, Carla."

Taking a deep breath, he looked out to the lake. "I'm sorry."

Clenching his hands into fists, he knew it was all pointless. Shaking his head, he walked away from the lake. That was the first day he'd been back to the lake since that night. He'd never gone there again.

Once he was in his car, he didn't make any unnecessary stops and arrived at home. It was no surprise to him that his mother's car wasn't in the driveway. After the scandal had broken, his father suffered a heart attack and so had no choice but to have 'round the clock care. Since he'd been that way, with a nurse attending to all of his needs, Axton had seen a marked improvement in his mother. She stopped drinking, stopped the drugs, and now did a great deal of charity work at the school.

Entering his home, he went straight to the old man's office, which had been converted into a bedroom.

Leaning against the doorway, he saw the nurse trying to feed him, but his father wasn't having any of it.

"Fuck off. I can feed myself."

"I've been told that you throw it away, Mr. Farris, please," the nurse said.

"I'll deal with it," Axton said.

His father glared. "You get the fuck out. Get out."

"He has these episodes of anger. I know it's tough. Go and have a break. I'll deal with this."

The nurse looked at him like he was saint or something. Waiting for her to leave, he closed the door and turned to face his father.

"Come to see how long I've got until I die?" Benjamin asked.

"Not long, I imagine. Not if you keep treating the nurses like shit. I'd smother you with a pillow, say you suffocated."

"You took everything from me, boy," he said. "You've got some nerve coming around here."

Axton snorted. "Please, deep down inside you're proud. I did to you what you did to Grandpa. You outgrew him. I did the same with you."

"You think you're ready for everything the Four Kings' Empire is."

"I took what you made, and now it's three times the company you had."

"But is it as good?"

Axton sat in the chair opposite, resting his head on his hand and staring at his father. "Tell me what happened the day of the bonfire ten years ago."

Benjamin burst out laughing.

"This is priceless. You're coming to pester me about a time so long ago."

"She was pregnant," Axton said.

"Ah, yes, pregnant. Trash as well. Her parents were not worth being mixed with the Longs. You know what happened on that night so long ago. Why the sudden interest?"

"No concern of yours."

"You know, Axton, this power play that you're going through, it's not going to last."

"It's not?"

"You see, the kind of power you have, you don't know how to deal with it. You're just a boy."

Axton got to his feet, grabbing one of the needles that was on the tray that the nurse left near the bed. "You didn't see it coming, did you? The takeover, the scandal. All these years you've been pissed about what I did. You don't even realize I'd been planning it for a long time. Longer than that night. Killing Carla Smith didn't set off your downfall, Dad. Your downfall began the day you threatened me."

With that, he plunged the needle into Benjamin's skin and watched as his father slowly fell asleep.

****

"Everything is going fine, Paul. You really need to stop worrying," Taylor said. "You've not heard anything from him since that day. Please, stop."

"I care about you, Taylor. I think this has gone too far for all of us." She heard him typing away. "I mean … we don't know for sure they were involved. This scandal regarding the fathers, I mean, if you look at it, it's just too much for words. Extortion, blackmail all that stuff."

"Will you do me a favor?" she asked.

"Along with the list of stuff you want to know?"

"A woman came into work today. Catherine Riley, I believe her name was. I'd like you to find out everything we need to know about her."

"Why?"

"Because of some of the stuff she said, and Axton was pissed about her."

"This is the same woman you said was caught with a dick up her ass?"

"Not just any dick. Easton's."

"I don't like this, Taylor. They're a big company. Axton, all of them, they know what they're doing."

"I know. I'm going to be careful. Please, just find out everything you can."

"On it. I better go."

He hung up before she could even say anything

else. Rolling her eyes, she dropped her cell phone to the bed, picking up the envelope that had been waiting for her. Inside was a USB key.

No note.

No way of knowing where it came from.

Just a key.

This had to be one of their tests.

Tests to prove loyalty to the company, to him.

She wasn't loyal to Axton.

She wasn't loyal to the Four Kings' Empire.

Her plan was to bring them down to the ground.

Sliding the key into her laptop, she waited.

Sure enough, there were files, some of them letters, and some were clearly fake.

Scrolling through the details, she knew without a doubt that one of the four had given this to her.

Clicking through all the details, she made a note of the companies she recognized, the details that concerned her. She couldn't copy or paste any of the information. She didn't know how thorough Axton was with his little tests.

Once she'd spent an hour going through the key, she disconnected it and pulled it out. She'd let them all know she didn't take kindly to this kind of shit. No, she couldn't do that at all. She had to remember to keep her cool, and that *didn't* mean losing her temper. She could do that without them knowing.

Leaning back in her bed, she pulled out the diary that after ten years showed significant signs of wear and tear. She'd tried to keep it in the best possible condition. This was all she had left of Carla before she'd gone.

Opening the book, she stared at the picture of the three of them together. Her, Carla, and Paul. The heading read "Big Plans for Our Future."

Tears filled her eyes, recalling the day it was

taken. There had been a career day at school. After spending all morning listening to people talk about their work, doing tests to see where they'd be most suited and just doing all the boring stuff, they'd decided to finish the day having a bit of a picnic, laughing, joking, teasing.

So long ago and yet not long enough.

Rubbing at her chest, she put it aside and flicked open the first page.

Dear diary, or imaginary person reading my diary,

Taylor totally got another rose and love letter in her locker today. It was such a cute note. Each one telling her that she's beautiful and if they could, they'd tell her to her face every single day. I know she's not sending them. Taylor wouldn't have the time nor would have that big of an ego to send herself shit. I don't even know if she likes them. When I see her, her face lights up like it's Christmas or something. Then when I talk about it, she's like, it doesn't matter.

How can it not matter? Someone cares enough to send her a rose and love letters. I think that's sweet.

In other news, I talked to him again today. We had to do it in secret, and he knows my number now. He's always texting. It doesn't matter what time of day or night, and each time I see his number, I can help but feel so fucking happy. He's so amazing. Of course, we have to keep everything secret. It always has to be secret. I hate that. It's like he's ashamed of me. He says not. If Taylor was to know, she'd tell me to cut him out. I don't know. Anyway, I hear Mom calling that dinner's ready. Bye.

Carla always kept her diaries. Each year she had a new one. Her parents still had the old ones, and Taylor had even taken the time to read through them all. It was this last diary that had the pregnancy, one of the four kings, and other little details.

The final moments before her death.

Putting the book down, Taylor stared up at the ceiling.

Closing her eyes, she slowly drifted off to sleep.

The sound of banging made her jump though. Rolling over, she saw it was a little after three in the morning.

The banging was getting louder, and she frowned. Climbing out of bed, she rushed through her apartment, freaking out.

Walking to the door, she jumped back as the banging started up again. Pressing her hands to the door, she saw Axton through the peephole. Rubbing the back of her head, she quickly ran back to her room and placed the diary in her closet out of the way before rushing back.

She opened the door, and he looked fucking pissed.

"What took you so long?" Axton asked, storming into the room.

"Hello, this is my apartment, and it's, like, three in the morning. What the hell?"

He grabbed her around the throat and pinned her up against the wall, shocking her with the sudden change inside him. He wasn't holding her too tightly, but the threat was there.

"What the fuck are you doing working for me?" he asked.

"I've told you, Axton. I'm there because I want to learn."

"Bullshit. I know you've got a reason. I will find out why, but it will end better for you if you tell me now and cut out all the crap." He stepped up close. "Or do you think you can take me on, is that it?"

"Paranoid much?"

"Tell me."

"What happened to you?" she asked. "This is my apartment, and you're here threatening me."

She held onto his wrist and arm, not that it would stop him from hurting her if he so wished. She felt the strength inside him.

Axton was the one in control right now.

He could hurt her.

"I want to know the truth. You think I don't know what is going on here? How you magically turn up when I need a PA."

"You didn't have to hire me." Deception wasn't something she was good at. In fact, she sucked. David had warned her trying to lie her way out of shit would only make things worse for herself. She didn't want to make things worse. It's why she'd decided to be herself, Just a more confident and sure version of herself. "You were the one that said yes to me. I don't know who you're talking about or what is going on here, but you've got to let me go."

He glared at her, his gaze moving once again down her body.

Her nipples tightened at that look.

The tension in the air changed. He stepped right up close to her, his body against hers, letting her know exactly how much he liked it.

"I *will* find out the truth."

"There is nothing to find out," she said, trying her best to lie. Staring at him, she remembered what Easton had told her. "Why did you help me out of the lake?"

He jerked back, his hand releasing her neck.

She didn't touch where he had, but she wanted to.

"I don't know what you're talking about."

"Easton told me what happened. What you did."

"You shouldn't be talking to him."

"Why not?"

"He's not the most stable guy. He'll say anything to get into your pants."

She laughed. "Then why was he talking about you and not himself? He wants in my pants, he's got to be the one doing all the stuff. Wooing me?"

"Don't overthink shit, and if I were you, I'd forget about what happened tonight."

"You can wait right there."

She stormed away from him, grabbing the USB key. The shorts she wore were small and with the way he'd been touching her, were riding right up her ass, making it uncomfortable to move.

Slamming the key against his chest, she glared at him. "I will say it over and over again if I have to. I don't take kindly to being manipulated. I'm there because I want the job."

He took the key from her.

"You can leave now."

She wasn't about to stop him.

He took the key and, without a word, left her apartment. Leaning up against the door, she felt her heart pounding. Her body was on fire.

Whenever he touched her, she went up in flames.

This was the complete opposite of her feelings for David. When he touched her, she'd cringed at first. It had taken so long for her to get used to him touching her.

Placing a hand around her neck, she touched where Axton's fingers had been. He could have dug his fingers in, but he didn't. He'd slammed her against the wall, but rather than be angry with him, she'd liked it.

Slowly, she ran her hand down her body, cupping one of her tits.

Opening her eyes, she realized there was a

camera in the apartment. A man or a woman watching her. If she stopped now, covered herself, he'd know. Axton would know that she did.

She was so close to winning their trust.

Easton, Romeo, and Karson seemed to trust her. They were happy with talking about anything.

Axton was proving to be the most difficult.

Closing her eyes, she ignored the possible camera watching her and everything else. Cupping her tit, she pinched the nipple, feeling the ache deep in her pussy.

Slick.

Wet.

Dripping.

Ready for a nice fat cock.

Not just anyone's.

Axton's.

She'd felt it for a few seconds as he pressed his body against hers. The pleasure had consumed her. She'd not wanted him to stop.

To keep on taking.

What would it feel like to be held captive beneath his touch?

Would Axton take what he wanted, or ask?

She didn't want him to ask.

No, she'd love for him to take.

Pulling her shirt down, she exposed her tits, ignoring that nagging feeling that someone was watching.

Let them.

Let them watch.

Let them show Axton what she did when he left her alone.

She let go of her tits, moving down to slide a hand beneath her low shorts. She now had one hand on her tit and another in her shorts. Finding her wet slit, she plunged a finger down, touching her cunt.

Wriggling out of her shorts, she spread her legs, still leaning against the door, playing with her pussy.

Her apprehension disappeared at the thought of Axton discovering what she was doing. He kept looking at her like he wanted to fuck her.

She couldn't deny her own feelings anymore either.

She wanted him.

Her body was ready for him.

Plunging two fingers inside her, she rubbed her thumb against her clit. Keeping her eyes closed, she imagined him here, holding her, spreading her wide as he took her. She'd be nothing more than a hole for him to take, to fuck, to use.

He'd make her dirty and fuck her so hard because that was what he liked.

There would be no pretending with him.

Just accepting, experimenting, playing.

He'd take, and she'd give with equal measure.

The two of them, riding toward that crest of pleasure.

Fucking, consuming each other.

She wanted him so badly. Her fingers were not enough, but they had to do. She rubbed her clit and fingered her tits, finding her release.

She moaned his name, and when it was all over, she slumped against the door.

Losing control wasn't part of the plan. Nor was it part of what she wanted to do.

Working her way into their lives, becoming necessary, gaining access to everything, she was willing to do whatever it took.

Opening her eyes, she stood up, bending down to gather her shorts in her hand.

Her heart raced as she walked away without giving a single glance to the window.

Entering her shower, she turned it on, and stepped beneath the spray. Resting her head against the cool tile, she took several deep breaths, feeling … terrible.

She knew the rumors about the four kings. What they were capable of.

Even in high school she'd been in the bathroom when girls whispered what was going on. How they'd shared all four of them. That they all liked to watch each other fuck and to take. How hot it was to be the center of their little gangbang.

David was aware of the rumors. He couldn't confirm if they were true or not. Only what he knew, which wasn't all that much.

She'd seen the video today of Catherine between them. Axton had to have been the one holding the camera.

"You've got to be willing to bend to their rules. They will test you. You want to go in deep with these guys, you've got to be willing to go all the way. Even if that means them filming you, or taking you, one after the other," David said.

"That's fucking crazy. This is all just … it's getting too much, Taylor," Paul said.

"I can do it."

Everything she was doing was for Carla.

For many decades the four kings had ruled, but no more.

No matter what she had to do, no matter how hard she hated it, she would do it.

She'd come this far.

Once it was all over, she'd deal with herself then.

Chapter Seven

Ten years ago

"He can't tell me what to do," Easton said. "I won't fucking allow it."

"What are you going to do, report him for abuse?" Karson asked with a laugh.

"That would be so fucking funny. Could you imagine the child protection workers turning up to his house? Seeing the car that is the cost of twice their salary. Yeah, Easton, that would be fucking classic. Spoiled rich boy claims abuse."

"Fuck you, Romeo."

"You do what you've got to do," Axton said, writing in his notepad. They were all in the library for English as their teacher had been suspended, pending an investigation for fucking a student.

Whatever.

Axton was bored.

He was always bored.

School didn't do anything for him.

The teachers were all afraid of him.

Apart from a couple of the chicks, he was so over it all.

"I'm going to fuck whoever I want, and I don't care what he says."

"Please, your dad will not care where you screw, Easton. You're being petty," Axton said.

"What if I fuck Taylor Keane or Carla Smith?"

Axton tensed up. Easton pointed across the library, and Axton didn't need to look to see the two in question sitting with Paul.

They were always together.

"Seriously, Taylor's fine," Karson said. "Dad

wouldn't have *that* much of a problem but Carla? She's, like, poor."

"Then that is what I'm going to do. I'm going to fuck Carla Smith. Maybe even knock her up. Let him tell me then what to do."

"Don't," Axton said.

"Why the fuck not?"

"You think that will end well? You think your dad, our dads, would allow that? We've all gotten the speech about bagging our shit up and being careful. They don't want any brats until it's the right time," Axton said. "We don't have time for your playing these games."

"Please, Axton, we've got all the time in the world. We're seniors."

"And if you knock Carla up? What then?"

"Not my problem. She'll be putty in my hands."

"Yeah, that's not going to happen," Romeo said. "I'm bored now, and this class blows. I'm out of here."

Getting to his feet, Axton left the library, along with Karson and Romeo. Glancing through the windows, he saw Easton approach Carla's table.

Taylor and Carla stopped laughing.

Axton knew Easton was making a mistake, a damn big one. He only hoped it didn't cost Carla or Taylor anything in the long run.

****

Present day

"I'm sorry about him," Easton said.

Taylor finished writing up her notes on all of his requests and glanced up. "Sorry?" She was a little distracted by the work she'd been doing. Today Easton had asked for her note-taking services while he'd been on a phone call. This wasn't all she did. Her job description ranged all over the place. From coffee lady, to lunch collector, note-taker, contract typist or whatnot. They were constantly working, constantly signing contracts, making new deals, building their empire.

She actually loved the work she did so much. One of the things she hated when it came to work was to become bored. Boredom was a curse, at least it was to her.

When she was at work, she didn't want to think of anyone else. The only problem she faced: as time went on, she'd need to get her shit together because she wasn't here to socialize. She'd currently been working for Four Kings' Empire for nearly two months. Axton hadn't made any more impromptu visits, nor had he given any sign of seeing her masturbate against the door either. Not that she anticipated him actually telling her he did that. Of course not.

At the moment she didn't have time to think as the company was currently in the process of two takeover bids of two different companies, both of which held varying interests. One was a media house that made and distributed things like DVDs, music and other means. They hadn't delved into the market of digital and so in recent years had been suffering with the change of how people watched and listened to movies and music. The other was an organic retail outlet that had seen a massive decline since several supermarket chains had opened, offering the same food at bargain prices.

Two bids, at the same time, work was 'round the clock. No time to investigate or even sleep. When she got to work, all four men were here, working hard. If she was even a second late, Axton was on her case.

They didn't have time for sloppy work, and he could find anyone to replace her. So, her gathering of information had stalled out completely.

"Axton. He told us what he did. The late-night visit and stuff."

"Do you guys tell each other everything you do?"

"We tell each other enough. We have to."

"Yeah, you've always been close."

"I remember you in high school," Easton said. "Always with … Carla."

She'd noticed whenever he said her name, pain flashed behind her eyes.

"We were more like sisters, actually." She looked down at the notepad. The truth was, she wanted to tie him to a chair, all of them, and demand to know her answers. Instead, she was having to take time.

What unnerved her a little was how secretive Catherine Riley seemed to be. She wouldn't give anything away over the phone and demanded a face-to-face. Paul, at her request, had arranged a lunch together. She'd said that it needed to be private. How the four kings were monitoring her every move.

Taylor herself found it increasingly difficult not to look around, not to wonder who was watching her.

She'd gone for a run in the park and seen so many people with phones or other devices and she'd freaked out. David now took her to his gym and helped her with a set routine. She'd been slacking lately, and the carbs were having an effect. A couple of her skirts were fitting too snugly around her waist.

"You know you could just abandon your plan. There's no shame in that."

"And let them get away with it?"

"What if there's nothing to get away with?" He held his hand up as she went to speak. *"I get that they hid some stuff. What if it was for her own good? You're assuming here that everything is bad."*

"I know it's bad, David. I know it. Carla, she's not … I mean, she wasn't like that. She'd never have done that."

"You don't know that, Tay. Even you said that she was keeping secrets. I just don't want you to put everything into this only to be screwed over at the end of it. I care about you."

"You know it was always strange," she said.

"What?"

"In the last few weeks before Carla … died, she'd been acting really strangely. Meeting someone in secret. She'd always tell me that she couldn't say anything, you know. How it had to be in private. I always thought it seemed a little cruel to me." She stared at him, seeing the frown on his face.

"Why?"

"If he was her boyfriend, he was too ashamed to admit it or go public. Kind of cruel, really."

"What if he was doing it for her own good?" Easton asked.

Taylor shook her head. "No. This wasn't for Carla's own good. It was for his."

"You don't know that."

"What I do know is whatever happened between them killed her." Taylor stood up. "If you'll excuse me."

"How can you say that?" Easton asked.

The desperation in his voice made her stop for a second. The diary never mentioned who Carla had been seeing, just that it was one of the four. She didn't have a clue, and narrowing it down seemed to be her best option.

The way Easton reacted, it was almost like he knew something. As if she was insulting him.

Turning back to face him, she raised a brow. "Say what?"

"That whoever she was with … killed her."

"She ended her own life. Suicide."

He nodded his head, face pale.

Interesting.

She would find out the truth one way or another.

"It's hard to talk about," she said.

There was a time to pry and a time to know when to back the fuck off.

"I will get these typed up for you pronto," she said.

Easton didn't stop her.

Walking to her desk, she sat down and got straight back to work. She didn't have time or the privacy to be able to write down what she'd discovered, if it was even anything of relevance.

Out of the corner of her eye, she watched as Easton slammed out of his office to go to Axton's. Within minutes Romeo and Karson appeared.

"You've not upset the little prince, have you?" Romeo asked.

"Not me. I'm just working."

"Yeah, yeah."

She watched them go.

If only she had some way of planting a listening device. She did ask Paul for one, but he refused. He'd already told her that he was out of this. That he didn't want to be part of it. He felt they were losing their own lives on this quest that could bring them back nothing.

It wouldn't bring Carla back.

It wouldn't bring them anything but pain.

But if she'd not killed herself, it meant someone else took her life. Ended it early.

Taylor paused in her typing. Did she really want to know that? Could she bring herself to know that kind of truth?

Carla had been her best friend in the entire world.

If she trusted you, she'd have shared everything.

She suddenly felt sick. Getting to her feet, she left

her desk, heading toward the bathroom. Moving up to the sink, she gripped the edge of the counter, taking several deep breaths. She couldn't think or focus or do anything right now.

In her mind she saw flashes of Carla as she pulled her out of the water. The pain that sliced through her from the cold but also knowing her friend was dead.

She held her in her arms.

Cold.

Lifeless.

Dead.

Turning on the water, she splashed her face, thankful she'd forgone the makeup today. David would pitch a fit if he saw her. Her hair was even pinned back into a bun and her face fresh and clear of makeup.

He'd once told her the way she looked was her suit of armor. She'd entered the lion's den without it on.

"What is your deal?" Axton said.

She looked up into the mirror to see him in the bathroom, his arms folded. He looked menacing.

"I don't know what you mean."

"Whatever you said to Easton, what is it?"

"He was the one to bring up Carla," she said, glaring at him.

He glared right back.

"Aren't you worried about me? About my feelings? You're coming in here accusing me of doing something? What exactly could I do? None of you knew Carla. None of you had anything to do with her." She turned around, staring at him.

She hated how she responded to him. The thickness of his arms. His muscular body. The way she knew he'd hurt her if given the chance.

There was something hard and rough about him.

He made her ache in ways she'd never

experienced.

He stepped into the room and she stayed in her spot, waiting, watching. He could pounce at any second.

Did she want him to do that? To take what he wanted?

Axton was a cold man to the core. She'd read the stories about him, and months later seen the news of how old kiss-and-tell flames had suddenly been met with huge bills, unpaid debts, and facing homelessness.

Going up against this man had consequences. If you didn't take him down, he'd push you into the dirt and leave you to rot.

He was, after all, a businessman.

Suddenly, he stepped up close.

She didn't back down, nor did she cower away.

Staring into his dark brown eyes, she waited.

"You didn't lodge a complaint about me."

"We weren't in working hours." She held in her gasp as his hand went to the counter beside her hip. His arm so close to her, and yet, he still didn't touch. They weren't touching at all, but he was close.

Anyone who came into the bathroom would think they were kissing.

"I don't know what you think you're up to, Taylor, but be warned, I'm aware."

"I'm not up to anything."

"I'm not a stupid man. Ten years have gone by since I last saw you. You magically appear out of thin air and you expect me to believe it's all down to wanting to work hard."

"You have a problem with my work ethic?" she asked.

"You're one of the hardest-working people I know."

She ran her gaze down to his lips, wanting them

on her. Licking her own in return, she stared back up at him. "Then I don't see the problem."

She gasped aloud as he gripped her hip and suddenly he was pressed against her. His solid body held her captive, keeping her in place. She couldn't move.

Placing her hands on his chest, she stared up at him. "What are you going to do?" she asked. "We are in working hours."

"Whatever the fuck you're doing, stop it. Whatever it is you think you're after, you won't find it."

She tilted her head to the side. "So much paranoia locked up in one package. Tell me, Axton, do you think the entire world is against you?"

He leaned in close, so close they shared the same air.

"I don't think it. I *know* it. Be careful here, Taylor. I'd hate to see anything bad happen to you."

With that, he was gone. She watched him leave the bathroom. The only evidence he'd been there was the scent of his cologne and the rapid beating of her heart.

She touched her hip where he'd held her.

Turning toward the mirror, she lifted up her skirt, and right there, red marks from his touch. Seeing them on her pale skin made her smile.

She could get to him, and she intended to have a whole lot of fun with this.

Putting her skirt down, she ran her hands down her shirt, pushing out any wrinkles.

Leaving the bathroom, she made her way to the desk and finished her work for the day. She didn't look toward Axton or give him the time of day when he passed her desk.

"Always keep them guessing. Always leave them wanting more."

When it came to this man, she didn't know what

she wanted. Getting close to Axton wasn't part of the plan, but if that was what she had to do, she'd do it.

****

"You do know it's not in my job description to pick out items of jewelry for your dates." Taylor watched as Romeo tossed a round, green tennis ball up into the air and caught it. Whenever she was in his office, rarely did he sit still. It often made her wonder if he knew how to do something that didn't require physical effort.

"We've done all the boring stuff."

"Yes, because employing people, going through health benefits is such a boring job."

"We're all about helping people," Romeo said, giving her one of his wicked smiles. He in no way did anything for her. It was like her body didn't exist for him.

She sat with her notepad on her lap as he held six different boxes in front of him.

"Did you buy all of these?"

"Yep. I kept staring at them for, like, an hour straight."

"I do have better things to do."

"I know. I work here as well, remember? You've got to see Karson soon, then on to Axton."

She nibbled her lip, feeling nervous about that one. It had been a few days since he'd invaded her bathroom break. The attraction for him was on a completely different scale. She couldn't think. She'd been at the copy machine once again, trying to figure out why it wasn't working. Axton moved up behind her, and with a flick of the button, it started working. The way his body felt, the heat, just all of it, she had to control her moan, to keep herself from begging him not to stop.

This had never happened to her, not once.

"Is there something going on between you and

Axton?"

"No, why?"

"He's been in a bit of a mood lately. You know, growling at everyone and stuff."

"Why do you put up with him? He seems to be awfully bossy to all of you, and you're all partners, right?"

"Axton is … the boss. If we're all honest. He was the one that set this all up for us, and he's the one that keeps us thriving. He's a fantastic guy."

"Now you're trying to sell me on him?"

Romeo chuckled. "I wouldn't do anything of the sort. Nah, Axton has always been a grownup. I even think he came out of his mother's womb ordering people around." This made her smile. "Yeah, even in high school, he was always like that. But then, he wasn't even allowed to have much time to be a kid, you know?"

She didn't, so she shook her head. "I don't remember much. You and the others weren't exactly in my circle."

"You may have not seen us, but believe me, Axton saw you."

This made her frown. "I have no idea what you mean."

"Then maybe it's a good thing you don't know." He winked at her. "Now, stop being a pain in the ass and help me."

She rolled her eyes and stood. Walking to his desk, she stared at the array of jewelry on offer. They were all exquisite pieces.

"What are they for?" she asked.

"For?"

"You know. Have you been naughty? Upset her? Is this for a first date? Second? The hope of getting her into bed?"

"How about all of the above?"

She shook her head. Glancing over the pieces, she blew out a breath. "Fine, do you know what color she'd like?"

"Nope."

"Then I'd go with the blue, it looks pretty."

"You're not an expert on diamonds?"

"Nope. I'm not an expert on much, and they don't impress me."

"Why not?" he asked.

"Diamonds don't keep anyone warm at night. Sure, they're a nice treat to have, but I guess I'm old-fashioned. I don't need the monetary gifts."

"What is it you need then?"

"To know that I'm wanted. That I'm loved. Needed. That kind of thing."

"You don't have a boyfriend though."

"Nothing ever worked out."

"How come?"

"I've got a lot of commitment to my work. Getting close to someone, it takes a lot, and I don't have that kind of time, you know."

"I get it."

She shrugged. "Not exactly a lot I can do to change the way my life turned out."

"Why do you say it like that?"

"I once had plans, you know. To go traveling all over the world. To see landmarks. Maybe even go bungee jumping."

"Now that does surprise me. Why don't you go and do all those things?"

"Because the person I planned them with is no longer here." She held her notebook to her chest like a lifeline. "I'd go with the blue. It's beautiful, and it doesn't look like you're trying too hard to get what you want. Is there anything else?"

He kept staring at her, and right now she'd already given him more information than she intended.

She felt stripped open once again.

Exposed.

Vulnerable.

You're here to do a job. Get it done.

"Thank you, Taylor." She moved toward the door. "For what it's worth, I think you make a great fit here."

She looked over her shoulder at him. Gone was the smiling, teasing, charming man. In his place stood someone serious, someone scary.

"Thank you."

Without giving him a second glance, she walked toward her desk. Looking up, she saw Axton had all the blinds in his office open. That's not what made her stop and watch. There was a woman, beautiful, blonde, without an ounce of weight on her. She wore a tight dress, revealing so much skin that Taylor had to actually look to see if she wore anything at all.

Axton was smiling, and he looked happy. His arms were folded, and he was listening to whatever the woman said. Jealousy sliced through her, and she rubbed at her chest, hating the strike of pain she got.

The woman, whoever she was, ran her hands up and down his chest, touching him as if she had a right to do so.

You don't own him.

You've got no claim to him.

Besides, you want to bring him down, to make him suffer.

You can't make him suffer if you want him.

"What are you glaring at?" Karson asked.

"Nothing." She hated that she'd been caught

staring.

"Ah, that's just Emily. She's one of the women he sponsored to help get a modeling contract. She's harmless. Just passing through and he always has a meeting with her. This happens around once a year, if that."

She hated that she'd been jealous when the woman wasn't anything special to Axton. Glancing at him now, she saw he wasn't being anything other than nice, supportive.

She wasn't used to feeling jealous, or possessive. Especially not about Axton.

Pushing those thoughts aside, she ignored the feelings that were building within her and got straight back to work. She didn't have time to be dwelling on what wasn't hers. He didn't belong to her in any way.

She had to learn to remember that.

****

"Hurry up," Karson said.

She quickly wrote down his notes that he was making for the current contract problem. They had hit a snag with another company they intended to buy out. Their business rival had offered a more compelling takeover bid, and since then, the Four Kings' Empire had been in an uproar over it.

Taylor couldn't even remember the last time she'd been at her home. She'd been forced to wash and change here as they needed 'round the clock assistance. Not that she minded. Going home only reminded her of everything she still needed to do.

Paul was constantly on her case about backing out of her plan.

David did nothing but warn her.

Her apartment was empty.

Lonely.

She hated being alone.

The sadness would always hit her hard during those times. The boxes that were filled with old pictures and memories would hold her down, force her to face reality that she was all alone.

"Done."

"Good. I want that typed up. No mistakes within the next half an hour. We cannot let those bastards win."

She nodded, getting to her feet.

"Why do you think they're thinking of going with Hammer Industries? It's not a done deal, but we pretty much had this shit in the bag."

Staring at Karson with his black hair and blue eyes, and deadly look, she saw the anger in his eyes.

According to her research and sources, he was the soldier of them all. The one that went into battle in the boardroom, the one everyone looked at. Axton was the one that manipulated everything. Romeo and Easton were the two charmers. They gathered information. She was always careful around everyone, especially Karson.

"I don't know."

"You have an idea. You didn't seem shocked when we got the update they'd turned down our bid and were planning to go with Hammer Industries. You must have an opinion?"

"I have one, but I don't think you're going to like it."

"Try me."

"Hammer Industries have a reputation for rebuilding the companies they take over. They push all money and resources to build each one back up. Creating a family and something that will thrive for all. Whereas you're … you're about changing it all. Tearing it down, creating a new brand. Doing something different."

"You don't like what we do?" Axton asked,

startling her. She hadn't even heard him approach.

He leaned against the door looking every bit as imposing as she imagined he intended to be.

"I don't have a problem with how you organize your business. You're at the top for a reason."

"But?"

"There's a reason Hammer rivals you. Their business is diverse, as is yours. Part of their company is to offer something long-lasting. Something different for the struggling business."

"What is it they offer?"

"Hope. Rather than being torn down or taken over."

Karson snorted. "Please. What they do is lose money."

"Do they?" she asked, forcing herself to look away from Axton. He started to make her nervous. "They may be losing money, but It wouldn't matter to the companies that they're buying, would it? We all know that being sentimental will only ever get you so far. It's not good business, but over the past few years, they've been able to stay afloat so they're clearly doing something right somewhere. The businesses that took time to rebuild themselves, to change with the ever-growing markets. They're finally coming into fruition. Hammer Industries are not just interested in making their books look solid today but investment for the future. I'll have these documents written up. I will leave you both to your meeting."

"I take it he's my three o'clock," Karson asked.

"You got it."

"I'll pass. Tell him I have a headache."

She chuckled. "Karson will see you now." She smiled up at Axton. He stood in the doorway but wouldn't let her pass. Holding onto her files tightly, she waited.

"You've got some good theories about Hammer Industries."

They weren't good theories. For ten years she'd watched them. Any company that rivaled the Four Kings' Empire she'd kept a close eye on. No one else had ever come close, but they had.

She had a great respect for them, too. She had this image that they didn't even look at Axton and his crew as any threat at all. Far from it, in fact. They were not in the market to take. They weren't interested in them.

Sitting behind her desk, she waved her mouse to bring the screen back to life.

Her cell phone buzzed, and she saw it was a message from Paul.

Paul: **Date arranged. Saturday. Ten.**

He'd finally organized the meeting with Catherine Riley. This was one of the biggest risks she'd ever taken.

Deleting the message, she pocketed her cell phone and got started on work.

She hated business so damn much.

When she first started her degree, she'd been tempted to change her plan. Nothing else captured her attention. She couldn't go back to doing English as that was something she and Carla were going to do together.

It's was on their bucket list of plans.

Doing them now felt like she was leaving Carla behind.

She couldn't bring herself to do that.

So, she got started typing, making sure there were no mistakes. No missing commas, apostrophes in the right places. Another perfect letter for her in a long line of them.

You can't keep doing this forever.

Time was ticking.

She couldn't allow herself to become complacent.

Sitting up straight, she placed her fingers over the keyboard and started to type.

Stick to the plan.

****

"You're settling in quite well," Axton said.

With a notebook on her lap, waiting for Axton to get started seeing as he'd asked her to his office on this very fine lovely Friday morning, she waited. "I'm enjoying my time here."

"You are?"

"Yes. Does that surprise you?"

"Some find it much harder to adapt to a more intense way of life."

"I don't find this all that intense. I like to keep busy."

"You've changed a lot over the years," he said.

"Not really. You didn't know me back then."

"I'm talking about your appearance."

She looked up from her notebook, confused. "My appearance?"

"You always wore your hair up in a ponytail, bigger clothing. You were never like this. Never fully on display."

"Do I make you nervous?" she asked, staring at him.

"No, do I?"

"Make me nervous?"

He nodded.

She held her finger and thumb very close together. "A little bit."

"Good."

"You like making people nervous?"

"It means I'm doing something right."

She tilted her head to the side. "Gives you the right edge?"

"Something like that." He winked at her.

Her body heated under his gaze, and she smiled. "I think we should get down to business, don't you?"

"Yes."

She started to make notes for a letter that he wanted, detailing what the Four Kings' Empire would consider doing with the current business that had decided to change tactics and go with someone else.

He continued to talk as she made notes to the relevant key points that he was making. She was rather impressed with the changes that he made.

"What do you think?" he asked.

"This is a huge change from what you were going to do." He'd intended to fire all existing employees, change the business, turn it into an online company, and turn the entire stores into warehouse facilities. The e-community was building fast, and she knew the impact of it would mean more work for everyone. She got it and even understood it.

"What's up?" he asked.

"Nothing."

"You seem … surprised. Will you go through with your plans?" she asked.

"I'm tempted."

"Oh."

"I'm kidding. You have to understand, Taylor, I won't make promises if I have no intention of keeping them."

"So, you make promises then?"

"Only the ones I intend to keep."

She stared at him, and something passed between them. She didn't know what.

"Go out with me tonight."

"Go out with you?"

"Yes."

"I'm your PA."

"Not after five."

She chuckled. "I work long after five."

"Then the moment you leave this building, you stop being an employee."

"Why?"

"To show you how to have a good time."

"I know how to have a good time."

"Then show me how you have a good time."

"I don't know."

"Come on, Taylor, what have you got to lose?"

She thought about it. This was what she wanted. To get close to him, to have access to all of his things, or whatever she could prove about the company.

"You're not going to think badly of me?" she asked.

"How is that even possible?"

"Simple. My kind of fun may not be your kind of fun."

"Let's have a deal then. The start of the night, I'll be in charge of the fun. The second part of the night, you will."

"You think we're going to last all night?"

"Hell, yeah," he said. "Come on, Taylor, we've got a lot to catch up on."

"I've got to ask. Will you be the boss here or someone else?"

"Oh, I'll be the boss."

"I'll pick you up at seven."

"How do you know I'll be ready?"

"I don't mind waiting in your apartment if you're not ready by then."

She sighed. "Fine. I'll be ready by seven."

"You can leave at four if that will give you plenty of time."

She turned back to look at him. "I'll be ready by seven, probably even long before then as well."

"I expect that done by the end of the day."

"It will be." She left his office with a smile. Everything was working incredibly well.

****

"What will a date give you that our PI hasn't?" Karson asked.

Axton had already watched Taylor leave for the day. Her office desk had given no inclination of what she had planned for either of them.

"Come on, she was getting off to him. The only reason he's interested in this date is to fuck her," Easton said.

He glared at him.

Easton held his hands up. "What? It's true. She looked fucking hot, and we all wanted a taste of her."

Axton clenched his hands into fists. He wanted to knock that fucking look off their faces. When the PI had given him the up close and personal details of her touching herself, he'd nearly lost his fucking mind. This had also made him … curious. Did she know she was being watched? Why had she come back after all this time?

He didn't trust her.

It was as simple as that.

Her secrecy.

The way she watched them.

Something just didn't sit right with him.

He didn't understand it.

"You're looking for something that's not there," Easton said.

"Something's not right," Karson said. "I believe

Axton. We've got to be careful around her. She's too curious about us all."

"And she doesn't bring anything up directly, but she's always waiting for one of us to mention something."

Easton shook his head. "When did you all become so fucking paranoid? I mean, seriously."

"What is your plan?" Karson asked.

"Get to know her. Find out if she's holding anything back. I don't know. Do whatever is necessary to make sure we're all in the clear. Until I say otherwise, be careful. All of you. What you say. What you do. All of it. Even down to memories you share."

"This is all bullshit," Easton said. "If you were so fucking worried why did you employ her? There are a million other people who'd be less of a headache than this."

"Easton, don't," Karson said.

"What? Don't admit that he's a fucking stalker? How he couldn't get enough of her in high school?"

Axton glared at Easton.

Each of them had come to blows many times, but never once had they gone for the kill.

"What? He can go around doing whatever shit he likes, but we've all got to go ahead and take it? To keep his shit."

"You know why we do that," Karson said.

"No, I don't know anything. You're all fucking bowing down to him as if he's some kind of god. He's no different from any of us," Easton said. "And I think it's time Taylor learned the truth."

Axton stepped forward.

Hands clenched into fists.

Ready.

Poised.

Primed to attack.

"What's the matter, Axton? You don't like the thought of your secrets being exposed?"

"Your secrets go far deeper than any of mine, Easton. Remember that," Axton said. "Or do I need to remind you once again what happened to your last little rebellion?"

Easton physically backed down, the fight leaving him.

The room grew tense, and Axton looked at his friends, not liking the way they were watching him, clearly waiting to see if he'd strike.

"Do any of you have a problem with the way I handle this?"

"Look, man, you've got to go what you need to do."

"The Four Kings' Empire is all of ours," Axton said. "When we took this over, I gave you all an equal share. You all demanded that I take a percentage from each of you, which meant I had the final say. That was what you guys agreed to. If you have a problem with any way I do business, speak now."

"We don't have a problem," Karson said.

"Romeo?"

"No problem."

"Easton?"

"No."

"No, what?"

"I don't have a problem with who you do fucking shit to. I know when we took over that we inherited a whole load of shit. Don't try and vet everything I've got to say to Taylor. Okay. I know I've got to be careful. I told *her* years ago that I had to be careful." He shrugged. "It doesn't matter though, does it? Are we done?" Easton asked. "I need a drink."

Axton stared at his friend. "For what it's worth, I am sorry."

"Doesn't mean shit right now, Axton. It doesn't end." Easton stepped out of the room, leaving him alone with Romeo and Karson.

"I'll go and talk to him. Make sure he doesn't fuck up or do anything stupid," Romeo said, leaving him with Karson.

"You've got something to say," Axton said. "Say it."

"Do you think you're worrying for no reason? Taylor's reliable, good at her job, and has never given us cause for concern, apart from that first day when she flew off the handle over a little thing."

"She's close friends with Paul and an escort, and I don't know, I have a feeling she's trying to figure out what happened to Carla all those years ago."

"How do you know that?" Karson asked. "There's no way of knowing that."

"Because I know her. Creepy stalker, remember. I know what she's thinking and how she operates. I knew back then she wouldn't let it stand."

Karson stood with a hand on his hip. "We've come a long way from being teenage boys."

"Doesn't matter. We're all in this together. Have been for a long time. I hope I'm wrong."

"You're rarely wrong. You said to Easton that this wasn't good for him. When we all discovered she was pregnant, we warned him."

"And she was found dead." He knew, as did Karson, Romeo, and Easton that she didn't die from her wrists being cut.

"Don't you think she has a right to know the truth? Maybe if you talk to her," Karson said. "I don't know, you two have this thing going on right now where you seem to fuck each other with your eyes." Axton simply stared at Karson, who eventually put his hands up in surrender. "Fine. This is your deal. Remember, we warned you."

Karson left his office.

Stepping up to his office window, Axton looked out across the city. It was a little overcast, not painting the city in the best light.

Hands on his hips, he thought about the pictures he'd seen. The way she touched herself. She'd been so fucking beautiful, and yet, he'd not even for a second believed she'd reached her full potential.

The lust that shone in her eyes, he wanted all to himself. He wanted to pull that lip that she had a habit of biting and show her what to do with them.

He wanted to make her dirty.

To take her down a path and show her what true carnal pleasure was like.

First though, he wanted to take her on a date.

Asking her had been a fucking mistake, but he'd done so because he couldn't help himself. Since hiring her, work had become a fucking chore. He found himself at the most inconvenient of moments, thinking about her. About the past, the sacrifices he'd made to be where he was right now.

No one knew the true extent of what he'd done to be where he was. Everyone assumed it had all been handed to him on a plate. In a way, it had. He'd always been expected to take over from his father, to be the one who took the Four Kings' Empire to new heights. Of course, his father never actually intended for that to happen.

When the takeover had happened, and he, Easton, Karson, and Romeo had taken their rightful places, they'd uncovered a whole shitload of trouble.

Trouble he hadn't been prepared for.

Trouble he'd inherited and now carried that burden with him.

He knew if given the chance, his father would try to destroy him. It was the only reason Axton kept the evidence of what his father, and all of their fathers, had done before they took over. For now, it kept their fathers quiet and out of the picture.

They were fighting a constant battle of wills.

Axton had no intention of losing.

Ten years ago, he'd known his own needs had to be put aside.

What he wanted didn't matter.

Only what his family needed, what his position was within the Four Kings. Everything else was null and void. So, he'd done things from afar. They knew what he'd done. No one else.

Rubbing at his temples, he felt the first stirrings of a headache.

This was not what he wanted to deal with.

When he hired Taylor, he'd wanted his concerns to not be valid. However, he was starting to feel that he was right, and with that created a whole new set of problems. She did damn good work, but now he had to make sure she never found out the truth about anything.

"Why couldn't you have stayed safe elsewhere?"

Chapter Eight

Ten years ago
"*There is no greater person on this earth than you. One day, I hope you see what I see,*" Carla said. "Is that it?"

"What?" Taylor asked. "It's sweet."

"It's getting kind of creepy if you ask me."

"What's getting kind of creepy, ladies?" Paul asked, moving up behind them, placing his arm across both of their shoulders.

Carla rolled her eyes and handed the single note to Paul. "This."

He read it over.

"Let's not forget the single rose either. It's always a different color."

"No, it's not. It's never the same color one after the other," Taylor said.

"You have an admirer?" Paul asked.

"Not me, silly," Carla said. "Taylor. She's been getting these weird letters and roses for some time."

"You have? How come I've only just heard about it?"

Taylor chuckled as Carla hit him on the arm. "I've told you so many times about them. This is the thing with men. They don't listen."

"Hey, I listen all the time," Paul said.

Taylor rolled her eyes. "I'd ignore her. She hates all guys at the moment. Don't know why though. Have you got a secret admirer you're not telling us about?"

Carla shook her head. "It's nothing, okay? Nothing at all. Men and boys—because that's what they are most of the time, right? Boys—are just childish and immature, and I don't like them. It's as simple as that."

"And you're *not* sounding immature right now?"

"I have a right to sound immature and a right to be a little jealous." Carla pulled Taylor against her chest. "Aren't you curious in the slightest who they're coming from?"

At first, she'd thought it was a prank. She'd tossed out the rose but kept the letter, keeping it in a safe box to read whenever she felt like it. Then, when no one made a big deal about it, she'd kept the rose in a slim vase until it died. She loved the flowers so much, and her mother hated roses so they weren't even allowed in the garden.

"I don't know. What if it's someone I don't like? Or don't know?" Taylor asked.

"What if it's the janitor?" Paul said.

Taylor burst out laughing. "Yeah, that would be creepy. I don't know. I like the roses, and the letters are always really sweet. I'm not freaked out yet. I imagine that will come much later."

"I've got to head to geography. Catch you at lunch," Carla said.

"Yep."

"That's my cue to go as well. See you at lunch," Paul said.

She walked down the long corridor going toward math. It was the only class where she didn't have either Paul or Carla. Inhaling the sweet scent of her rose, she hummed to herself all the way to class. She was the first to arrive, so she took a seat, one from the back. It was her usual chair.

Pulling out her books, she flicked her pencil on the table, looking out across the field. The track was closed as they'd had a huge rainfall, which had made the grass way too slippery and a hazard.

"Nice rose."

She frowned, looking up to see Axton pass. "Thank you."

He ran his fingers over the white petals. She held her breath, but he didn't say or do anything as he took the seat behind her, like he always did in math. Actually, whenever they had classes together, he always sat behind her.

****

Present day

Pulling her heels on, Taylor listened to Paul and David once again berating her. At least this time they weren't in her apartment. She wouldn't have to do the introductions for Axton when he arrived.

"Are you kidding me, right now? This has gone on for long enough. You're clearly not going to find anything," Paul said.

"I'm starting to think Paul is right on this, Taylor. Don't put yourself in danger. You've not found anything out."

"Because I've not been given the chance to," she said. "I know I'm onto something. I know they're hiding something. I'm going to find out what it is."

"But how?" Paul asked. "It's not going to change anything."

She was getting tired of his moaning and no good attitude. "I'm trying here, Paul. I want answers."

"Then why don't you come out and ask them, Taylor? Why not just say, 'what did you have to do with Carla's death?'" Paul asked.

David chuckled. "You really think he'd come out and tell her the truth if they were in fact part of it?"

"I don't know, okay? I don't know fucking jack squat anymore," Paul said. "All I know is it has to be better than her sleeping with the man."

"There's not going to be any sleeping involved,"

David said. "Not if I taught her right."

"Guys, these calls are getting boring now. We're all arguing over the same old stuff," Taylor said. "I'm doing this whether you like it or not, Paul. I've told you this. David, thank you."

"Remember all the warnings I've told you about."

"I know. I know." She wriggled her boobs in the bra and ran her hands down the dress. "The clothes are starting to get a little tight again."

"Go back on your runs," David said.

"I can't. Someone is watching, and I freak out just by being here. I don't want to make a mistake out there. It's bad enough as it is." She had to purposefully walk to the car as if she wasn't thinking about someone watching her, stalking her every single move.

"You're going to be okay, Taylor. You've got this."

"I think you're both fucking fools," Paul said.

The knock at the door silenced them all.

"I've got to go," Taylor said.

"If I don't hear from you by tomorrow morning, I'm coming looking," David said. "I've been doing some inquiries about the Four Kings' Empire, and I don't like what I've heard."

"You didn't have to do that."

"I'll do whatever is needed to keep you safe, Taylor. You're my friend."

"Believe it or not, I agree with him," Paul said. "Catherine was difficult out of fear of what they had on her. She's not to be trusted, Taylor. She wanted to sell their secrets to the highest bidder. No one likes a rat or a sell out in business. And no one wants to get hit by the Four Kings' Empire. They're capable of ruining everyone who dares to stand up against them."

She took a deep breath. "Wish me luck."

Hanging up the call, she pocketed her cell phone in the small bag and made her way toward the door. Pushing her raven hair off her shoulders, she released a breath. "You've got this."

Opening the door, she smiled, seeing Axton dressed in a tux. She saw him in a suit every single day, but this was far more dashing than she thought was possible. He was cleanly shaven. The suit molded to every single muscle, and the look of it just screamed wealth. He looked out of place in her modest apartment.

He'd always looked out of place in King's Ridge.

"Hey," she said.

"I brought you a gift."

She watched as he pulled one hand from behind his back to reveal a single red rose.

"Oh, wow," she said. Her heart pounded. Could he have been the rose leaver all those years ago? Staring into his dark eyes, she had to wonder for just a second it if was him. No, it couldn't be. Axton Farris would never, ever, leave her something like this. She was getting way ahead of herself. The rose was left by a mystery man. Axton couldn't. Pushing those thoughts aside, she breathed in the scent. "It smells lovely." Closing her eyes, she felt relaxed and calm. "Will you wait while I put it in some water?"

"Sure."

He stepped over the threshold into her apartment. Taking a deep breath, she turned away about to leave, but he caught her arm, stopping her. "You don't have to be afraid of me."

She looked at the hand on her arm then up into his eyes once again. The promise within them tightened something deep within her.

"I'm not afraid of you being here, Axton. Make yourself at home."

He released her arm, and she missed his touch instantly.

Stepping into her kitchen, she found a small vase and placed the flower inside it. When she got home tonight she'd move it to her bedside.

She walked back into her sitting room and smiled at him. He stood in her sitting room, looking at her artwork. The apartment had come fully furnished, and she'd only added a few pieces to make it more "her."

"No pictures?" he asked.

"I don't keep much around, to be honest." She folded her arms beneath her breasts, stepping up beside him. "I'm not much for personal touches. You?"

"You've seen my office."

"It's the only thing I've seen."

"That's true. To get to my apartment you have to be a really good girl."

This made her chuckle. "You say that to all the women you're taking on dates?"

"Who said I'd ever been on a date?"

"Come on, Axton. You can't pretend that you've been celibate all your life."

"I didn't say anything about fucking, Taylor." He leaned in close, his lips near her ear. She closed her eyes as his breath fanned across her neck. "I take what I want and I fuck who I want, but I don't date."

"Then I must be special then," she said, grabbing her bag. "Because you're taking me out on a date." She stood at her front door. "After you."

"I remember a time when you'd have run away."

"I've never been afraid of you."

"In high school?"

"Not even then."

"I don't believe you."

She smiled. "There are a lot more things that are

scary in this world than four little boys who think they controlled a town. The world is a lot bigger than King's Ridge, Axton. Surely you know that."

"I know a great deal, Taylor. More than you'll ever know."

"We'll see."

They stepped out of her apartment, and for a few seconds, she was nervous. This was taking things to the next level. Work wasn't there to keep her safe, nor were David and Paul.

She was on her own, going out with him.

No one would be there to help her, or to stop him. *Are you really afraid?*

Stepping onto the elevator, she chanced a glance at him, and the truth was no. She wasn't afraid of him, had never been afraid of him.

Most people in high school had done whatever they could to avoid him or to steer clear of him.

She'd never felt like that. If he sat behind her, he sat behind her.

If they crossed paths, they crossed paths.

She never treated him like a king, nor would she now.

He wasn't a king, not to her, not yet.

Neither of them spoke as the elevator descended to the underground parking lot. One of the reasons she loved this apartment block was the tight security.

Stepping out of the elevator, he took hold of her arm once again, moving toward his car.

She recognized it.

"Isn't that the car you had years ago?" she asked.

"Yes."

"Can't you afford to buy, like, a fleet of cars that are all different?"

"I can afford to have a car in every single make,

model, and color. Not going to happen. I like my car."
He opened the door. "Climb in."

"I never thought the day would come when I
climbed into your car," she said.

"You're the only woman I've ever allowed in my
car." He slammed the door closed, and she frowned,
watching him round the vehicle to climb behind the
wheel.

"What does that mean?"

"It means what it means. I don't take women out
in this car. This is always saved for special occasions.
Buckle up."

She quickly strapped herself in as he pulled out of
the lot, heading onto a main road, going further into the
city. There was a lot of traffic, so she relaxed back
against the leather.

"Where are we going then?"

"I thought a little Italian would be right up our
street."

"I like Italian. Love pasta, all kinds of it."

He glanced over at her. "I know."

"How?"

"I have my means."

*"You're getting in too deep. Axton is not known
for letting people get away with hurting his business.
This could end badly for you."* One of Paul's many
warnings flittered through her head, once again
reminding her of all the trouble this could cause.

She has a right to know.

Carla's parents had a right to know the truth.

"That's not creepy at all."

"Everyone loves pasta, Taylor."

"All of your dates love pasta?"

"Nope, and I told you, I don't do dates."

"You never took them out for a meal?" she asked.

"I've never needed or wanted female company unless I want one thing."

"So I really am special." She batted her eyelashes.

"What about you?" he asked.

"We've already had this conversation, remember? You asked me why I wasn't seeing anyone. Yada, yada, yada."

"I did, but surely that's not the whole story?"

"What can I say, I never really got a lot of attention."

"And now?" he asked.

"I get some. It's all a lot of fun."

He pulled up outside of a very well-known Italian restaurant. Paul had taken her to it for her twenty-first birthday and also to celebrate the success of his latest technology deal. That had been one of the few occasions they spent together. There were times she'd wanted to reach out to him over the past ten years, but studying and life got in the way. Whenever they were nearby though, they hung out for a few days, and then something would pull them away. Paul's company was a massive success, and she was working on her own career as well. The time Paul had taken her here, he'd talked all night long about his company, and for a short time she forgot about her plan. There had been a few times over the years where she had thought about forgetting her plan, of moving on. Then she'd have a dream or a memory, and she couldn't do it. She couldn't bring herself to forget.

The waiting valet opened the door. Taking the man's hand, she climbed out, but Axton was there, removing his hand and taking over.

"She's my date, and I know how to handle her, thank you," Axton said, his tone telling the other man not to even argue.

"That wasn't very nice," she said. "I'm not a thing for you to handle."

"I wanted to help you out of the car."

"Does it really matter who helps me out so long as someone does?" she asked.

"It matters to me."

"Bossy." She tucked her arm against his, pressing her breasts close.

Axton didn't show any sign of interest. They walked into the restaurant, and she tried not to be disappointed. She was following all of David's advice to lure him in. Showing temptation, offering herself up, flirting, all things he said worked. Axton wasn't impressed though. He wasn't falling for it.

Be yourself.

She was only ever herself around Paul.

Even David didn't get to see the real her. She spent most of her time practicing with him.

Paul had known her since they were kids.

Releasing her hold on Axton, she decided to do this her way. Tonight, the plan needed to be put on hold. Axton suspected something. She couldn't ruin all of her hard work by falling now. Flirting didn't come naturally to her and especially not in David's way. If Axton suspected something, she'd have to be extra careful about what she let slip. If he thought something was wrong, the other three would know.

Before leaving, she'd seen all three go to Axton's office.

There hadn't been a scheduled meeting.

This had been for something new.

Pushing some hair out of her face, she nibbled her lip as the maître d' showed them to their table. Axton took charge once again, pulling out her chair, and she slid into it, smiling up at him.

"Thank you."

He stared at her for a few seconds before finally taking a seat.

Picking up the menu, she opened it up, and her mouth watered. Chicken alfredo, fettucine, Italian meatloaf, pot roast, risotto. From comfort to luxury to impressive, everything was there with a little note on the bottom to say that they were made on request.

Oh, yum.

"See anything you like?" he asked.

"The entire menu."

He laughed. Glancing over her menu, she liked that she'd been able to make him laugh.

"I do love Italian food. It has been a long time since I had some pasta though."

"Why?"

"I'm not a very good cook. I've been focusing on my career and other things. I didn't take the time to learn how to cook it. There was this little Italian place near the college, and believe me, their meatballs were heaven. I think if I lived there any longer, I'd have turned into a meatball."

Staring at the list of tempting food offers, she couldn't believe she'd just done that, told him about herself and about her life. She had to keep remembering her plan.

The plan.

Yes, of course. It always came back to the plan.

"You've always had a killer body, Taylor. You shouldn't hide it, meatball or not."

"You're speaking like you know me," she said.

"I do know you."

"We were never in the same circles."

"Didn't mean I didn't notice you, Taylor."

The roses?

The letters?

"If you've got something to ask me, just ask. Remember, be prepared for the answers."

"Why did you help me out of the lake?" she asked. "Why did you make it seem like it wasn't a big deal?"

She saw his jaw clench at her question. She wouldn't be pushed down again, not over this.

"I don't think you're ready to know the answers to that."

"You said you'd tell me the truth."

"I will."

"Then tell me what happened that night," she said.

"I helped you out of the lake, Taylor. I was the one that heard you when you screamed. That's what I did." He shrugged. "Nothing more. I had no idea who it was that you were holding or what had happened."

She stared at him.

"I can't imagine what that must have been like. I've got Easton, Karson, and Romeo. I'd never want to pull them out of a lake."

She swallowed past the lump in her throat. "It wasn't easy, that's for sure. I found it really rather difficult, especially after. Even now, I sometimes get nightmares."

"What happens?"

"This is not really date conversation." *Keep it about him. About sex. About the temptation. You want to lure him to do what you want.*

"I want to talk about it. I don't believe for a moment you really talked to anyone. Did you see a doctor, a shrink?"

She shook her head. "No."

"I was there. This is something we share. It's a

bad thing, but it's still something."

She glanced around the restaurant before taking a deep breath. "She's screaming for my help. In my dream. We're at the lake. It's cold and dark. She's in the water, and I'm there watching. Seeing her start to drown, only she's screaming for my help. I dive in, and no matter how hard I swim, she's always far away. I can't get to her. When I finally do, I wake up." She stared down at the menu, licking her lips.

"I dream that you're pulled under," Axton said, making her look up.

"What?"

"I pulled you out of that water, but for a split second, I didn't think I was capable of doing it. You slip through my fingers, and you're pulled under. I don't help either of you," he said.

"You dream about it?"

"Yes."

Could she have been wrong about him? About all of them?

She pressed her lips together, trying to figure out what the hell was going on. Nothing made sense to her right now.

"Would you like the alfredo?" he asked.

"I'd love it."

"Right, let's talk about something more interesting."

"Oh yeah, what is that?" she asked.

"What you're going to do with the remainder of our date."

The waiter had brought them over a bottle of wine. She watched him as he poured the clear, sparkling liquid into her glass.

"I figured we could go to a club. I love to dance. Really love to dance."

"You do."

"Yes, and it'll be the perfect way to work off all of these calories," she said.

"Funny, I can think of another more useful way."

****

Taylor was like two different people. Axton enjoyed his meal and watched the façade slowly slip. Of course, it helped that he'd plied her with a lot of wine.

Wine, jokes, and good food.

Gone was the woman pressing her tits against his arm, not that he minded that so much. He'd rather liked it in fact, feeling her against him. She had an incredible body. All full hips, large tits, the perfect hourglass figure. The dress she wore showed off her body to absolute perfection. She'd always been a bigger woman even in high school. Food was her weakness.

What he found interesting was the way she'd pull a little on the dress as if she wasn't comfortable.

The more he looked into Taylor's life, with the PI doing a thorough background check, the more he knew something wasn't right. He'd never been wrong about anything like this before, and it was only a matter of time before he found out the truth.

When he made to pour her another glass, she covered it up and shook her head. "I've had more than enough, thank you."

"Another glass won't hurt."

"I'm not going to have another glass. Besides, I think we're getting to the part of the date that's mine."

He paid for their meal and refused her money as she tried to pay.

Walking out of the restaurant, he was moving toward his car when she pulled him away.

"No, not yet."

"Where are we going?" he asked.

"Come." She took his hand in hers. He watched as she removed her heeled shoes, and she suddenly dropped about four inches. Her eyes were once again level with his chest. She tugged him in the opposite direction of his car.

Following her as they quickly ran across the road, he couldn't believe that she'd gone without her shoes and was tempted to stop as she opened up the gate to the center park.

She stepped off the hard path, onto soft grass. "That feels so good."

"I thought we were going dancing."

Taylor pressed a finger to his lips. "If you're quiet, you'll hear them."

"Hear what?"

"Them." She winked at him, her finger over his lips, and then he heard it. The soft sounds of music. "There's a small band that plays on the opposite side of the park. I think they got a contract or something with the city to offer tranquility or something like that. It's beautiful, and I love coming here."

It was already dark. He saw a couple of people walking, hand in hand, gazing up at the stars. He'd passed the park many times. Not once had he taken the time to visit.

She released his hand and held hers up in the air. "I love coming here. It reminds me a little of home."

"You miss King's Ridge?"

"I miss the time I was there, growing up. Doing the whole adult thing gets boring after a time." She spun in a circle and stopped to smile at him. "Do it."

"What?"

"Let go, Axton. Surely there's someone there that can relax for you. Right now, you're not the boss." She stepped up to him, placing his hands around her waist.

"You're just Axton, no one else. Come on, for me. This is my portion of the date."

He rolled his eyes. "What do you want me to do?"

"Prove you're not a stick in the mud."

"And how do I suggest you do that?"

She threw her hands up in the air and spun. "Try it. Come on, Axton, relax. Nothing is going to hurt you."

He didn't want to. Watching her do it, he felt like he was seeing the old Taylor. The one that hadn't lost anything.

One night wouldn't hurt.

Throwing his arms up in the air, he copied her. Closing his eyes, he spun, and when he turned full circle, he stopped, opened his eyes, and found her smiling at him.

"See, that wasn't so bad, was it?"

"It could have been worse." He tugged her close, wrapping his arms around her. "What are you up to?"

"What's wrong with having a little fun every now and again, Axton? You don't need to be so serious all the time."

She pulled away from him but grabbed his hand at the same time. "Come on."

Before he knew what was happening, she was pulling him through the park and they were running. Light filtered on the ground from the lamps, and he kept looking to check her feet. He didn't want her to hurt herself.

Suddenly, she stopped, resting her back against a thick tree trunk. "That was fun."

He was shocked to find that he was smiling along with her. "Yeah, that was fun."

He stood right in front of her, placing a hand against the rough bark. She tilted her head, her long, black hair falling back. "You look beautiful tonight."

"Thank you. You clean up rather nicely yourself." She placed a hand on his chest. "It's nice to get you out of the office. You've not growled at me once."

With his other hand, he placed it at her hip, loving the feel of her curves, especially as she released a little gasp when he did touch her.

"You like it when I touch you."

"I like a lot of things."

She moaned as he pressed his cock against her stomach.

"Why do you keep teasing me? You're messing with the wrong man."

He stared into her blue eyes, so tempting, so dangerous. He wanted to lose himself in her gaze and never come back out.

"What's the matter, Axton? Can't handle the heat?"

"You think you've got what it takes to mess with the boss?" he asked. Moving his hand from the tree, he sank his fingers into her hair, tugging on the length. She groaned hard, her body softening against him. He pressed his thigh between her legs, not even caring that anyone saw them. All he cared about was her.

"So far you do a lot of ordering around, Axton, not a lot of follow-through."

He cupped her cheek, using his thumb to tilt her head back, staring at her lips. They were so plump. "These would look good wrapped around my cock."

She ran her tongue across her mouth. "You want my lips on your dick?"

Gripping her hair, he tugged her to the floor so that she knelt before him, her mouth in alignment with his dick. Opening the front of his pants, he reached inside and pulled out his cock.

"Look at you, Axton Farris in the park getting his dick out. Whatever would people think?" she asked.

"What about Little Miss Angel? Taylor Keane, on her knees, mouth ready to take my cock. You tell me what people would think."

She wrapped her fingers around his length, flicking the tip with her tongue. "Why don't you stop thinking what others would and tell me how to suck your cock."

Tightening his hand around her hair, he saw her eyes dilate and heard the gasp in her voice. Pressing the tip of his dick to her mouth, he thrust inside, watching his length disappear. The warm, wet heat wrapped around him, swallowing him down until he hit the back of her throat.

She moaned, the sound vibrating up his length, tightening his balls. It had been a long time since a woman sucked him, and fucking hell, Taylor was everything. She kept her teeth at bay and worked her tongue like it was made of magic. Thrusting his hips, he slammed into her mouth, using the tree to hold himself up as he fucked her mouth.

He stared down into her eyes. Taylor was looking at him, moaning as she did so. He heard a couple of people passing, and he groaned. Her eyes grew wide, and he wondered just how wet her tight little cunt would be. Would she be dripping for him?

"When I come, swallow every last drop. You don't let any escape and I'll let you come, right here, right now."

She worked her hands and mouth over his cock. Pushing her hand out of the way, he continued to work her mouth, hitting the back of her throat each time. The first couple of times she gagged but finally got used to his invasion.

Her lips did look so pretty, the way they stretched around him, trying hard to take as much of him as she could.

In. Out. In. Out.

His length glistened with her saliva.

She slurped him up, and he saw stars when her throat swallowed him down.

He was so close. Gripping her hair tightly, he fucked her face, not holding back, giving her everything, expecting her to take all of it.

When he finally came, he pulled out so only the tip was inside her and watched as she swallowed every last drop. He quickly released her hair and felt her neck, feeling her work his cock until there was nothing left, his seed completely drained with her magical lips.

Stepping away, he watched as she licked her lips, removing every last trace of semen.

Helping her to her feet, he pressed her once again against the tree.

"My turn."

"You don't want to take this elsewhere?" she asked.

"No. I want to watch you come apart, right here, right now."

Kneeling down on the ground, he lifted her leg up, tracing a finger inside. Finding her panties were already soaked, he tugged them from her body, pocketing the evidence. They were going to be his trophy for the night.

Sliding a finger through her slit, he touched her clit, giving it the lightest touch before moving down to plunder inside her tight heat. She cried out his name. Her fingers sank into his hair as he leaned forward and licked her pussy. She tasted so fucking good, just as he knew she would. Spreading her lips wide, he sucked her clit before tracing down to where his fingers were fucking her.

She was so tight and wet. Staring up at her, he saw her head was thrown back, her chest heaving. She looked so sexy and so wanton. This was how he wanted to remember her and never forget. How he'd imagined her to be.

So giving.

Once again, another couple stepped past them, and this time, she gasped. More of her sleek cream covered his fingers, and he smiled against her cunt. His little angel liked the thought of being caught. She was no innocent, and he fucking loved that.

In that moment, he wondered what he could do to push her over the limit. To test her boundaries. To see what else she was capable of.

He wanted it all.

Pulling his fingers from her pussy, he brought them back, teasing her anus.

She moaned this time.

The people had already passed, which was a shame. He wondered if she'd make him stop or to keep on going? Not that he'd stop in the first place. He wanted to feel her coming on his tongue, riding his fingers, and giving him exactly what he wanted, and there was no way he'd stop that. Not now, not ever.

"Please, Axton," she said.

Sliding his fingers across the puckered hole of her ass, he continued to lick and taste her sweet clit as he teased her, seeing just how far she'd be willing to go with him. She'd already surprised him by not pushing him away. He liked it. He wanted to push her to places that she never for a second thought she'd go. Teasing her ass, he pressed against the tight ring of muscles at the same time he bit down on her clit, bringing her just the right amount of pain that made her gasp. He watched as her hands covered her mouth, trying to keep the scream inside. He didn't want her to hold back.

Pushing a finger into her ass, he knew it would burn, but he soothed it out by ravishing her clit. Within seconds she came, giving him that scream he wanted. So beautiful. All of his, given to him.

She didn't stop as he finished off her orgasm, licking and soothing her pussy, before pulling his finger from her ass. Using a handkerchief, he wiped his fingers and stood. Licking his lips, he smiled at her.

Taylor grabbed his jacket, slamming her lips against his, kissing her taste.

"My place?" he asked.

"Yes. Please."

Chapter Nine

Ten years ago

"What did he say?" Karson asked.

Axton didn't need to hear Easton's reply to know what his father said. They all knew what their parents would say if they got a girl pregnant. Not just any girl either, but the "wrong girl." A girl from the wrong side of the tracks.

"He told me she was to get rid of it. That I had to encourage her to go for an abortion, as otherwise he'd deal with it," Easton said.

"And?" Romeo asked.

"And I came straight here with you guys. I don't know what the hell to do."

"Simple, get her to get rid of it," Karson said.

"When did you become this fucking cold, Karson? That's my kid."

"I thought you were only using her to get back at your dad?" Axton asked.

"That shit went away a long time ago, okay? I like her."

"Wow, someone get out the violins. Easton actually loves someone," Axton said.

"Screw you."

"No, not screw me. You've got to figure this shit out. Do you understand?"

"I don't have to figure anything out. I'm not going to ask Carla to get rid of the baby."

"Your dad will do something," Karson said, speaking up. "We all know if he doesn't alone, they all will together."

Karson was talking about all of their fathers.

"You know the drill. One heir, Easton. And it

can't be with someone they don't choose." Axton wished he could say something else, to give his friend better advice.

"This is bullshit," Easton said. "She's pregnant with my kid. I love her. I'm not going to let her get away. I don't want to let her go. I promised her I'd take care of her. I can't *not* do that."

Axton stared at his friend, seeing how clearly devastated he was. "If you don't they'll 'handle it,' and you'll never see Carla again."

"They wouldn't hurt her. They wouldn't." Easton didn't sound so sure on that part.

Easton was the only one who didn't seem convinced about what their fathers were capable of.

"You've got to handle this, Axton. At least talk to him or something. I don't know. Give me some more time," Easton said.

"There's not a lot I can do, Easton." He ran fingers through his hair. "Come on, we've got to go. They'll be arriving soon to start the bonfire, and I have no interest in being here until it's fashionably late to do so."

****

Present day

Entering Axton's apartment, Taylor wasn't surprised by the sheer size of it. Her full place could be fit three times into his. The luxury that surrounded her wasn't lost on her either. Not that it would be easy to miss. The elevators that also had men waiting to greet them. The security around the entire building.

Everything seemed perfect.

Pristine.

And it just made her want to mess it all up.

Stepping into his main sitting room, she looked over at his floor-to-ceiling windows. That she struggled with. Being afraid of heights didn't help her one bit.

"I don't know how you can stand that," she said, spinning around to see him staring at her ass. "You were checking out my ass."

He moved up to her, his hands going behind her back, squeezing the cheeks. "You've got a fantastic ass. One day soon, I'm going to fuck it."

She cupped his face, pulling him down to kiss his lips. Her pussy was slick, and she felt desperate for more of his dick. She couldn't control herself around him. He was like a drug to her system, and she was desperate for him, begging for more. Needy for all of him.

He plundered his tongue into her mouth, and she moaned, sinking her fingers into his hair, pulling his head back as she broke the kiss, nibbling down to his pulse, and the opening of his tux shirt.

Axton kneaded her ass, drawing her close. She felt the hard ridge of his cock pressing against her stomach.

Within a matter of seconds, he had her pressed up against the wall, tugging her dress up to her hips. He pressed a hand between her thighs, sliding inside her pussy. She released a moan, this time not doing anything to be quiet. She was desperate for every single part of him, yearning for more.

He added a second finger, then a third, stretching her out, and she whimpered, needing more, wanting his cock sliding in deep, fucking her hard.

"I want your cock," she said, voicing her needs.

"You'll get my cock soon." His fingers withdrew from her pussy, and she moaned as he grabbed both her wrists and pinned them up above her head. She felt the slickness of her own cunt as he held her hands with the one he'd been touching her with. Staring into his dark eyes, she felt herself falling, desperate for him.

In this moment, it wasn't about finding out the truth, or trying to win him over, or anything. This was all about pleasure. What they could both give and receive from each other. He turned her so that she was facing the wall. The zipper at the back of her dress slid down, exposing her. He flicked the catch of her bra and released her arms, pushing the dress from her body until it fell at her feet.

Stepping out of it, she kept her heels on, which she'd stepped back into on the way back to the car. He turned her again with her hands above her head, his gaze on hers. She breathed in deeply, and he started to look down at her body.

"You're beautiful," he said. "So fucking beautiful."

She gasped as his hand cupped her tit. His thumb skimmed across the nipple, teasing her, playing with her body as if it was his and only his.

It is his.

Only for this moment and not for much longer.

Again, she focused on Axton's touch. Not on the guilt she felt for enjoying herself or anything else. Just his touch and how he looked at her.

She could get used to the way he stared at her, as if he was hungry for her and only her. No one had ever looked at her like that.

"Spread your legs."

"You're very bossy."

"I like to get what I want."

"And what else do you want?"

"At the moment, for you to be quiet."

She pressed her lips together but still smiled, watching him, waiting. He traced a finger between her breasts, circling each nipple before sliding down. Going past her stomach, after dipping into her belly button, he moved down a thigh, then up again, going down the other one. He reached around, gripping her ass cheek, and she cried out, knowing there would be bruises from his touch.

"I want to fuck your ass," he said, kissing her shoulder. "There's so many dirty things I want to do to you, Taylor."

She pulled her hands from where he held them, ignoring the burn from his grip. Pushing his jacket off, she released a few of his top buttons then pulled his shirt apart.

"The only way to do dirty things to me, Axton, is to be naked."

Within seconds she had his clothes off, and they stood naked. His ink surprised her. He wasn't covered by it at all. There was one on his arm, his top left shoulder, his stomach, and one across his heart. The one on his heart she recognized. The crown with four points for each of them.

Stroking a hand down his chest, he caught her hands, holding them away from his body.

"You don't want me to touch?"

"I want a whole lot more than that." His gaze stared at her. "Turn around. Bend over."

She raised a brow but didn't question him as she turned, giving him her back. Bending over, she waited for his next instructions.

"Grab your ass, spread your cheeks open. I want to see your ass and pussy." Gripping her ass cheeks, she wasn't in any doubt that he'd see her. When he turned the light on, he'd be able to see every single part of her.

He moved up behind her, and she gasped as his finger slid in deep to the knuckle.

"Hold yourself still."

Axton added a second finger, pushing in and out.

She closed her eyes, enjoying the way he teased her body. When he pressed a second finger within her, she moaned, rocking back against him.

"How long has it been?" he asked.

"What?"

"Since you've been with a man? How long?"

"Erm, a couple of years."

The only person she'd ever been with was David. How pitiful was that? She'd used him, and he'd showed her everything. She had also paid him for the pleasure of his teaching.

Axton gripped her tit as he continued to finger-fuck her, stretching her open.

"I like to do a lot of dirty things, Taylor."

"Like what?"

"It depends on what you're willing to do, how far you're wanting to go with me."

This was the opening she needed.

She wanted this, was curious about what he wanted.

"Then take me on this ride with you, Axton. I'm not going anywhere."

He pulled his fingers from her pussy and spun her around, dropping her to her knees. "Suck them." He pressed his fingers to her mouth, and she sucked each one. When he had all three fingers in her mouth, she couldn't help but drool, but he still didn't stop, pushing into her mouth, making her take it all.

When they were clean, he took his fingers, sucking her saliva from them.

"Open your mouth."

She opened her mouth, and he placed his cock inside, and she sucked him hard, moaning as he plunged all the way in, making her gag.

He fucked her mouth for several thrusts before

pulling out.

Axton took her hand and started to pull her into his bedroom. Within seconds he had her bent over the bed, ordered her to hold her ass wide open, and she watched as he pulled out a condom, and then a dildo. It made her giggle to see him with the large fake cock in his hands.

He moved toward the bed, his cock covered with the condom.

She gripped the sheets beneath her as the tip pressed to her entrance. Just by feeling him there, she knew he was a big man.

Slowly, inch by inch, he sank deep inside her. He stretched her wide. She'd not had a cock like his before, so long and ready to take her. She gasped as he gripped her hips and slammed to the hilt.

At first, she did experience a little pain, which shocked her. The pain mixed with the pleasure, and she didn't want it to stop. She felt each pulse of his cock as he filled her. She clenched around him, desperate for more, needing more of his cock, hungry for it.

He pulled out of her, and he wrapped his fingers around her hair and jerked her up. She stared across the room to see the mirror. She'd not seen it when she entered, but there it was now, showing the two of them. He pulled out so only the tip remained. The condom ruined the visual. She wanted to see his dick, the thick vein, all of it, sliding in deep. Axton slammed inside her, and she cried out, watching it and feeling it all at the same time.

"Watch me fuck you, baby."

He took her, fucking her hard, taking her to the next level of pleasure.

She couldn't get enough. He suddenly stopped, pulling out and releasing her.

She moaned. "Please, don't stop."

"I love hearing you beg, baby, but right now, I want something else."

She looked over her shoulder as he picked up the dildo, and he began to coat it in some lubrication.

Biting her lip, she stared at him.

"Do you want it?"

Yes.

No.

Fuck.

I want this so badly.

"Yes."

"Don't worry. I'll go slow. I'll make sure you love it."

She turned back to looking at the sheet.

Not once had she ever been honest with David. She'd always told him the answers he needed to hear. The desire she thought she was supposed to have. She didn't tell him once that she'd craved to feel a man holding her down, taking what he wanted. How she wanted to hold herself open as he brought her pleasure. Being fucked in every single hole, and then held afterward.

The top of the cock pressed against her ass, and she couldn't help but tense up. Axton soothed her ass, stroking the curve.

"Shh, it's okay."

She chuckled. "I don't think you should be soothing me when you're trying to get a big fat cock inside me." She cried out as he pushed the dildo past her tight ring of muscles, filling her ass with at least half of it.

"Watch as I fuck your ass with this, baby. One day soon, I'm going to fuck it and fill it with my cum. Watch it run out. I may even film it so that I have it with me for a long time to come."

She whimpered. She liked the thought of him taking his pleasure, of watching them fuck. She'd love to watch that video as well.

He pushed the cock inside her ass, and she gripped the sheet beneath her as it filled her, stretching her.

When it was all in, Axton stroked her ass once again, moving his finger between her thighs to tease her clit.

"So pretty." He gripped her ass and moved her so that her ass was in front of the mirror. "Look."

The dildo he'd used had been dark. As she stared at her ass, she saw just how filled and stretched she was.

Axton didn't let her watch for long. He pulled her back into position, and this time as he plunged inside her, there was more of a burn, the dildo in her ass making her smaller. She heard him moan and then tighten his grip on her hips as he fucked her hard. Each slap against her butt rocked the dildo within her, and she ached for more, desperate, needy, wanting it all.

"Please, please, please," she said.

"Yes, that's right, you're all fucking mine, Taylor. You're not getting away. When I say, you will come to me, and I will take what I want, and you'll love every single thing that I do to you."

She pushed back and cried out as he started to stroke her clit. With the dildo in her ass, his cock in her pussy, and his fingers on her clit, she just couldn't stop. The pleasure was so intense, the next level of pleasure, of pain, of everything she ever wanted and more. She'd dreamed about this moment, of being completely taken over by her own needs, of wanting an orgasm and feeling him come. There was no time for anything else. He fucked her hard, showing no mercy as he took and took, and she gave him willingly. There was nothing she wouldn't give to him. He could have everything. She wanted to give him everything.

"Please," she said.

"You want to come, my beauty," he said.

"Yes!"

He teased her pussy, bringing her to the edge, making her whimper and beg for more. "I'm the one that controls your pleasure. I'm the one that says what you can have. Me and only me."

"Yes."

She would agree to anything just so long as he'd let her come.

Axton pushed her over the edge, and she came, screaming his name, begging him not to stop, to do anything but to keep the pleasure coming. Her orgasm was so intense that it pushed him into his own. He held her hips tightly as he pounded away, taking what he wanted from her, and she gave it to him.

There was nothing she wouldn't give to him. Every single part of her belonged to him and him alone.

As the pleasure started to ebb away, she didn't feel anything other than being absolutely sated.

"That felt amazing."

"That's just the start."

He eased out of her pussy, and she watched as he wrapped up the condom, then tied it together, but he didn't throw it away in the trash.

"What are you doing?" she asked.

Axton didn't say. He walked out of his bedroom and her curiosity was piqued. Following him to the balcony, she watched as he placed it in a trashcan, and then set fire to it, using a small amount of fuel. She couldn't bring herself to step out, to look over at the city. Axton looked unfazed by his surroundings.

The cock inside her ass was still there, rock hard within her.

Minutes later, he came back inside. "Why did you burn it?"

"A lot of women will go to great lengths to have our cum. Think about the amount of child support they'd get. The cushy lifestyle."

"I have no desire to have kids. That is … insulting."

"I've walked in on women who've tried to push used cum inside themselves. If Easton, Karson, or Romeo left a condom … believe me, we don't allow anyone to take advantage."

"You fuck a woman together?"

"Sometimes. Sometimes we just watch each other."

"The bond of brotherhood?"

"You sound pissed."

"Of course I'm pissed. Seriously, as an after-fuck moment, Axton, that one sucked. You grabbed your special condom and burned it. Newsflash, not every single woman wants your kid. Wow, I can't. You know what, I want to go home."

She was so angry right now. How dare he assume she was after his money or his kid?

"I do this all the time. No need to get upset."

Taylor laughed and snorted. "Just compare me to all of your money-grabbing whores. Huh. After all, we only want you for your money. It has nothing to do with actually having a good time." She grabbed her bra, quickly putting it over her tits and strapping it up. "I don't want your kid, Axton, or your money. I mean, I get that there are women out there, but believe me, I don't want any of that crap. When I have a child, it'll be with a man who loves me. Who'll want to spend time with my child and with me. They won't look at him or her and think about how he's been trapped or used. That's not the kind of life I'd ever want any children I have to face."

He stepped up to her, grabbing the dress. "Good."

"Give me my dress, Axton."

He grabbed the dress and tore it in half. "You're not leaving."

"Wow, you really don't know how to behave like a gentleman."

"I never claimed to be one. Don't mistake me for one either."

"Oh, believe me, I won't." She folded her arms, glaring at him. "Take me home."

"No. I'm not done with you yet."

"You're not going to get done with me. I don't want to be here."

He cupped her cheeks, tilting her head back. "My dildo is still in your ass. Let me help you out of it, and then if you still wish to go home, I'll take you."

She pressed her lips together. It was on the tip of her tongue to shout all manner of things, to finally tell him her accusations. Was he the one to get Carla pregnant? The way he handled the condoms it made her wonder if he wasn't willing to take that risk for that reason. She'd meant every single word she said. She didn't want his money or his children, just the truth.

"Fine. But I want to go home."

He took her hand, and she expected him to push her to the bed and start to remove the dildo.

Axton led her to the bathroom.

"What are you doing?"

"I'm not just going to yank that thing out of you. I put it in when you were highly aroused. With the way you're looking at me right now, I doubt you are. You're also tense. I want you to relax."

He filled the bath, and she watched as he placed some soaps into the water, swirling them around with his hand.

It all seemed a little surreal to her that he was doing this, that she stood in his apartment. They'd just fucked, and it had been raw and fantastic. She'd loved every second of it. Now though, she felt a little empty, a little lost.

David had warned her about this, had told her that she'd struggle not to feel that connection, to keep the barrier up where he was just another man.

"It's ready." He took her hand, and she didn't fight him.

Climbing into the water, she slid down so that she didn't jar the dildo inside her.

She went to ease back, but Axton stopped her by climbing in behind her. She wanted to protest, but he pulled her against him, gently, his legs down either side of hers.

The sheer size of him surprised her. In this moment, she felt small, delicate, and she didn't want to be a hard-ass. Not right now. She'd just had mind-blowing sex. Even though she hadn't lost her virginity, something had changed inside her. This was the first time she'd had sex just to feel good, not for any other reason, and she was worried that she couldn't go back. That she'd ruined everything.

"I'm sorry," he said. "With you I seem to be putting my foot in it."

She didn't say anything. Right now, she was too exhausted.

He ran his hands up and down her body.

Even though she didn't want to feel anything, his touch did spark her arousal. He made her ache, and she didn't want him to stop when he kept on touching her.

She wanted him so much.

He wasn't a job right now.

Axton was something else.

"I don't like being accused of stuff I'd never do."

"I'll try to remember that. You'd be surprised what some women would do to have an easy life."

She sighed. "That's not me. I like working hard."

"I noticed."

"You did?"

"Well, I notice your ass the most."

She chuckled.

"Are you still mad at me?"

She held her hand up so he could see. "Little bit."

"Well, I'll have to make it up to you."

He lifted her legs up so that they were on either side of the tub, spreading her open. His fingers teased down her body, moving between her thighs. She watched his hand as it moved between her slit, stroking her clit.

Everything was becoming clouded around her. She had to stay focused, but the moment he touched her, she wanted to forget everything else and simply bask in the pleasure of his touch and push everything to one side.

Couldn't she have a little time to herself?

"Give me everything, Taylor."

As if the devil himself had spoken.

She pushed past the guilt and took for herself, letting herself go to the pleasure of his touch.

****

Taylor opened her eyes, staring across Axton's bedroom. After he'd made her come hard in the bathroom, he'd taken out the dildo and admired the hole of her ass. It had been dirty and sinful, and then they fucked again before falling asleep, his arm wrapped around her waist, holding her close.

She had to leave.

It was nearly four in the morning, and she had to get home, or do something to get to her meeting.

Besides, she didn't want the awkward morning-after routine. Slowly, rolling over, she took her time, moving away from him. He let out a grunt, and she stilled. His arm didn't pull her closer, and she quickly slipped out of it, easing out of his bed and standing on the floor. In her apartment she knew where every single squeak was.

Tiptoeing away from the bed, she hoped that he didn't have any creaking noises.

She moved quickly through his apartment toward the door. She pulled on her dress, only to realize that it was fucking torn. He'd torn it from her. He owed her for a new dress. Gritting her teeth, she passed his kitchen and paused. As if by some miracle there was a laundry basket filled with clothes. They were neatly folded and placed as shirts or sweatpants. Not a suit in sight. It kind of made her curious to see him in this kind of clothes. The hanging-out clothes where he didn't have to be the boss. Taking a shirt and a pair of sweatpants, she quickly pulled them on, gathered her heels in her hand, and was about to leave. The temptation was too great though.

Stepping down one of the corridors away from his bedroom, she saw a plain white door. Twisting the doorknob, she opened the door, and came face to face with his office.

Right now, she didn't have time to rummage around, but one day soon, she'd have to get back here to have a look. Closing the door, she turned and heard a noise. Holding her breath, she waited.

No more sounds came out, and without waiting around, she rushed out of his apartment toward the elevator. The man was waiting, and she refused to look at him as she bent down, putting the heels on.

A definite fashion statement.

Heels with sweatpants and a shirt.

Totally classy.

The elevator pinged open, and she quickly rushed out of the building. Her face heated at the shame that suddenly swamped her. She felt all of their gazes on her, judging her. She shouldn't have run out, but she also wasn't going to stick around.

Axton's apartment building wasn't too far from Paul's. She didn't bother with a taxi.

Walking the twenty minutes to his building, she went into reception and smiled at the woman waiting.

"Could you call up to Paul Motts for me?" she asked.

"The name?" the woman asked, not recognizing her. Taylor couldn't remember the last time she'd come to Paul's apartment. It had been so long. They either met at her place or for dinner.

"Taylor Keane."

She waited as she put a call through to Paul. He was going to be so pissed that she woke him up, but they were friends, right? They weren't perfect. Paul would never replace Carla. It's why she didn't try to replace her with him.

She wished it had been different these past ten years. That they didn't spend so much time losing touch. Each time she saw him, she vowed to stick around, but then something would happen, and months would go by, even years before they saw each other again.

The woman finished on the phone.

"You may go up."

She thanked the woman and walked toward the elevator. The man didn't say a word as she stepped onto it, taking her up to Paul's floor.

Her friend was waiting for her when she stepped

off.

He raised a brow at her attire. "David would totally have a fit if he saw you."

Paul wasn't wearing a shirt, and he rubbed the back of his head. "Your date went well?"

"Really, really well."

"Need some coffee?"

"Please."

Following him down to his room, she stepped inside.

He closed and locked the door, and she waited for him to lead the way into the kitchen. She followed behind him as he started to make some coffee. She noticed he liked the cheap stuff for some reason.

"He ruined my dress," she said, filling in the silence. "It's why I'm dressed like this."

"I gathered."

She didn't say anything, staring into the cup. Paul sat opposite her, waiting.

This was her first "morning after."

"This is your first time, isn't it? Where you weren't being taught what to do or what to say?"

She nodded. Words failed her right now.

"Are you okay?"

She shook her head. "No, I'm not okay."

"What's wrong, Taylor? Talk to me."

"I knew it would be different, but I didn't think it would be like this. It meant nothing with David."

"I still think it was a stupid idea to bring him into it."

"I couldn't go there without being prepared, Paul. You know that."

He held his hands up. "You and I both know you didn't have to do this."

The tears she'd been keeping in started to fall.

She didn't know what the hell to do anymore. Everything felt so raw, so open. She didn't know what to do or what to say.

"You like him?" Paul asked.

"David?"

"Axton."

She shrugged. "I don't know."

He sat down opposite her, cup in his hands, waiting.

"Yes, I like him." She nibbled her lip. "You probably think I'm so stupid right now."

"I don't think you're stupid at all, actually. Do you love him?"

"I don't know, Paul. I barely know him. All I know is what I've been paid to know. What I've seen."

Paul reached out and placed a hand on top of hers. "You can't keep doing this. You've got to come clean or let it go."

"I can't. I've got to know the truth."

"I wish I didn't go and check that damn report."

"Aren't you curious about it? Don't you think we have a right to know?"

"Yes, I do, which is why I'm helping you, but I'm scared for you, Taylor. The four kings, they're deadly. Even I've heard rumors."

She frowned. "What kind of rumors?"

Paul withdrew his hand. "I didn't want to tell you."

"Tell me."

"Before Axton and the others took over, there was talk of underhand practices. How they manipulated and circulated rumors to bring companies down so they could snap them up for cheap prices. There was also talk of possible blackmail as well. Deals with politicians, that kind of thing."

"You're saying this all happened *before* the takeover bid by Axton, Easton, and whatnot?"

"Yes."

"What about the rumors now? What are they all about?"

"I don't want you to go hunting for this, Taylor. I want you to stay out of it."

"I can't. Not yet. Not until I know the truth."

"Will that kind of truth really set us both free? I know David's on your side, and he makes you believe you can do anything. That you're justified in doing what you think is right."

"This isn't about being justified, Paul. I want the truth."

"At what cost?"

"Justice. For Carla's parents to know that their daughter wasn't keeping secrets from them. All of it."

"You feel guilty," he said. "Because you enjoyed your time with Axton."

"Don't do that, Paul. Seriously, don't do the whole looking deep inside me. I'm really not interested right now or anytime."

"You can pretend all you want. It doesn't change the fact you had fun, and now you feel like you didn't deserve that fun."

"Can I stay here tonight?"

"You know you can use the spare room." Paul rubbed at his temple. "I've … erm … I've got a date tomorrow."

"A date?"

"Yes."

"Wow, congratulations. Who is she?"

"A lawyer. I've known her for a few years."

"Wow, congratulations," she said again. What else could she say?

"Thank you."

"Don't worry, Paul. I won't be here. I appreciate you letting me use the spare room."

She finished her coffee, stood up, and hugged him. "You're a really good friend." She turned away about to leave.

"Be careful, Taylor. I don't want anything to happen to you."

"I know, Paul."

****

Keeping the baseball cap down, Taylor entered the coffee shop. She was way too tempted to have a look around her, to see if anyone was paying her attention. Instead, she ignored that niggling feeling that someone was watching her. She'd gotten a couple of hours' sleep in Paul's spare room and changed into a pair of jeans and a shirt.

She saw Catherine, dressed in a similar style, in the back booth. Taking a coffee to sit with, she sat opposite the other woman without saying a word.

"I know you," Catherine said. "You're the Kings' PA."

"Taylor Keane." She held her hand out.

"This is bullshit. I thought this was a legitimate meeting. Paul said it was."

"It is." When Catherine went to go, Taylor caught her hand. "I honestly just want to talk."

"You're going to go back to your bosses? Tell them that you've seen me."

"They don't know I'm here."

"Ah, so are you fucking them yet? Last I heard they didn't fuck their PA."

"I'm not here to talk about that."

"I did. Well, I fucked all but Axton. He didn't do fuck all with me. I guess he believed he was too good for the likes of me. You know, the small folk."

Taylor tried not to squirm, but with how roughly Axton had taken her last night, every single part of her felt sensitive. Catherine was too busy looking away and not paying her any real attention to notice.

"Why did you want to talk to me?"

"You know why. Paul gave you the relevant details of why I want to talk to you. You can trust me."

"I spoke to Paul. You tell me what it is you want."

"I want to know what information you've got on the four kings."

Catherine burst out laughing. "You think I'm going to tell you so you can go back to your bosses. I've already lost my job, and I can't find another one thanks to them blacklisting me."

"You were going to blackmail them though. You weren't exactly an innocent party."

"Is this your bartering speech?"

"You were using them as much as they were using you. The only difference is, you didn't see it. They won."

Catherine chuckled. "I can see why they like you. Don't hold anything back, do you?"

"You can get a job. I've got a friend who'd be willing to help you." Paul had told her what to offer before she even came here. She'd told him not to bother that if Catherine wasn't willing to talk. Then they didn't have to offer anything. He'd told her what he wanted her to offer and even lost his temper when she tried to refuse.

"What are the conditions? You see, I'm not new to this, little girl. I know what is expected of me, and I know what is expected of you. So, let's cut the bull and get straight to it."

"You'd have to leave the city. Be willing to start

up somewhere new. He'll help you, but it will mean being quiet for some time and changing your ways. If you don't agree, you're on your own."

Catherine snorted. "Starting over."

"It's either that or wait for whatever savings you've got to dwindle, then homelessness."

"And in return?"

"Tell me what you know about the four kings."

"And what makes you think I've got anything?" Catherine asked, leaning in close.

"Because no one in this world goes out of their way to ruin a person's reputation or career unless they've got something to hide. I've got no interest in what you've done or what they've done. I want to know what you had on them. Simple as that."

Catherine sat back. "You do surprise me."

"I get that a lot."

"When I give you this information, what then?"

"I had a friend … a long time ago. Something happened, and people need to know the truth."

"You think the four kings are involved?"

"I know they are. I just don't know how much."

Catherine laughed. "This is just too good. They've hired a PA intent on bringing them down."

"I want to know the truth."

"And you think I can help you."

"You've got something, and I want to know what that is. Clearly, it was enough for them to silence you. To make you a laughing stock and so no one would believe any story you tell about them."

Catherine folded her arms. "I'm intrigued."

"Just tell me what you know. You've got nothing to lose and a job to gain."

"Ten years ago, the rise of the current four kings was something of a media frenzy. A scandal broke the business world. Nearly brought the empire and all those connected to it down on its knees."

"I know all about that. The father was in some unscrupulous deals and manipulating facts, buying off press. That kind of thing."

"Yeah, but not a lot of people know it was Axton to bring it all crashing down around his dad."

This made her pause. "What?"

"Axton, Easton, Romeo, and Karson are four points of the crown. The Four Kings' Empire, the crown. They had access to every single kind of information possible. They leaked it out to the press. To keep them safe and to allow future access the people they dealt with kept their sources quiet."

"Okay, so why do you think they're still dirty?"

"Because the dads that ran it before Axton and the others, they had a whole dirty way of running the business. They may not be dirty now, but they're keeping secrets about it. We're talking cover-ups and at one time even mob hits."

This made Taylor laugh. "Now you're lying."

"I'm not lying. For a long time, the four kings ruled everything, and if anyone so much as blinked at them the wrong way, they ended up at the bottom of a river."

That last statement made Taylor freeze. Catherine kept talking. In the back of her mind, she flashed to the bonfire, to a time gone by.

"Wait, what do you mean river?"

"Look at the Ellie Andrea case."

"What?" Taylor asked.

"Do your research. Ellie Andrea was an escort. Last known customer, Nial Long. They have secrets that cannot stay buried. For the right price, I wanted to get the right information to be made for life."

"Easton's dad. What happened?" She didn't care what Catherine wanted. Just the facts.

"She was found dead, face first in a river. Apparent suicide. They reckon she got pregnant. Tried to kill herself."

This couldn't be a coincidence. Pulling out her cell phone, Taylor quickly typed in the name and saved it.

"If you're going after the four kings, be careful. I mean that. You won't come out of this a happy woman."

She nodded. "You have absolutely nothing of any worth at all."

"Excuse me?"

Taylor burst out laughing. "I can't even for a second believe that I thought you had something. I mean, the name of a prostitute that their parents hired doesn't help me. Pregnant or not, a prostitute sleeps with lots of men and women." She shook her head.

"It was enough for them to be worried, so fuck you," Catherine said.

Even though none of the information she got was on the current four kings, the name was something for her to look into. She'd never gone back to look at the fathers. She'd done as much research as she could on the current four kings, but that was all. That was her mistake.

"You were going to sell your body and their secrets. Regardless of what you think, it's their company. It's not for someone like you to sell those secrets."

Catherine stood. "You think you're better than me? You're not. You have your own agenda here. There has been a lot of talk with some of the four kings' enemies. You see, using my body gets me in on a lot of secrets. Some of those men that the four kings have ruined like to talk. There's files on a lot of bad deeds, and you can bet the current generation have them in their keeping, just in case a need arises."

"How do you know that? Who told you?"

"Easton likes to talk a lot when you suck him dry. Work his cock and get your answers. That's what I did." Catherine grabbed her bag. "Good luck. You're going to need it."

Taylor had no intention of fucking Easton.

Chapter Ten

Ten years ago
"You ever thought about having a baby?" Carla asked.

Taylor flicked through the catalogue that Carla had. The clothing looked amazing, but there were none in her size. "No, why?"

"I just … I saw a woman in town today, and it got me thinking about kids."

"Aren't you a little young to be thinking about kids and that kind of stuff?"

"I don't know. I'd love to have one or two," Carla said.

Taylor paused. "One day I want a family. A massive flock of them. You know, running around my feet. I can bake cookies and be the perfect mom. One day, maybe. First I'd need a boyfriend."

She heard Carla sigh. "Yeah, a boyfriend."

Taylor frowned and sat up, moving toward the bed. Carla was rubbing her stomach, looking worried. "What's wrong?"

"Nothing," Carla said.

"You keep saying that, but you're not acting like nothing is wrong. Talk to me, weirdo."

Carla chuckled. "Honestly, I'm fine. Just a few … cramps."

"I thought you said you started the other day. It's why you couldn't come swimming."

"I don't want to talk about this anymore. Did you see anything at all?"

"Carla?"

"I mean it, Taylor. I don't want to talk about anything, okay? I'm fine. It doesn't matter."

Taylor stared at her friend. Carla had been yelling at her a lot more lately, whenever she tried to pry.

"You know what, I'm heading home."

"Taylor?"

"No, Carla, I'm sick and tired of this … whatever it is you're doing. I'm not your punching bag or someone for you to yell at because you're not happy. I'm out of here."

****

Present day

Axton didn't like that she'd sneaked out of his bedroom or that he didn't feel her leave. He must have been fucking exhausted not to have stopped her. He was normally a light sleeper, a really light one.

It was the first time in a long while that he could ever remember falling asleep and sleeping the whole night so soundly.

She'd not answered any of his calls, and when he stopped by her apartment, she'd not been there either. He knew without a doubt she'd been with Paul, but he'd not gone to Paul. He didn't want him to know how fucking desperate he was to talk to her.

By Monday, he sat in his office and waited. He'd arrived at six in the morning, knowing she always came to work early. It was what he'd been planning on.

There's no way he'd let her back the fuck out, not now. Not with knowing how good her pussy felt wrapped around his dick, or how hot she looked with the dildo up her ass. She'd looked perfect in every single way to him, so beautiful and ready for anything. He wanted her again. These feelings she inspired within him wouldn't go away, not that he wanted them to.

He wanted her, plain and simple.

Axton heard the elevator doors open, and he stood from his chair, moving toward the door.

Taylor appeared, but she hadn't seen him yet. Her hair was pulled back into some kind of loop bun at the base of her neck. She looked … stunning. She wore barely any makeup, and he wondered if that was because she'd stayed with Paul over the weekend.

She put her bag near her chair, fired up her computer, and removed her jacket. The black dress she wore molded to every single curve. It had a belt around her waist, enhancing those full tits and hips.

"Did you have a good weekend?" he asked.

Taylor released a little scream. "Axton, you scared me." She placed a hand to her chest. "I didn't think anyone would be here at this time of the morning."

"I've been waiting to talk to you. I called you several times."

"My phone died."

"Don't lie."

She nibbled that lip again, making him ache. What was it about that simple action that seemed to undo him? It was like she took all of his focus away, and he just wanted to suck on that sweet lip.

Stepping up close to her, he wasn't surprised when she took a step back. He didn't stop until her back was pressed against the wall, her chest heaving with each of her indrawn breaths. Her nipples were already rock-hard, pressing against the front of her dress.

She liked this.

"You've got to stop," she said. "Right now, you're my boss."

"Why are you so wet for me then, Taylor? Why is it you want me to touch you, right here, right now?"

She groaned. "We're not supposed to do this."

"You want to though, don't you?" He cupped her hip. "You feel this too." Pushing her dress up to her waist, he lifted her thigh over his hip, thrusting his cock against her core. She let out a gasp, pressing against him as he pushed against her.

It wasn't close enough. He needed inside her again.

Grabbing her hand, he didn't ask for permission as he dragged her into his office. Slamming the door closed, he pulled her into his arms. Sinking his fingers into her hair, he took possession of her lips, sliding his tongue across her mouth. She opened up with a gasp. Her fingers gripped his shoulder tightly, pushing at his jacket until it fell to the floor. She started to attack his shirt, shoving him down onto the sofa.

He sat down and pulled her into his lap, lifting up her dress, tugging her panties off. He threw them across the room.

"Please tell me you've got a condom."

He reached into his pants pocket and held one up. "It's right here."

She took it from him, tearing into the foil. He was already taking out his cock, and together they worked the latex over his dick. Once he was covered, she lifted up. He held his cock at her entrance, and she thrust down onto his length. They both moaned as he filled her. When he was a couple of inches inside her, he grabbed her hips and, giving her no time to prepare, he thrust up and pulled her down, filling her tight cunt.

He couldn't wait. His need for her was too great. Lifting her up, he slammed her back down, fucking her.

Taylor held onto his shoulders and started to ride his cock. He wanted to see her tits bouncing as she took him. Reaching for the dress zipper, he slid it down, and her tits were covered by thin cups of lace. He quickly lifted them out of the cups and moaned as they started to bounce.

Returning his grip to her ass, he watched her ride

him.

Sliding a hand between her thighs, he stroked her clit, feeling her tight heat clench around him the moment he did. For the first time in his life, he wished he didn't have the fucking condom on. He wanted to feel every single pulse and clench as she fucked.

"You're going to get on the pill. I want to fuck inside you."

"Can't," she said, gasping out as he pulled her down, not letting her get away with anything. He wanted to completely consume her.

"Why not?"

"They make me ill. I can't take them." She cried out as he pinched her clit.

"Fuck!" He lifted her up, pushing her down onto the sofa. Lifting her legs up, he watched his cock fill her tight cunt and the fine hairs of her pussy as it was split open, and his condom-covered cock was slick with her arousal.

He'd love to fill her with his cum, to watch as it dripped out of her pussy.

He'd have to keep that pleasure for her ass.

She reached between them and started to stroke her clit. He watched as she took her pleasure at the same time, and he continued to fuck her hard, giving her everything. He'd wanted to do this over the weekend, to have his fill of her so he could finally put whatever need he had away.

With the way she felt around him and how much he loved seeing her beneath or above him, riding his dick, once or twice wasn't going to be enough. He had to get in charge of this. To get himself under control.

She came hard, her cunt squeezing his cock as he fucked her through her orgasm. Only after she'd come and screamed his name did he finally allow himself that pleasure, filling her up with his cum.

When it was over, they were both panting.

He didn't know what time it was.

"You've got to stop ruining my panties," she said.

"You've got to stop wearing them. Don't wear them, I won't ruin them."

"This shouldn't be happening." She pushed some hair off her face.

"It's happening."

She chuckled. "I know it's happening, but it shouldn't. You're my boss."

"One of four."

"Oh, so you'd like to share me out between your friends?" she asked.

Never had he been so overcome with jealousy. "No. They don't get to touch you." He wrapped his arms around her, holding her tight. "They don't get to know just how good you are. You're all mine."

"I get it. I'm all yours. I had no idea a Four King could be possessive."

"There's a lot more to us than what they paint in the news."

"I get that. I can see that," she said. "I'm going to need to go back to work."

"I don't want you sneaking out again."

"I'm not very good when it comes to the morning-after thing."

"Had a lot of experience with that?"

"Not as much as you'd think." She stroked over his chest. The crown he'd gotten inked stood out. "This place means a lot to you, doesn't it?"

"I've gone through a lot to get to where I am today."

"I can see that."

"I know a lot of people think I've got this handed

to me on a silver platter, Taylor, but I didn't. I got this through a lot of hard work." He didn't even know why he was telling her this.

"I get it."

He pulled out of her pussy. She didn't wait for him. She rolled out from beneath him, and he watched as she put herself together. She eased her tits back into the bra and wriggled the dress into place. Next, she turned toward him. "I don't suppose you'd do my zipper."

He'd have loved to see her naked all day long, but he wouldn't have liked any of the others to see what belonged to him.

Just the thought of them seeing her made him want to fucking blind them. She inspired these feelings inside him. He wanted to protect her, to not let anyone or anything hurt her.

"I like you like this," he said as she tucked her hair back into a bun.

"Like what?"

"No makeup. Just like I remember you."

She paused. "Did you ever put anything in my locker ten years ago?"

"I have no idea, why?"

"You say certain things, and I don't know. Just reminds me of something I got."

"I have no idea what you're talking about," he said. "Where were you this weekend?"

"At a friend's. I needed to clear my head."

"Paul's?" He didn't like feeling jealous, especially as he knew Paul and Taylor were nothing special to each other.

"I was with him, but he had a hot date on Saturday. So, I went to see David."

"You've got a lot of male friends."

She shrugged. "I better get back to work."

He caught her wrist, stopping her from walking away from him. "Have lunch with me today."

"I work through lunch. I have four bosses that like to keep me busy."

"Tell the other three to fuck off."

She chuckled. "I can't. You've all got a conference, and I get to eat my lunch and take notes."

She tried to pull away again. He caught her wrist and kissed her lips, sliding his tongue across her bottom one until she opened up. He plunged inside, not wanting to let her go.

Finally, he released her, watching as she pulled away. She left his office, closing the door ever so gently before leaving.

He had to get his head in the fucking game once and for all.

****

"Anything else happen?" David asked.

"No, nothing. It's been all work. When we're there and have deadlines and stuff, it's like I don't exist."

"You'll exist. The only difference is you'll become the dessert."

She lay back on the weightlifting bench. Reaching up, she lifted the bar, doing a couple of pumps and putting it back onto the holder. David stared down at her.

Since she was sure she was being followed, this was where she came to work out, rather than be alone in an empty park. David was good company as well, and at least here, she could try to forget for a few hours what was going on. She hated working out. Most of the time, she'd work out, and then feel like a treat for all of her hard work, which was why David often took her to dinner after.

"Have any new clients lately?" she asked.

"A couple. I don't kiss and tell, you know that."

"Business is good."

"You're trying to change the subject. If I didn't know straight away that you don't have feelings for me, I'd even think you were jealous. I know differently. You're avoiding, why?"

She grabbed the bar again and did a couple more pumps.

"Does this have to do with Paul?" he asked.

She paused with the bar pressed against her chest. "I don't want to talk about it."

"You slept with him."

She didn't say anything. Putting the bar back into rest, she sat up, and moved toward the running machines. Clicking the speed she wanted to run, she tried to block out David. As usual though, he stood by her side, helping her, training her.

"I know it's hard."

"I don't want to talk about this. I mean it."

"Taylor, I know you're having all these kinds of feelings."

She clicked pause. "I don't want to do this, okay?"

The desire to run left her. Stepping off, she glanced around the gym and felt completely out of place. This wasn't her scene.

Memories came, of her hanging out with Carla, eating snacks, watching movies, planning for the future by looking through catalogues.

You stopped being that to be this.

You chose this.

Tears welled up in her eyes, and she felt herself panicking.

David grabbed her arm and pushed her into a room. It wasn't as bright as the rest of the gym.

"Calm down." He placed a hand to her chest, and he started to do some deep, even breathing. "Focus on me. Calm down."

Breathing in, one, two, three, breathing out, one, two, three. She kept on doing it, finding that calm that had been about to leave her.

"He was the first man I had sex with. The first man I had to leave in the morning, and right now, I just … it's hard."

"Because you want to hurt him?"

She covered her face.

"Paul's been getting to you. I know he has. He's been against this plan from the start. I don't even know why he agreed to help you."

"He couldn't have been completely against it."

"Why?" David asked.

"Because he helped me."

"Then I guess he wants to move on but you're not letting him."

She glared at him. "I don't want to talk about it."

"Here's the thing, Taylor. You're going to have to talk about it if you like it or not."

She stopped and whirled around to look at him. "Why though? I don't want to talk about this."

"Because having sex with someone doesn't cut you off, okay? You can develop feelings for that other person."

"You're telling me that you have feelings for me?" she asked, knowing he didn't.

"I care about you, Taylor. I'm one of your best friends, and I don't want to see you get hurt. Your plan was a good one, but sex and feelings brings a whole new grey area and you've got to be able to deal with that."

"I'm sticking to the plan, David. I'm not going to back down. I wish everyone would stop treating me as if

I'm some kind of a child. Like I don't know what I'm doing."

David covered her mouth as she started to yell. "What you're doing right now, that is childish. All we want to do is help you. You've got to learn to accept our help. We all care about you. We all worry."

"I don't know who I am anymore."

He pulled her into his arms, and she held him, needing his strength in that moment.

"You're Taylor Keane. Kickass friend and one hell of a woman. Remember, own your shit. It's who you are."

She nodded, pulling away. Taking another deep breath, she smiled at him. "I'm sorry."

"I need to know. You can stop this at any time. Just quit, and it will all go away."

"I can't quit. Not now. I need to know the truth. I don't even know if it's about bringing them down anymore. I just … I need to know the truth."

"Then let's get back out there. Work your ass and get back to work."

They left the room, and she went straight back to the treadmill. Putting in the speed she wanted to run, she got started once again, repeating stuff through her head.

Find the truth.
Prove Carla's death wasn't a suicide.
Deal with the kings.
End them.

The last one she wasn't so sure about anymore.

She'd done her research like Catherine suggested. If it wasn't for Catherine, she'd have never found this. She'd spent so much time over the past ten years, not only planning this, between college and then making a life for herself, but also watching the four kings now, that she'd not delved into their fathers. She'd found the old newspaper article online. There had been a picture of Easton's and Axton's fathers with the woman. It didn't help her. She had so many questions and not enough answers.

Part of her believed if she was just to ask Axton what he had, he'd tell her. Then of course, she figured he wouldn't tell her the truth. Who would? She was a no one. They had sex, but that was as far as it went.

After her run, they went to the mats, and David helped her do some stretches.

"Taylor," Axton said.

David had her leg pushed up near her head and was stretching her out. This gym was one of the best in the city as it had many different facilities. Not once did she think it would be where Axton would work out.

Looking up, she saw Axton, Easton, Karson, and Romeo, all slick with sweat, clearly coming out of a workout.

"Hey, guys." She forced a smile to her lips. "What a surprise to see you all here."

"Who is this?" Axton asked.

She didn't like the look in his eye. He wasn't happy at all.

"This is my friend, David. David, these are all my bosses. Romeo, Easton, Karson, and Axton."

"Nice to meet you guys." He released her leg and shook each of their hands. She noticed Axton shook the longest and hardest, refusing to let go.

David went to grab her leg when Axton stopped him. "What are you doing?"

"I'm helping her stretch out."

"I can do that."

"You know how?"

"Yes." Axton pushed him out of the way, and she stared up at the man that had her entire mind and body all over the place. She couldn't think clearly at all.

He touched her thigh, bringing it up, and she stared into his eyes, seeing how dark they were. He wasn't happy. Rather than be afraid though, she found his deadly look highly arousing.

"So, what do you do, David?" Karson asked.

She tuned them all out and focused on the way Axton held her leg, pressing it up against her body. She felt him move between her thighs. The intent was there, and everything disappeared and the only thing she felt was him.

Between her thighs felt really, really good.

He released her leg and did the other one, staring at her. "I didn't know you came to this gym."

"Oh, this is the first time I've been here."

"Why?"

"I usually run."

"What made you change your mind?"

Oh, shit!

"I felt like a change. Besides, it's not always safe."

He leaned over her, putting his hand beside her head, and he completely surrounded her.

"Is that all?"

"Of course."

"I think she's done enough," David said, suddenly there.

Pulling away from Axton, she smiled up at David, holding her hand out toward him. Axton caught her hand, stopping David from helping her. He helped her up.

"He's my ride tonight." She pulled her hand away from him, but Axton wouldn't let her go.

"I want to talk to you."

Before she knew what was happening, he had

pulled her into one of the changing rooms. It was only a small room, and Axton had her pressed up against the wall.

"Who is he?" Axton asked.

"Jealous?"

"Don't be fucking coy with me, Taylor."

"He's my friend."

"You fuck him."

"You've fucked most of the female population. Now is not the time to get angry with me for having a life."

"He's a fucking escort."

"How do you even know that?" she asked.

"I heard him. I know my dick distracted you, but I can do two things at once. I can listen to your *friend* talk and fuck you."

"Screw you, Axton. You're not the boss of me. You'll never be the boss of me."

He wrapped his hand around her neck, tilting her head back with her thumb so that she had no choice but to look into his eyes.

"I *am* your boss, Taylor. And I will screw you until you can't think of anyone else. You've fucked him, haven't you? The escort that has been with so many women. I'm surprised you're friends with him."

She wasn't going to bite.

"Got no answer for that?"

He pulled her thigh up against his waist and began to press his cock to her pussy. The shorts she wore didn't exactly hide her from him, not that she wanted to.

"You're wet for me, Taylor. You want me to push my dick deep inside you, fuck you right here, right now. How long has it been since you were with him?" he asked.

"That's none of your business."

His other hand pressed between her thighs, and she moaned.

"You're hot for me, baby, no one else."

He shoved his hand down her pants, and she spread her legs wide so that he could find how wet she was.

"There we go. That's how wet you are for me, baby." He touched her clit, and she closed her eyes. His grip tightened around her neck. "Look at me when I touch you. Know it's me that's making you feel good."

She didn't fight him.

He slid his fingers down, pushing inside her, working two fingers in deep, and she moaned, needing more.

"You want my cock, don't you?"

"Yes!"

"I'm not going to wait." He shoved her pants down as she attacked his, pulling them down. Wrapping her fingers around his length, she groaned as he lifted her up. In the next second, his cock was inside her, and she couldn't believe for a second that she was fucking him in a gym.

He pulled out, only to slam to the hilt inside her, making her ache and moan for more.

Resting her head against the wall, his lips brushed her neck, and she cried out, wanting more, desperate to feel him. He fucked her hard, and she loved that he didn't hold back, that he took what he wanted without any remorse.

She hated that her body wanted him so badly. That she couldn't bring herself to stop this pleasure or this need that built between the two of them.

Glancing down at where they were joined, she saw his cock, slick with her cream as he took her. Cupping his face, she kissed his lips, desperate, hungry for his kisses. She couldn't get enough of him. She felt completely taken over.

"Does he make you feel this good, baby? Does he give you what you need?"

"No."

Axton pulled out of her, taking her to the floor. He tugged up her shirt and unhooked her bra. He shoved it to one side, she pulled him down, kissing him again, only breaking from the kiss so that he could remove his own shirt.

His cock slid back inside her, and she wrapped her legs around him, but it wasn't enough. Rolling him over so that she was above him, she leaned down, kissing him again and moaning as his tongue traced across hers.

She touched his with hers, tasting him as she rode his cock, driving up and down his length. His hands cupped her tits, pressing them together. His thumbs teased her hardened nipples.

When she was with Axton, nothing else mattered. All her troubles ceased to exist, and all that she saw was him, everything about him.

"You drive me fucking wild, baby," he said.

"Please, don't stop."

He ran his hands down to her hips and began to help her, showing her exactly what he liked and just how deep he wanted her to go. He was so big, long, and wide, so open and exposed, and there was no way to control him.

In that moment, every single part of her belonged to him.

He pumped inside her, and everything fell away as it always did. She forgot everything and stared at him. Axton Farris, the man who was turning her world upside down.

"Come for me. I want you to fucking come, baby.

Come all over my cock."

She reached between them, finding her clit, touching herself as he thrust up inside her, fucking her. She took every inch of his cock, needing more, desperate, hungry, wanting everything he gave her, not wanting it or him to stop.

"Yes, please, yes."

"Come for me, Taylor. Come for me." He kept repeating the words and staring into his dark eyes, and she came hard.

His cock pounded within her. She felt him thrust in deep and the pulse of each wave of his cum as he filled her up.

"You're not to be alone with him again," he said.

"I hate to break it to you, Axton. You're not the boss of me."

"With my dick inside you, I'm your fucking everything."

Chapter Eleven

Ten years ago

"Easton really fucked up this time," Karson said.

Sipping at his soda, Axton looked up. He was working through another English assignment that had to be turned in. He could pay any number of people to do the work for him, but he wasn't a cheater. Over the years he'd done many things and he was by no means a good guy, but he did his own schoolwork. Those grades were all fucking his.

"What could that fucker have possibly done?"

"He went and knocked up Carla."

"We know this," Axton said. He was very much aware of Easton's little obsession with the girl. It wasn't something he needed to deal with. That shit wouldn't fall to him.

"He's planning on running away with her."

This made Axton pause and look at his friend. "What?"

"You heard me right. I heard him talking about it. He's planning on running away. Wants to start a family with her."

"That's not … possible."

"We need to talk to him before he goes to his dad."

Axton closed his books and got to his feet. "Or before his dad does something that Easton can't control."

Leaving the bench where they'd been hanging out, he made his way around the school building and saw Taylor in the parking lot. She was on her cell phone, biting that lip that she always seemed to be biting whenever she was nervous.

"Come on, man, you know you can't have that."

He didn't argue with Karson.

He wasn't allowed to have, didn't mean he couldn't look.

****

Present day

Tapping her fingers on her leg, Taylor stared out the window, wondering what the hell to do. How he could just barge into her workout session, fuck the life out of her, and order her around. She knew he'd done it quite easily in fact, and she'd been hot for him, no denying it.

When it came to Axton, she couldn't think straight. No matter what he wanted, one click of his fingers and she was putty in his hands. Now, instead of heading home, he had her in his car, taking her back to his place.

She wore her workout clothes, and David had looked a little confused when she let Axton do all the talking.

"You're quiet."

"I'm just waiting for my next lot of orders, sir."

"Don't be a smartass."

"Yes, sir. Sorry, sir. What else would you like, sir?"

"What are you doing being friends with a male escort?"

"You've got a problem with that?"

"It's you, Taylor. I don't see that happening, like, ever."

"Hate to break it to you, Axton, but you don't really know me."

"I know a hell of a lot more about you than you'd even care to think about."

"Now you're just being creepy."

"I'm stating it like it is."

"Fine, I'll bite. How do you know a lot about me, and here is another thing, what exactly do you know about me? You say stuff like that, but I don't believe it."

"I've got my sources."

She had a feeling this was more than the PI that was on her case. She'd asked Paul to try to figure out who was following her or who Axton had employed. As yet, he'd come up with a blank—even if he was looking at all, which she wouldn't know.

Paul was very much anti-plan right now.

He was so worried about her, and she got it.

So far all they really knew was one of the kings got Carla pregnant. Her being pregnant was covered up in the death report, and a lot of money was paid to the guy who'd written up her report.

She knew the kings had a history of blackmail and extortion.

Now, that could only go back as far as the last generation, their fathers, but they had taken over the company, which also meant they must have known of at least some of their parents' bad practices. Did that mean they were following in their footsteps? She'd not seen anything of the sort during her time thus far.

She'd gone hunting all over the company, going to past files and contracts, and there was nothing there. Whatever they were hiding, they were doing so close to home, and she intended to find it.

She only hoped this wasn't all in her head. She'd come all this way. There *had* to be something.

The main question for her was should she continue with this at all? Should she ignore everything she'd been doing, and just go on? Accept that Carla in some way killed herself, that no one was to blame. Could she do that after all this time? This was what she'd been wanting to find out. The truth. To finally know what happened to Carla. To have some closure on this. The Four Kings' Empire was once flooded by scandal of their fathers' creating. Would Axton be the only one out of all four of them to protect that kind of data or would it be divided so nothing made any sense to anyone?

Ten years she'd waited. Planning, changing her entire future to find out the truth. There's no way she could back down now. Even if she didn't like what she found, she would at least know, or that's what she hoped.

Glancing over at him, the way he held the steering wheel told her he was the one in charge, the guy in the lead, and everyone else had to do as he said.

"I like David. He's fun."

"How are you friends with him?"

He trained me to fuck so that I can take you out.

"The usual way. I was getting tired with all the fuss and hired him, why?"

"Why did you hire him?" he asked.

"For the usual reason you hire an escort, Axton." She pushed some hair off her shoulder, hoping he didn't see her embarrassment.

It was one thing to hire David to teach her, quite another to admit it to Axton.

He pulled up in his parking space, and she didn't wait for him to get out of the car. Climbing out, she moved toward the elevator and he caught her hand, slamming her up against the wall.

"What the hell are you doing?"

"Why?" he asked.

"Why, what?" He surrounded her once again. His fingers were beneath her chin, head tilted back, and she waited.

"Why did you go to him?"

"I wanted to."

"Was he your first?" he asked.

She gasped, totally taken back by his question. She hadn't been expecting it.

"He was, wasn't he?"

Taylor didn't say anything.

"You paid for your first time? You let him slide into your pussy, take your tight little cherry."

"Enough. I want to go home."

"You're not going home." He'd already grabbed her bag from the trunk of the car and had it flung over his shoulder. He took her hand, and before she knew it they were in the elevator, heading toward his floor. Staring at her reflection in the metal doors, she looked a mess. Her hair was out of place, and the clothes she wore were the least sexy out of everything she owned.

All of David's training was screaming at her to make him go home so she could sexy up.

No.

She wouldn't back down.

Squaring her shoulders, she waited as he pulled her down the long hallway to his apartment. The moment they were through the doors, she pulled out of his hold.

"Will you stop tugging me around as if I'm a damn ragdoll?"

He threw her bag onto the floor, then pushed her up against the door, taking hold of her hands, and capturing them beneath one of his own. "I will do whatever the fuck I like."

"Just like always, one of the kings doing and saying whatever the hell he wants."

"Why go to an escort to lose your virginity? That seems pretty fucked up to me."

"Last time I checked, you weren't the boss of me and you're still not, so let me go."

"Why?"

She stared at him, not wanting to give him any

answers.

In that moment, she hated him.

Hated what she was doing.

How she had to work.

The danger she'd put her friends in because of this stupid fucking idiotic plan.

She'd wanted to back out, to end this so many times. All it would take is a thought about Carla and she couldn't do it. She had to know the truth.

"Why, Taylor?"

"Because I wanted to. I don't like dealing with boyfriends. That's the truth you want. I've never had a fucking boyfriend in my entire life. No one to date. I worked, and I did so every single second of every single day. I didn't have time for that. So, I hired an escort to fuck me and to show me everything I've been missing. I can suck your dick like a pro. Take it in my pussy and even in my ass, and I can give you orgasms not a lot of women can even dream of giving you. He taught me how to fuck and to get what I'm due. He's also my friend."

Lying didn't seem right.

Gritting her teeth, she stared at him.

"Your first time shouldn't have been paid."

"Relax, Axton, he gave me a discount."

He slammed the door beside her head. She didn't flinch, just stared at him.

"Are you jealous right now? Is that what this is? You don't like that I found someone to take care of that little dilemma?"

"Your first time should have meant something."

"You're confusing me now."

"You think I don't know what it means to lose that first time? What it's like to have it taken from me?"

She frowned, staring at him. "What?"

Axton laughed.

"No, you don't get to laugh right now. I made my choices. That wasn't taken out of my hands."

"Would you have done it with someone you cared about? Someone who wouldn't have taken your money."

She frowned.

Don't fall for this.

"I don't understand."

"If it was me, and you were still a virgin, would you have taken me up on my offer? Slept with me."

"Axton, we were never in the same circles, so it's kind of not the point."

"We were very close in ways you don't even understand."

She closed her eyes, trying to think.

Right now, her brain was refusing to do anything basic, like thinking. She didn't know what to do or what to think, and right now she was freaking out.

Sex was just sex.

"How did you lose yours?" she asked, biting her lip.

He groaned, his hand cupping her cheek. His thumb pulled her lip out. "So fucking sexy. You have no idea how much that made me want you."

"I'm really confused right now, Axton."

"I know, I know."

"Answer me," she said. "How was your first time 'taken'?"

"My father wouldn't have any kid of his that didn't know what he was doing. So, one night, he made sure to watch as I fucked my way through whore after whore."

"What?"

Axton smiled. "Most kids would have loved it. As a present to themselves, their dad getting them a chick or as many chicks as money can buy. Putting you in a hotel room, sitting there, watching as you fucked. I had an instruction by the end of the night that I had to bring at least one woman to orgasm. To scream my name as if I was the only thing that mattered in the world. That sick fucker watched while I did."

"Did you want to?" She was fucking mortified for him.

"Do you hate that, Taylor? Hate that I was forced to fuck just to appease him? Because he didn't want a pussy for a son. He wanted a boy that he could be proud of."

"I don't know what to think right now."

"It's okay. I was a good boy, Taylor. I passed all of his fucking tests with flying colors. It's why I rule now. I didn't question anything he told me. I just did. Like a fucking machine."

"And now you're paying the price?"

"There is no price to pay for being on top. What you learn to do is sit, wait, and watch. You can never have anything for yourself in this world. You can always look but never touch. The most precious jewels in this world are usually the ones that you can never have."

His gaze was on her mouth.

His thumb caressed her lips, and she closed her eyes. Tilting her head back, he pushed his thumb into her mouth.

"That asshole should never have fucked you, Taylor. Should never have sunk his dick inside you. That was something you should have given."

He pulled his thumb from her mouth and started tugging her shirt.

She shouldn't let him do this, but she couldn't stop it, nor did she want to. She started taking his clothes off, throwing them to the side.

With his shirt on the floor, she ran her fingers

down his back, scoring the flesh.

He leaned forward, taking her nipple between his teeth, biting down on the bud.

She cried out from the pain and the instant hit of pleasure.

He consumed her body.

She forgot to think about anything and everything but the pleasure of his hands.

The moment she was naked, he lifted her up, and she wrapped her legs around his waist, holding him as he carried her through to his bedroom.

He didn't let her go.

He followed her down to the bed, his body wrapped around hers, making her ache for him to be inside her.

His lips took possession of her own, and she cupped his face, kissing him right back.

He leaned up, reached between them, and his cock pressed to her core.

She moaned his name as in one smooth thrust, he filled her to the hilt.

Axton didn't have a small cock, so she felt every single inch as it filled her, taking her to a new wave of pleasure.

She wrapped her arms around his back, scoring the flesh with her nails. He grabbed her hands and pinned them either side of her head. He was the one in control. Not her.

Slowly, he pulled out of her, only to slide back in.

He took his time making love to her. This wasn't a cold, hard fucking, but something more. Something deeper. Something with meaning.

It terrified and delighted her all at the same time.

Axton kissed her hard as he made love to her. Every inch of her body belonged to him and what he could do.

Suddenly, he pulled out and moved between her thighs. He lifted her up, his hands beneath her ass, and she cried out as he licked her pussy, circling her bud before moving down to plunge his tongue inside.

The pleasure was intense, and she didn't want him to stop.

"Please, please," she said, moaning his name.

He gave her exactly what she wanted.

The orgasm started to build, and she begged for him to push her over the edge, to let her come.

When he did, it was like she was floating.

Axton didn't give her a chance to come down from that high. He slid deep inside her, his arms around her, filling her.

This wasn't fucking.

Axton Farris was making love to her. He was becoming her first, and she relished it.

He drove inside her, taking his time, kissing her.

She'd never had this. It was all new to her, and she was somewhat startled by just how good this felt, how ready she was for his cock.

How desperate she was for more.

He shattered her soul as he showed her something beautiful.

This didn't have room for revenge or justice.

For the first time since entering his life, she was finally getting the real Axton. The real man that he hid from the entire world. No one got to see him like this. But right now, he was the only person in her life.

"I think you're the most beautiful woman, Taylor Keane."

He spoke the words just as he moaned, filling her once again with his cum. They were not lines to get what he wanted but something more.

Axton was trying to tell her something, but as the pleasure filled her, she couldn't think what it could be.

****

"We should have taken a bath before we … erm…"

"Made love?" Axton asked, finishing her sentence.

She giggled. "Yes."

"Well, I didn't want to wait and ruin the moment. Waiting around for everything can ruin a lot of shit. I have no interest in doing that. I've already wasted enough." His fingers traced down her shoulder, and she leaned back so that she could look up at him.

"What have you lost?"

"Nothing to concern yourself with."

"You're always mysterious." She rested her head against his chest, closing her eyes.

There were no words, nothing that could help her in this situation.

David hadn't prepared her for this.

Being made love to.

It was … so new. Her body felt open, exposed, ready for more.

She wasn't there to bring him down, and her plan seemed to be falling all around her. Nothing felt right or normal.

"It'll keep you interested."

She giggled. "You make yourself sound like a book. Believe me, I don't see me getting bored any time soon. That was a lot of fun, and I have no intention of letting you get away from me." She knelt up in the bath, spun around, and straddled his legs. "I see there are a lot of benefits to having a tub this large."

"So many benefits."

She kissed his lips, running her hand down his

chest, cupping his cock. He was flaccid, but with a few touches, he was soon rock-hard. His hands caressed her back, one sinking into her hair, the other cupping her ass.

Just as she was about to lift up and take him inside her, his cell phone rang.

Taylor groaned. He'd brought it into the bathroom with him.

"I've got to take it."

"I know." She reached over him, her tits smashing against his face as he handed him his phone. "Here you go."

"Farris," he said.

One of his hands still cupped her ass, and she watched as the playful smile left his lips.

"That's not fucking acceptable. No. We'll talk tonight. You get him there, and I'll be in the office within twenty minutes." He snapped his cell phone shut.

"Do I need to get dressed to go to work?"

He shook his head. "I can deal with this." He kissed her neck. "I've got to head in though. Just a few problems."

"You don't need your PA?"

"Nah, I want you to stay here. Keep the bed warm. Order takeout."

"You know I was in the gym earlier today."

"Or cook yourself something. Just relax. I'll be back." He climbed out of the tub, and she leaned back, watching him.

Closing her eyes, she listened to him getting dressed. His cell phone went off once again. He was always working, which was never usually a problem. Now though, she felt a little jealous at just how quickly he could leave.

When she heard him enter the bathroom, she smiled up at him. He cupped her neck, kissing her lips.

"I'll be back."

"I'll be waiting."

He left the room, and she listened for his main front door.

She was once again alone.

Alone in Axton's apartment.

He'd made love to her.

Biting her lip, she tried not to think about what she should be doing.

The stuff she should be searching for.

Running her hands back and forth within the water, she tried to think of something else, anything else that could make sense, but she couldn't do it. His office was right down the hall.

Axton wasn't here, and she needed answers.

"Sex makes you blind. Feelings make you foolish. No matter what, you cannot combine the two."

Getting to her feet, she wrapped her body in a robe and her hair in a towel, giving it a good rub to dry it. Once it was dried, she dumped the towel to one side. She stepped inside his room.

The scent of him surrounded her, and she felt the instant hit of guilt.

Pushing past that, she walked through his apartment, checking to make sure this wasn't one of his many tests.

The apartment was completely empty.

She walked down the carpeted floor to his office.

Licking her dry lips, she took a deep breath.

"You can do this."

Pushing some hair off her face, she counted to ten and opened his door.

Sliding inside, she quickly closed it behind her.

His office seemed like such a personal space.

Her heart pounded at what she could possibly

find.

She walked up to his desk and checked each of the drawers. All of them were locked. There had to be a key of some kind. Checking beneath the desk, she found the small hideout and took the key. Sliding it into the lock, she twisted and the desk drawers opened.

She saw several files and quickly glanced through them.

There were pictures of each of the board members but also of his friends. Karson was there, Romeo, and Easton, flicking them open, she quickly glanced over the information.

Easton was described as a weakness.

She closed the files. They were not what she was looking for. Rummaging around in his desk, she found nothing.

Locking it up, she put the key away, and glanced around the office.

"A safe."

She checked everything and then thought about safes.

Checking the pictures, she found one that didn't move in a slide action. Pulling it open, she saw the safe hidden behind. There was a combination, and she cursed.

"Fuck!"

With hands on her hips, she tried to think of all combinations it could be.

She started with Axton's birthday.

Nope.

Easton's birthday.

The day the scandal broke out.

The bonfire's date.

Nothing.

A combination of numbers.

Time was passing and she didn't know what the

hell to do, and so as one last stupid effort, she put in her birthday numbers.

The click of the lock surprised the fuck out of her.

Axton had used *her* birthday as a code.

How?

Why?

How long?

She stood staring at his safe, wondering what the hell was going on.

Why would he use her birthday?

She didn't think for a second that it would … do anything.

"You're here now. You can't back down." Opening the door wider, she saw several thick files. Reaching inside, she read the name on the edge. It was Nial Long, Easton's father. Flicking it open, she saw several pictures. Moving the file to the table, she read several reports of missing women. Last known whereabouts and who was paid off.

Her hand shook as she found his copy machine.

It was a risk to do this, but she needed these files herself. There was no way she was going to be able to expose all of their hidden secrets without proof.

She moved onto the next file, and it was like reading a damn soap drama. Tales of extortion, rape, cover-ups, the lot was hidden within these files, and she had somehow been able to get access to them. It was fucking insane. There's no easy way to do this.

One by one, she copied the files that had the most relevance to her. The stuff that wouldn't be brushed aside, waiting for proof. The moment she was done, which wasn't enough time, she wasn't willing to risk her life another second.

Closing up his safe, putting the picture back in one place, she turned toward the door, and rushed out.

She took one last look around the office and saw nothing out of place.

With all the documents in her hands, she rushed back to where he'd dumped her bag.

Opening it up, she found the small secret compartment in the bottom. Her bag wasn't small, as she liked to carry a change of clothes just in case, along with her lunchbox and other items. It wasn't a fancy bag, and now it came in handy. Lifting it up, she quickly placed the neatly copied pages into the bottom and put her bag together.

She didn't know why Axton kept these files like this. Maybe he was worried that anyone could hack into a computer system and steal them. Hard copies were normally harder to find, even if they were easy to steal once someone found them. He was normally so careful. Guilt hit her at abusing the trust he'd given to her. He'd left her here alone, trusting her with his stuff.

Biting her lip, she was tempted to put them back. *No!*

She was doing this, even if she didn't like the sick feeling in her gut. Whatever reason Axton had, that wasn't on her. That was on him and his friends.

With her cell phone in hand, she dialed Paul's number.

"Hello," he said.

"Shit, I woke you up."

"Taylor, it's, like, two in the morning. What the hell?"

That meeting must have run on a lot longer than Axton thought.

"I got them," she said, licking her dry lips.

"You got what?"

"The files. I have them. I have copies."

She heard him moving around, doing something.

"Are you sure?"

"Yes. I need you to do one more thing for me, okay?"

"I'm listening."

"There was a woman or a girl at the time mentioned in one of the files. Will you find her? Find out what happened to her. I'd love to talk to her, if that's at all possible."

"Sure."

She gave him the details.

"That's it now?" Paul asked. "You're done. You're quitting."

"Not yet."

"Taylor…"

"I didn't find anything on *her*," she said.

"Maybe he doesn't have it."

"Or maybe it's back in King's Ridge."

"No, Taylor. You got what you came here for. Evidence about the Four Kings' Empire. Isn't that what you wanted? Who cares that it isn't about Axton, Easton, and the others? This is about the empire, not about them."

"This isn't about that. I need to know the truth."

"Dammit, Taylor. If what you're saying is fucking true, you do realize that this will put you at risk? That there's a chance they'll come after you?"

"Don't you want to know the truth? To find out what happened?"

"Of course I do. I don't really have much choice in the matter. You've been on this mission for as long as I can fucking remember."

Tears filled her eyes. She'd been on this mission since she read Carla's diary.

"I need to know the truth."

"Some things are best left in the past."

"I've got to go." She hung up.

Yes, she had enough to create a scandal, but the evidence in these files was all about the previous four kings, not about Axton or the current controllers of the Four Kings' Empire. She didn't know what to do. She was so torn right now. Carla's death was no accident. She was convinced of it. But what if they didn't have anything to do with it? Was Carla really pregnant? Did one of their fathers knock up Carla? The information she had proved Nial Long's involvement in cover-ups. If she brought this out now, Axton would know it was her.

The problem?

She needed to know the truth before she did that.

This wasn't over yet. Not by a long shot.

Chapter Twelve

Ten years ago

"Would you walk over broken glass to help me?" Carla asked.

"Yes."

"What about a steaming pit of molten lava?"

Taylor thought about it. "Do I have superpowers?"

"No, you're a human."

"Then no, your ass is doomed."

Carla burst out laughing.

"Wait, why would you be near molten lava?"

"I was put there by an alien."

This made Taylor laugh. "Then I totally get superpowers and save you from those pesky alien creatures."

"I'm bored."

"Then find something else to read," Taylor said.

"When did Paul say he was coming again?"

"How should I know? It's you he loves." Taylor placed a hand to her forehead. "Oh, Carla, I love you so much."

"Stop it."

"I just want to be around you and kiss you." She spoke in a very high-pitched tone, even though Paul had a deep voice.

"You're so bad."

"He totally has the hots for you."

"Yeah, well, I think he's sweet, but I don't see him like that."

"Why not? He's sweet, and he totally adores you. I'd say those are two pretty good things in his favor."

"There's no competition. He's a good friend, and

being boyfriend and girlfriend blurs that line."

Taylor snorted.

"I'm serious. Have you seen the way the four kings treat—"

"Not the four kings again. Please, Carla, your obsession with them is so weird. They're guys that think they own everyone."

"They do own everyone."

Taylor rolled her eyes. "Not me they don't, or you."

"I'd like for them to own me." Carla sounded all dreamy.

"Ew, you have a crush on one of them."

"I do not. Besides, they'd never look in my direction anyway. I'm the town loser."

"No, you're not. You're awesome."

"Ah, I love you."

"Yeah, yeah, get back to reading, weirdo."

Taylor flicked through the book she was reading.

"I think Axton is kind of cute."

Taylor wrinkled her nose. "Get over it."

"What about Karson? Or Easton?"

"Carla, I'm not interested in them. Please, let's just wait for Paul to get here and no more weird questions."

Silence fell between them, but like all things with Carla, it didn't last.

"Would you ever avenge my death?" Carla asked.

Taylor frowned. They were out at the lake, and she lay on the ground staring up at the sky. It was so bright and blue and clear. She was sucking on a lollipop, trying not to think of all the spiders and bugs crawling in her hair.

"Did you hear me?"

"I heard you. I was just wondering what's with

the morbid question." She turned to look at her friend. Carla was rolled onto her side, head resting on her hand. "Why would you want to know if I'd avenge your death?"

"You're like a sister to me. We're so close, and I was listening to this book on the radio—I can't even remember what it was called but it spoke about justice and revenge. If anything was to happen to you and I was to lose you because someone took you away from me. I'd do anything I could to find out the truth."

"You know this is all a little weird right now," Taylor said. She didn't even know why Carla was asking it.

"Would you? Come on. This is just like me asking you if you'd sleep with my husband or take in my kids if I died."

"Let's not forget the time you asked me to tell you if you're getting too fat, if you had a giant spot on your face. If I'd help you get a job or if I'd tell your mom you were with me when you weren't."

"See, I ask weird things all the time."

"That last one wasn't weird. Where were you?"

Carla rolled her eyes. "Nowhere. I told you. I just needed some alone time."

"Is this when you were listening to a weird book?"

"It wasn't a weird book. Answer me," Carla said.

She sighed. "First of all, I'd have to see if your death was suspicious. Then of course, I'd have to weigh in if you deserved it or not, because I know you can be a pain."

"Taylor!" Carla gave her a little shove, and she burst out laughing.

"What? I can have a little fun with all your morbid talk. Besides, I know for a fact you're a pain in the ass. Like, a royal pain in the butt. If your death was justified, then no, your fault."

Carla was laughing.

"Of course I'd do whatever I could. We've got a plan, Carla, and I for one intend to live our lives to the fullest. So, we've got to go traveling and do crazy-ass stuff."

She took her friend's hand, and they locked fingers. United forever. Best friends. Sisters.

"I love you, Taylor."

"I love you too, Carla. You're going to live a very long life. We've got stuff to do. Places to visit, and everything. We've got our entire lives ahead of us. Nothing bad is going to happen. Now, can we please go back to relaxing?"

Carla chuckled. "Yes."

"And stop listening to morbid tapes. Go back to reading romance. They are much more fun." Taylor pulled her friend in for a hug, and they started laughing.

****

Present, one week later

"So what is tonight all about?" Taylor asked.

Axton glanced over at her, admiring the full curves in the tight dress that she wore. "Tonight is a celebration."

"What about?"

"Success. Hammer finally lost our contract. We have the deal, signed and sealed, and now we're moving on to the next step." He was so fucking happy right now. Hearing that Hammer was going to win one of his contracts had pissed him the fuck off. No one beat him, no one.

"Are you going to stick to your promises?" she asked. "Or were they all just part of winning the contract?"

"We'll stick to them. The Four Kings' Empire makes sure we have an exceptional reputation." He glanced over at her.

The past week had flown by. He'd not been able to spend as much time with her as he'd like. Last-minute planning and negotiating had seen to that. Also, as she worked for all four of them, he couldn't demand her attention.

She seemed off.

"Are you okay?"

"Sure, why wouldn't I be?"

"You just seem … different."

"Nah, I'm fine."

She kept on looking out the window.

Did she even realize that she was trying to pull down her skirt? The dress wasn't overly glamorous, just a simple black cocktail dress.

The more time he spent with her, the more little details he seemed to notice.

The confidence fell just a little as she pulled on her skirt, trying to get it to cover more of her thighs.

He loved her fuller body. To him, she didn't need to spend her time in the gym as she was perfect already.

Something wasn't right with Taylor and hadn't been all week. She seemed a little distant, and he found it impossible to read her. It was like she'd taken a step back or something had happened. More often this week than any other she'd seemed lost in her own little world.

Even Romeo, Karson, and Easton had recognized it.

"Do you ever go back home?"

"Home? You mean King's Ridge."

"That is home, isn't it?"

He ignored the attitude. "Yeah, I still go home. My father is still there."

"You care for him?"

"He has a nurse."

"I'm sorry."

"Don't be. He probably deserves it. What's with the sudden interest in my family life, Taylor?"

"Can't I be concerned or show an interest?"

"I don't know. Can you?"

She crossed her arms beneath her breasts, and he didn't want to fight with her.

"You know, when I was younger my locker was broken into."

"So?"

"I was always left these roses and secret love letters. I think they were love letters. I never found the person who sent them."

He glanced over at her.

"Huh," she said.

"What?"

"Ignore me. I'm in my own little world right now. Sorry. It has been a long week. I don't even know what I'm saying half the time."

He didn't get her or understand her. She was so confusing right now. Pulling up outside the nightclub, he climbed out and shook his head at the valet about to open her car door. Stepping in his place, Axton opened it up and took her hand.

No one touched what belonged to him, and Taylor was all his.

Putting his hand at her back, he led the way inside. The music blasted off the walls, vibrating the large dance floor. He loved this club. It was one of the best that they owned. Of course, not many people knew they owned clubs. This was more of a private venture.

"Wow," she said.

When she started walking toward the bar, he took

her hand and led her toward the VIP section. They walked to their own private booth, which overlooked the club. They were surrounded by protective glass, which meant they could see out, but no one saw in, the perfect kind of privacy.

Easton, Romeo, and Karson were already there, drinks in hand. A couple of women were giggling over Romeo and Easton.

Taking the only available seat, he pulled Taylor into his lap.

"Four seats, really?"

"We don't do business here. This is our own private booth."

"No room for anyone else at your big ol' table."

"No need for others when we're more than enough as a foursome," Karson said.

"Ladies, leave," Axton said.

The women started to pout, but Karson showed them to the door, closing and locking it.

"That was rather rude," she said.

"What can I say, I like my privacy."

"Well, seeing as I'm not part of that foursome, I think it best I leave." She made to stand up, but he caught her around the waist, pulling her down into his lap.

His cock was already rock-hard, wanting inside her. He couldn't get enough of her perfect, tight pussy.

"You're part of me."

"So you two are exclusive now?" Easton asked.

"I didn't know we were meeting you guys," she said, wriggling on his lap.

"We're together. She belongs to me."

"You sure about this, Axton?" Karson asked.

"She's mine."

"Wow, possessive much?" Taylor asked.
"Besides, I've not said I want to be yours."

He banded an arm around her waist and pulled her back. With one hand wrapped around her pretty neck, he brought his lips to her ear.

"You want to belong to someone else, Taylor? You and I both know I'm the only one that can make you come so fucking hard you forget who you are."

"I'm sure anyone else could make me come," she said.

The wicked glint in her eyes made him smile. She didn't fool him one bit. Something was going on with her, and he was going to find out what.

"You know, you keep daring me, baby. You need to learn that when you play with fire, you're going to get hurt." He'd placed a hand on her knee and slowly started to draw it up underneath her skirt until he touched her pussy.

She gasped, arching up against his hand.

"She's so wet for me right now, boys. I bet you're all hard right now. Wanting to know just how tight and wet she is."

"We shouldn't do this," she said, pressing against his hand. The fight within her was not very strong at all. In fact, he didn't for a second believe she was even trying to get away from him.

"Why not?" He slid a finger beneath her panties. "You're already so wet. Don't worry about them. They know who you belong to, and besides, they like getting off to things they can't have."

"I'm not a thing."

"No, you're all mine, and none of them will ever know just how fucking sweet you are. How tight your cunt is as it's wrapped around my dick." He pulled her dress up and tore her panties off, placing them in his pocket.

He put her legs over either side of the chair so she

was open, exposed, and everyone in the room could see just how wet she was, and they would all know it was for him and him alone.

Sliding a finger through her pretty cunt, he let them watch as he placed a finger knuckle deep. That wasn't enough, so he added a second finger, then a third, stretching her pussy, working her open. Teasing her clit with his thumb, he stared down at her bunched-up dress.

Removing his fingers from her neck, he lifted her up, and eased the zipper down, pushing it so that the straps of her dress kept her arms bound to her sides.

"Fucking beautiful," Romeo said.

Glancing over at his friend, he saw all three of them had their dicks out and were working their lengths.

"You see that, beautiful, that's what you're doing to them. You're making them want to come over here and fuck your pussy. But you and I both know they're never going to do that. This pussy belongs to me and only me."

Drawing his fingers up to stroke her clit, he wished he had a mirror just so he could see how wet she was. Her ass wriggled against his suit pants, and he wanted that as well. Not in front of his friends though. That would be something he took in privacy without any of them watching.

"You want my dick inside you?"

"Yes."

"Beg me."

"Fuck you."

He pinched her clit, getting a scream from her. "Beg me."

She groaned, and he pinched her again.

"Please, Axton, I want your cock."

He moved her out of the way, pulled his cock out, and then moved her back in place where her pussy was in perfect view. Sliding inch by glorious inch within her, he seated himself to the hilt, and they both moaned.

Romeo, Karson, and Easton did the same moaning. Lifting up the dress and throwing it to the floor, Axton pulled her back against him, and cupped her tits, stroking her nipples. She wrapped her arms around his neck, pulling him down and kissing him lips. She moaned his name, and he began to thrust inside her, showing his friends exactly who owned her. He never took a woman first or brought a woman here. If a woman was here, it was usually through business, and he never made a point of claiming her.

In front of his friends, he was marking her as his, and as such, they would have no choice but to leave her alone. Every single part of Taylor belonged to him, and it always had. No matter how much she tried to deny it.

She was his.

He made sure of it.

For a long time now, he held himself back, and he wasn't going to do that any longer. She was his.

Taking her hand, he placed it on her pussy and got her to play with herself, to tease her clit, to bring herself to orgasm as he kissed her, driving inside her as he did.

She whimpered his name, and he couldn't get enough.

After the week of nonstop work, he didn't last long, shooting in deep just as she found her orgasm, her pulsing cunt drinking up every single blast of his cum.

Afterward, they were both panting, and he stared into her eyes, completely struck by her. She licked her lips, and he wanted her again.

Easton was the one to clear his throat.

"Bathroom?" she asked.

"Through there."

She climbed off his lap, grabbed her dress, and without looking at any of them, disappeared inside.

"Wow, man, you're claiming her?" Romeo asked.

"She's always been mine."

"You're playing a dangerous game," Easton said. "Remember your father won't approve. I know firsthand what that feels like."

"He's not the boss. Taylor's mine, and one day soon, I'm going to tell her the truth."

Easton paused with his drink pressed against his lips. "Excuse me?"

"You heard me. She has a right to know."

"I hate to break it to all of you, but he also came inside her. There was no condom," Karson said. "How many times have you done that? I know you, Axton. That kind of shit you don't forget."

He stared at his friend, refusing to answer.

"It wasn't that long ago that you didn't trust her," Easton said. "Now you're making plans long-term. Have you lost your fucking mind?"

"Keep your damn mouth shut, Easton. You don't know what the fuck you're talking about."

"I remember all too well."

Silence fell at the pain echoing around the room from Easton's voice. After ten years, he'd never gotten over it.

Even now, Axton saw it clear in his friend's eyes.

"We all agreed that there would be no women interfering. That we all had a say," Easton said.

"You want to take a vote on this?" Axton asked.

"She know about the letters?" Karson asked, drawing his attention toward him.

Axton stared at his friend.

"You can't even be fucking honest with her after all these years. This is pathetic, Axton, even for you,"

Easton said.

Before he could speak, the door to the bathroom opened.

Her cheeks were a beautiful shade of pink.

"I think it's time we joined the crowd and danced," Axton said. He stood up, took her hand, and led the way out of the room.

"This isn't over, Axton," Karson said.

"Oh, yes, it fucking is."

"Why do I feel like I stepped into a warzone there?" she asked.

"You didn't."

"Really? Because that sure as hell sounded like it. You guys aren't falling out because of me, are you?"

"No."

"You're sure?"

He pulled her into his arms as they got to the dance floor. "I mean every single word." He put his hands on her ass, holding her close. The music changed as it always did to a slow number.

She rolled her eyes, putting her hands on his shoulders. "You're not even going to give me a hint of what that fight was about?"

"Just guy stuff."

"Wow, sexist much?"

"We all seem to think we can meddle into each other's lives."

"That must be nice. Paul's always trying to give me advice. I don't take it though. I probably should. There's no probably about it, I know I should take it," she said, smiling.

He loved her smile.

Not the fake thing she tried to pass off as a smile either. This was a full-on smile with dimples. The one he'd seen many times from afar but never actually gotten to see up close.

"I've known best for so long."

"And you don't take their advice?"

"I do when I need it."

"Which is?"

"Rarely. I told you, my dad didn't raise a son to be a follower. He raised me to be a leader."

She stared at him, the smile dropping from her lips. "Do you respect your dad?"

"No."

"Do you follow in his footsteps?"

"I'm my own person, Taylor. I don't do what my father says or does."

"But you protect him."

He paused, staring at her. "I have to."

She nodded.

The moment was broken, and her gaze was on his chest. That niggling feeling was back once again, and he didn't know what to say or do to make it fucking stop.

****

A week later

Taylor hated sneaking into his office, especially as he always seemed to know the perfect time to interrupt her. The one good thing about Four Kings' Empire, there was never a dull moment. All four of the men had to go out to meetings, and she'd been left alone to keep track of each new development.

Which sounded perfect on paper. A week of being alone in the office. The perfect chance to sneak around, but alas that didn't happen much. They kept her busy, and between dealing with calls, sitting in via video link on meetings, writing up contracts, handling lawyers and just doing her job, she didn't have time.

This had been the first chance she had this week to check through Axton's drawers. With his mention of his father being sick, she intended to take a trip to King's Ridge. To do so required her to lie to get into his home. The guilt was there. She didn't want to do this, but her need for the truth kept driving her. Her feelings for Axton were making it hard for her to do this. Lying was something she hated doing, even on that first day at the interview. She tried not to think about it. She had to be prepared for everything. Carla had secrets, and they got her killed.

Paul had already come through in regard to the woman who had been raped by Nial Long. At his home, she'd gotten details of what happened. The woman had been passed around to each of the four kings like a fuck toy, used and abused until they'd thrown her out. It had been next to impossible to find the details. A report had been filed, and after some investigating, her statement had been withdrawn. The case had closed, but it had been filed as completed on the computer, which is why he'd been able to find it. The medical examiner's report hadn't been removed though. Paul had been able to find that even though nothing had been acted upon because she'd withdrawn her charges. The woman may have been lying, sure. But medical reports didn't lie. Evidence of rape didn't lie.

The more she found out, the harder it was for her to respect people of the law. They were paid to do a job, but it seemed the right person lined their pockets and that job became null and fucking void.

It pissed her off.

Just like it pissed her off about Carla and what happened to her.

The phone on her desk started to ring. Cursing, she closed up Axton's drawers and rushed out to see who it was.

"Four Kings' Empire, Taylor speaking, how can I

help you?"

"What's up, Taylor?" Easton asked.

"Oh, I was just taking a quick bathroom break. I didn't know how long the phone had been ringing. Kind of panicked and ran."

Easton chuckled. "I was just checking in to make sure everything is set up for my red eye tonight."

"Red eye, yes. You'll be arriving quite late, but not to worry, I already have a driver picking you up. He'll have your name on a card. No need to worry."

"Excellent."

"Can I ask you a question?" she asked.

"Sure."

"Axton spoke about his father the other week and how he's really sick."

"Yes." Easton spoke slowly, as if he wasn't sure he was allowed to speak.

"I was wondering, you know, how I'd go about sending maybe a gift basket or something. I don't know."

"I wouldn't worry too much. Axton has 'round the clock care for the old man. Besides, he's in the peak of health, Axton just likes to make sure that he's … safe."

"'Round the clock care?"

"Yes, nurses are there. A couple at a time."

"Okay, thank you."

"I really wouldn't worry about the basket though. He wouldn't appreciate it. Axton's dad is a funny old bastard, and he wouldn't take kindly to any … erm, gifts."

"Why not?"

"He just has an expectation of what he thinks his son should be and who he should be with."

"I don't make the cut."

"I better go."

Before she could say anything more Easton hung up the phone, leaving her confused. Paul was also not taking her calls. David had told her he had to get back to work. Only she seemed to be with the program right now.

It worked for her though.

If Axton's father was having treatment or something like that, it meant she could get inside his home.

She released a gasp as someone covered her eyes with his hands. The scent of Axton surrounded her.

"Surprise," he said, his voice whispering against her ear.

"I didn't know you were due back today."

"Don't act so happy to see me," he said.

Spinning around in his arms, she smiled. "You know I'm happy to see you. So damn happy."

Throwing her arms around his neck, she moaned as he kissed her back. His hand sinking into her hair made her melt.

This was the problem she had.

Her need for him seemed to be growing, and she didn't want it to.

Not only did she desire him, something else was happening between them. Staring into his eyes, her stomach twisted, and she nibbled her lip.

"What is it?" he asked.

"I missed you."

"Don't sound sad about that. It's good that you missed me."

"Did you miss me?"

"Yes. It's why I came straight here."

Without waiting for permission, he lifted her up, and she wrapped her legs around his waist. Entering his office, he went straight to his desk. He put her on top and shoved his computer off the surface.

She laughed at the mess he was creating.

"I'll have to clean all of that up now."

"Don't worry about it, I have a cleaning crew."

"You do?"

"Yeah."

She grabbed his tie and pulled him close, kissing him hard on the lips. He rested his hands on her knees and slid them up underneath, touching her pussy. As he made to pull them off, she lifted up so that they glided down her legs and he was able to throw them across the room.

"Finally, you save my panties."

"Don't worry. I won't be in the habit of doing that." He winked at her.

Suddenly, he picked her up and flipped her over so that she was leaning over the desk. He lifted up her skirt, and his hands caressed her ass, spreading the cheeks wide.

"You have no idea how much this beautiful fucking ass has distracted me. I want it."

"I'm all yours, Axton. To do with as you wish." She looked over her shoulder and smiled at him.

"Oh, baby, it is on." He pulled out his cock and placed it at her entrance. She moaned as inch by inch he sank in deep. He took his sweet time, making her feel every single pulse as he filled her, stretching her pussy to accommodate him.

She closed her eyes, thrusting back against him, desperate for more of what he could give her.

He wrapped her hair around his fist, drawing her head back. His lips kissed her neck, stretching her as his other hand ran down her body.

He owned every single part of her.

Axton set her on fire as he started to tease her clit,

stroking it just the way she liked, making her whimper, moan, and beg for him to keep on going.

"I want you to come all over my cock, and then I'm going to take your ass, beautiful." He rocked inside her, going ever so slowly, torturing her with his thrusts.

She was already soaking wet, but with the way he teased her, he deepened her arousal, making her slick with sweat as he did.

Anyone could invade his office, but in that moment, she didn't care. All she wanted was him to give her what she needed and then to fill her ass with his length.

"I love fucking you, Taylor. I knew it would be like this. Always be like this."

In and out, he took her, taking her pleasure to new heights as she begged him for more. There was no stopping him, not that she wanted to.

"That's it, baby. Come for me."

The moment he ordered the command as a growl against her ear, she couldn't control it. Her body became his, and she came, screaming his name, shuddering and pulsing as he fucked her.

He kept on teasing her clit, making her come harder until he released her. He pushed her to the desk so that she was flat against the surface, her tits smashed against the cool wood.

Axton pulled out of her pussy, and his fingers teased some of her cream back to her ass. She closed her eyes as he stroked over her anus, preparing her.

When the tip of his cock pressed against her ass, she was so ready for him.

Slowly, inch by inch, he began to sink inside her, pushing past that tight ring of muscles, taking her to new, dizzying heights. When several inches of his cock were inside her, he gripped her hips, and holding her still, he slammed balls deep within her ass.

He leaned over her back, his lips grazing her neck.

"Fuck, you feel so good."

She tightened her ass around his dick, and he groaned.

"You're so fucking perfect, just as I always knew you would be. All mine. Always."

He pulled out of her ass until only the tip remained. She cried out as he sank inside her. The pleasure was far more intense than when he took her pussy.

This was dirty, hot, and she trusted him that he wouldn't hurt her.

Axton ran his hands up and down her body, stroking her as he fucked her ass. She was spread out across his desk like a sacrifice for his pleasure only.

He reached between her thighs and began to tease her once again. "Every time I sit at this desk, I will remember this, and it's going to be impossible to work, you know that."

She giggled. "You're going to be so anal."

They both chuckled, and then groaned as he started to fuck her just a little bit harder. She pushed back on his cock, taking more of him inside her, needing him in ways she never thought possible. His lips were on her neck, kissing her, devouring her.

There was nothing of her left.

Axton owned every single part of her, and it scared her.

The power he held over her shook her to the core, especially as she denied it. She couldn't have feelings for him. This was just for some fun. It wasn't supposed to be anything serious.

It couldn't be.

She had plans.

Long term wasn't part of it.

She couldn't start thinking about a relationship with him.

Not now. Not ever.

As he rode her ass and she came all over his fingers and cock, she knew she was stuck. She couldn't back down, not now. Not after she had come so far. There was just a small piece she needed to unravel her puzzle, and then she could go back to her little hidey-hole and never come out.

Axton came, his cock pulsing his cum deep into her ass. He wrapped his arms around her, holding her close. She felt the rapid beating of his heart against her back, or it could have been her own.

"You're going to be the fucking death of me."

She felt tears fill her eyes, and she shut them quickly, hoping he didn't see.

In the back of her mind, she saw Carla's smiling face. The picture she wished she could always have of her, and never let go. Like always, it didn't stay that way. It morphed into the cold corpse she'd pulled from the lake.

Turning back now was not the answer.

Chapter Thirteen

Ten years ago

"You are perfect to me, and one day I hope more than anything to be able to tell you that to your face. Seeing you calms the beast burning inside me. Never change who you are, Taylor, you are everything." Taylor finished reading the note and inhaled the single white rose that had been left in her locker.

She had lost count of the number of roses and letters she'd gotten.

Carla took the note from her. "You don't think this is a little creepy?"

"I don't know. It's kind of fun to see them." She loved them all. Every time she found one she couldn't help but smile or feel a little sparkle in her life.

Yes, in a way it was super creepy. She didn't have a clue who had actually sent them, but on the plus side of things, she loved them. They were not scaring her. If this person was writing letters about wanting to wear her skin or cut out her eyeballs, she'd have a problem.

They were beautiful notes.

Sweet.

Kind.

Caring.

It made her believe someone, a mysterious someone, actually liked her in this school.

"You've got that glazed look again," Carla said.

Taylor slapped her friend on the arm and laughed.

Putting the note into her bag, she closed her locker and noticed her friend tense up.

The kings were walking past them, paying no attention whatsoever to anyone. Of course, people moved out of the way as they passed.

Carla though, was strange. She kept on staring at them.

"What's wrong?" Taylor asked, placing a hand on her friend's arm.

"It's nothing. Must be nice to go everywhere and have people move out of the way, you know."

"I don't know. I think for the most part people are afraid of them. I wouldn't want that."

"You're not afraid of them?"

"We've already agreed, I'm weird."

****

Present day

Taylor parked her car and stared up at the large mansion. The drive into town had taken forever, but now she was here, there was no turning back. She needed to know this. Paul had told her she was mad to do this and begged her not to go. Of course, she ignored him and did what she wanted to do.

If she didn't try to find out the truth now, she never would.

She owed it to Carla for others to know what poison lay at the core of the Four Kings' Empire. Axton, Easton, Romeo, and Karson knew what had happened before they took over. She had the proof she needed, and all it would take is sending them to the right paper, and boom, done. Their parents would have to answer for the crimes they had committed. She didn't know what would happen to their sons, to Axton and his friends. They had covered this up by not letting their parents pay. But they shouldn't have had to live with this either. What kind of monsters had they been living with, even in high school? She couldn't think about this now.

Biting her lip, she thought about what she was going to do. This would end everything she had started with Axton. There's no way he'd trust her. She wouldn't blame him. After all this, she wasn't a good person. At any point in the last ten years she could have changed her path, and she hadn't. There was no turning back now. She didn't know how she was going to get inside, only that once she did, this would all be over. Axton would know the truth, one way or another that she'd turned up at his home.

Do you want to be with him?

She refused to answer that question.

There's no way she could bring herself to even think about it. Not right now. Not yet.

"Just get out of the damn car."

Opening the door, she climbed out and made her way to the front door.

Drawing her hand back, she gave it a knock. She didn't wear her suit but had opted for jeans and a shirt.

A nurse opened the door. She knew from bits and pieces of information that nurses took care of his ailing father, that his father wasn't the best of patients, and she was just going to try and wing it from there.

"Hi, my name's Taylor Keane. I'm here to speak with Mr. Farris. I'm Axton's PA, and he said you needed someone with regards to an incident." Her heart pounded as she spoke the lie. She hoped that she'd not screwed everything up. She'd come this far, and she didn't want to turn back. Paul had been able to find funds given to nurses who'd been working for Axton. She didn't even want to think about why.

"Oh, shoot, yes, of course. Cathy must have forgotten to leave a message, but that's okay. We've been having a few episodes of late. Come with me."

She was being led down a long corridor.

"Mr. Farris isn't the easiest of patients, but Axton always makes sure we're well compensated for our work.

Unfortunately, Mr. Farris struck out yesterday, and Angela is missing a tooth. It has just been crazy here."

She didn't catch the woman's name. There was an almighty bellow from above. The nurse looked nervous.

"I'll be back. Please, make yourself at home."

Biting her lip, she clasped her hands together and moved quickly. She opened every single door, finding a sitting room, game room, and then one of the last doors was the office. Entering the office, she went straight toward the desk.

She didn't like being in this house.

Her nerves were completely shot, and being caught would take all decision and choice out of her hands.

With shaking hands, she opened drawers to find them all empty.

Slamming the last door closed, she quickly started moving around the room, but came up empty-handed. Moving the pictures produced nothing for her.

The office was a complete bust as it had nothing but musty old books inside.

By the time she got back to the corridor the nurse who saw her in looked a little frazzled as she came downstairs.

"While I was here, Axton told me to bring back a file. He mentioned where he kept them located, but I can't remember where. He figured while I was here I may as well, you know, rather than him stopping by while he's so busy."

"Oh, yes, of course. Everything is in the basement now. I'm sorry. I'll be back to answer any questions in a moment."

The basement.

Heading into the kitchen, she located where the

basement was. It wasn't exactly hard to guess.

Again, heart still pounding, she opened the door and made her way downstairs. The basement was huge. It was like it covered the entire length of the house.

Closing the door, she switched on the light and saw that everything was all neatly stacked up. There were so many filing cabinets that it would be like looking for a needle in a haystack.

Going toward the first one, she saw a date that was marked over twenty years ago. Moving from one cabinet to another, she found the one marked 2008. Ten years ago. When Carla had died.

Opening the cabinet, she stared at the files with names. Her hands started to shake as she saw one with Carla's name on it. Pulling it out, she felt sick to her stomach. Opening the file, she saw pictures of her best friend.

Closing the file, she shut her eyes feeling pain unlike anything she'd ever felt before. They had a file on Carla.

"Who the fuck are you?"

She spun around and saw a much older man who she didn't recognize.

"I'm so sorry. Axton asked me to come and get some files for him." She held Carla's file close to her chest. This man looked really scary.

"Well, little lady, you better run along because we don't want Axton getting pissed off that he missed his deadline or shit."

She held the files in her arms wondering who he was. He seemed familiar. "Are you Axton's father?"

The man laughed. "Please, I taught my boy a lot better than that. I'm Easton's father." He tilted his head to the side. "I recognize you."

"I'm sorry. You're right, I better get these and go.

Axton will be waiting." She wasn't about to add that Axton knew where she was because that was a total lie, and besides, she didn't need a babysitter.

As she was about to pass a long desk, a notepad caught her attention. It was plain white, but it was the symbol of the rose at the top.

She stopped and lifted it up. The notepaper felt exactly like the one that used to come to her locker every single day.

"What's this?" she asked, looking up at the old man, who'd not stopped watching her.

"That's our old notebooks. An order went wrong at the stationers. Instead of making a crown with the four kings, they came back with a rose with four thorns. We rather thought it was appropriate."

"Were they all the same?"

"No. Farris always had to have the best to stand out. He kept the roses and thorns. We all made another order and got the crown."

Axton was the one to send her those letters all those years ago, but why? He didn't treat her like he even cared. Why would he do this now?

"I'd better go."

****

A couple of hours earlier

Axton finished up the last of his contract signings before checking through his emails. He wasn't interested in anything to do with work right now. When he heard some commotion, he got up from his seat and went out to the main floor where Taylor still hadn't returned, but he saw Paul being held by security.

"What's going on here?" Axton asked.

Easton, Romeo, and Karson came out of their offices.

"I need to talk to you, but these fuckers wanted

ID. I don't have time for this shit. I don't want your damn company, Farris. I need to talk to you. It's important. It's about Taylor."

At the mention of Taylor, he didn't like the look in Paul's eyes.

"Leave." He ordered the security, and they all waited until they were alone.

Paul sent out a sigh of relief.

"Now, what about Taylor?"

He saw Paul was struggling. His hands were fisted, and he growled. "She's not here to be your PA."

Axton wasn't surprised by that.

"What the fuck are you talking about?"

"Carla." Paul looked at each of them. "She's here to get justice for Carla."

"How the fuck would working here do that?" Easton asked.

"Because working here brings her close to the files, right? The rumors, the scandal," Axton said.

"Look, ten years ago…" Paul paused. "I promised her I would help her. Do you understand? Carla was dead. Killed. We both know that it wasn't an accident."

"What do you know?"

Paul sighed and reached inside his jacket. Easton grabbed him as they thought he was reaching for a weapon, but Axton saw him pull out a book. A very old book.

"This is Carla's diary," Paul said. "Inside, she says how she had a relationship with one of you. How she ended up pregnant and how one of you said it had to be kept quiet. Taylor … she asked me to hack the morgue's systems and files. I did, and I discovered that her pregnancy wasn't on her autopsy."

"You also know money was filed to the morgue director at the time to look the other way?" Axton asked.

"Yes."

"What is Taylor's big plan?"

"To get your secrets. The ones that you've kept locked up tight for your fathers. The secrets that seep poison into this fucking place. What keeps you on top."

Axton stared at Paul.

"Where is she?"

"Taylor has enough to take your fathers down. Not only will this send your fathers to prison, it'll create a scandal that will shock you and the entirety of the Four Kings' Empire. It will expose the company to the practices of the past and mean you'd be investigated. That would affect shareholders, not to mention the ramifications of what your fathers have done."

"She hasn't done anything yet, right, so what the fuck is this all about?" Romeo asked.

"She wants the truth," Axton said. "About what happened ten years ago."

"Do you blame her? You and I both know Carla didn't kill herself that night. We all know that."

He stared at Paul, and he saw the truth in his eyes. "You saw?"

"I know what happened. I know … what I wasn't supposed to. I had the truth."

Axton didn't even realize that Paul had known. "Why didn't you tell?"

"He threatened my family, Axton. Told me I wasn't to say a word otherwise he'd slit their throats and then come after me. I wasn't willing to risk that. Taylor, she doesn't even care. She wants the truth and will do everything she can to get it."

"When did she leave?" Axton said. He knew for a fact if she was in King's Ridge, her life was in danger. He had to keep her away from there.

"Thirty minutes ago. I got her text."

"You're coming with us." Axton went straight for the elevator. He didn't even wait to see who followed him.

Karson grabbed Paul, and they made their way down to the parking lot. No one stopped them. Who would? They were kings here.

No one else could ever touch them.

Climbing into his car, Easton joined him at the front while Romeo and Karson trapped Paul in the back of the car.

"It's a long drive, and you better hope nothing happened to her," Axton said.

They all had secrets to protect. His father would hurt her for what she knew, and if the nurses didn't keep him properly restrained like they'd been paid to, he would be a fucking poison on the town.

He wasn't about to think of what Taylor was going to do to him and his company. Not until he knew she was safe. Those damn files were a fucking curse. He remembered the first time his father showed them to him. It was always with a warning that in life you'd make enemies and the key to success was to keep those enemies down, to have everything on them so you could use it when you needed to. It's why those files had never been destroyed. They were always there to keep each other in line. It was only he, Easton, Romeo, and Karson that had changed those ways. They didn't see each other as enemies but as allies. They were best friends.

For a long time, silence filled the car until Paul started to talk.

"Which one of you was it, huh?" Paul asked. "Who kept Carla's relationship a secret? Who knocked her up?"

Glancing at Easton, Axton saw his friend was having a really fucking hard time right now keeping himself in check.

"I'm curious, how did Taylor know that I was in need of hiring her?" Axton asked, changing the subject.

"It was pure coincidence. Holly has a great mind with writing codes. I acquired one that she's been working on. I wasn't aware of her past until she came in for an interview. I wanted Holly's great mind, and in doing so, it opened up the role for Taylor to take."

"What's David in all of this?" Axton asked.

Paul stared at him, and he glanced in the mirror before returning his gaze to the road. "He was part of the plan."

Axton chuckled.

"The one that helped her to seduce. That taught her everything she knew."

"He fucked her?" Karson asked.

"It was her idea. This was all business to her, and David helped her to get past those insecurities. To be able to do what she needed."

"To seduce us," Axton said.

"I don't know if she planned to seduce all of you or just one. From the moment this started though, you've tested her in ways that no one else has."

"You know, buddy, you're a really fucking useless friend," Romeo said. "You know what we're capable of, and yet you're spilling all of her secrets as if we're your best fucking friends."

"You won't hurt her," Paul said. He stared at Axton. "Because I also knew who left the messages and roses. I saw that too."

Axton gripped the steering wheel. "You're the all-fucking-seeing eye. Maybe we should pluck that out."

"No one gave a fuck about me, Axton, but then my father wouldn't bow down to yours, would he? You see, I knew for a fact that there were originally five points to that crown. Because my dad wouldn't bow down to the shit they wanted him to do, they tossed him out."

"And you as his son made sure you came back fighting for more."

"I made sure that I stayed on the right side of the law."

"I'm done talking," Axton said.

He drove all the way to King's Ridge, breaking the speed limit and not giving a fuck if anyone tried to stop him. He'd take them all fucking on, but right now, he intended to get Taylor to look him in the fucking face and tell him the truth.

Do you blame her?

She didn't want it to be you.

It didn't matter.

He had to make sure she didn't release those fucking secrets. Not yet. Not until he had everything in place. He would not go down for his father's sins, nor would he let Taylor either. She'd stolen, lied, and manipulated her way into this information. With Paul's help, they'd hacked security systems, and Axton didn't want anything to happen to her for this.

Like always, he'd do whatever it took to protect the four kings. It's what he'd always done.

****

Stumbling out of Axton's home, Taylor quickly rushed over to her car, not looking at anything. Her eyes were blurry from tears, and her entire life felt like it was falling apart. She felt broken, shattered. Everything she thought she knew was a lie. Axton didn't do anything. Those damn letters and the roses. He'd been the one to leave them all those years ago. Why? What the hell was going on? Nothing made sense anymore.

What the hell was she going to do now?

Unlocking her door, she went to open it, but she was suddenly grabbed from behind. A hand covered her mouth, and an arm banded around her waist, holding her captive. She tried to scream, but no sound could come out as she was forced backwards. She wasn't able to see anything, and then she was dumped in the trunk of a car. The file on Carla was thrown inside.

The light blinded her, so she couldn't see who it was that had taken her.

The trunk slammed shut, and she held onto the file like a lifeline.

She felt the car moving, and tears kept filling her eyes, slowly falling down her face. Fear consumed her, and as she closed her eyes, she thought of Axton, his face changing from that of someone serious to the few smiles she'd gotten from him when they were both alone together. He wasn't trying to pretend to be someone else.

This was just who he was, and she'd loved every second of being alone with him because he made it worthwhile to care.

Dammit.

She didn't want to have feelings for him.

He was part of the problem that she was constantly fighting.

Her sole reason for doing what she did. She couldn't fall for him, and fucking refused to allow herself to even think of doing that.

Closing her eyes, she gritted her teeth, gasping as they went over a speed bump. Her body felt so exhausted. She didn't know what was going to happen to her.

The car was suddenly parked, and she heard voices. None of them she recognized but then everything was muffled in the car.

Just as she was about to start hitting the trunk

roof the catch released and opened up. She blinked from the sun and stared up at Paul.

"What?"

"Hello, Taylor."

"What the hell, Paul? You scared the hell out of me." She sat up and came to a stop when she saw the four kings all standing just a few feet away. What made her a little sicker was the fact they'd ridden down to the lake.

Staring past where Axton stood, she saw the spot where Carla's phone had been. When she'd stared out and seen the body.

"What the hell is going on here?" she said.

"We could ask you that same question." Axton stepped forward and pushed Paul out of the way.

She let out a gasp as Axton grabbed her arm and was suddenly tugging her along. She wasn't wearing heels, so she was able to keep up as he threw her to the ground. He glared at her, and she knew in that moment that Paul had told him everything.

"That's right, sweetheart. Your little friend came through with the truth. I know everything."

Taylor didn't like his sneer or the way he stood over her. In her mind she thought about all those damn letters and they came from him. Everything she had learned had only confused her more.

Getting to her feet, Axton made to push her again, but she shoved him hard.

"You don't know everything." She got to her feet, glaring at him.

"Why is she pissed?" Easton asked. "We're the ones she's been spying on."

"Why didn't you tell me the truth, huh?" she asked. "Why leave all those damn letters for me to find? Was it all just a game? Was Carla a game? Knock her up and then kill her."

"I had nothing to do with Carla," Axton said.

She went to push him again, and he caught her arms, crossing them over her body and spinning her so that she facing the rest of the kings.

"But he did," he said.

She stared at Easton. "You're lying. It was you, Axton. Always was. You were the one that is always in charge. You make the decisions." She was sounding stupid, even to herself. Those damn letters. The roses. That was all Axton to *her*, not to Carla.

"Nope. I couldn't give a fuck about that bitch. She meant nothing to me. Nothing at all. Easton here, it started out as a game, didn't it, Easton?"

"Axton," Paul said.

Taylor looked toward her friend. Anger unlike anything she'd ever felt consumed her. "You stay out of this. You picked your side."

She hated how she liked Axton's arms around her.

How he felt holding her.

The pleasure that seemed to fill her just by being near him.

"Tell her the truth, Easton. Tell her how it started out as a game to piss your dad off."

"Axton," Easton said.

"You see, our fathers always had a plan for each of us. A plan that meant we had to marry someone suitable. Someone who they thought was worthy to be a queen to our king. We rule this place, just like everywhere we go and everything we touch. It all belongs to us." He spoke the words against her ear, and she saw Easton fighting. "Tell her the truth. After all, she's done nothing but be honest with us, right?"

She hated that, hated that he was using her own

failing against her.

Not once had she been truthful. Not to him, not to anyone. They didn't have to be honest with her.

Heart pounding, she watched as Easton nodded. "It was a game. It started out as a game. I thought Carla was cute, but I knew she'd just be a bit of fun."

Taylor gasped, thinking about her friend. The pain of knowing she'd been used and all this time she'd not known. Carla had kept his secret.

"You bastard!" She tried to get away from Axton, but he wouldn't let her go.

He was stronger than she was.

Harder.

She couldn't get at Easton to kill him.

"We had fun for a long time. She was different than a lot of the women I was with, or girls. They were normally all the same. Joking and laughing at boring shit. Not Carla. She was different. She didn't allow me to pacify her. I was the one that knocked her up."

"I'm going to fucking kill you."

Easton took a step forward. "And I was the one that fell in love with her," Easton said. "You can believe this all you want, but I did love Carla. She was my everything. I didn't want this. I didn't want this life. The money, the title, and shit. I couldn't give a fuck."

"You killed her."

"No. I wouldn't ever hurt her. I loved her, and I … I was going to take her away."

"He was going to run with her," Axton said.

"Will you shut the fuck up?" Easton asked. "I can handle this."

"No, Easton, you fucking can't. If you could have handled this, Carla would still be alive," Axton said.

"You think you're any better? Sending love notes and roses like it was fucking Valentine's Day."

"I kept her alive, didn't I? What did you do? That's right. You got yours killed."

Taylor cried out as Axton shoved her out of the way just as Easton charged him. Dazed a little, she watched as Easton and Axton fought.

This wasn't what she wanted. Moving back to the car, she rummaged about in the trunk looking for something to stop the fight. Pulling back a lever, she opened up a case and saw the gun, just a small pistol.

"Taylor, I'm sorry," Paul said.

"Fuck you, Paul. You made your choices right now, and I for one, don't give a fuck what you have to say." She didn't like swearing, but right now, hands shaking, she was nervous.

Loading up the pistol, she stepped forward, took aim and fired. The sound of the gunshot stopped Easton and Axton from fighting. Karson and Romeo had been trying to break it up.

They all turned toward her, and she pointed the gun at Easton.

"Now tell me what the fuck happened."

"You won't shoot that," Axton said.

"I spent the last ten years getting into shape, changing the person I am, and getting an escort to teach me how to fuck. How about you stop underestimating me right now? Tell me what the fuck happened!"

****

Ten years ago, the night of the bonfire

"What are we going to do?" Carla said.

Easton cupped her face, pressing his forehead against hers. "You said you didn't care about the money or that shit, right?"

"I don't. I've lived without money all my life, Easton. Why does it always have to come down to that?"

He kissed her head. "Because I am so fucking

273

used to it always being about money. About power. I want you, baby. I want only you."

She smiled. For a long time, she really didn't think this was going to happen. When Easton showed her any attention, she'd always thought he had another reason for playing her. Like he was treating her as a bit of fun, but she loved the attention. That had been some time ago, and they were still together. She'd given him her virginity, and now they were making plans for the future.

"What about Taylor? Can I tell her?" she asked. She hated lying to her best friend but also knew she didn't have much choice, not if she wanted to keep this with Easton. He valued his privacy, and because of that, it meant she kept their secret. Not that Taylor would have a problem.

"You're going to have to let her go. If we do this, we have to run and not look back. You, me, and our baby." He placed a hand against her stomach. "Just the three of us. You have to make a choice."

"Then as always, I will choose you and our family." She felt guilty for not thinking about Taylor. They'd been the best of friends for as long as she could remember.

"Okay, I will call you as soon as I'm ready. Pack what you need and nothing else."

"You're sure?"

"Hell, yeah, I'm sure." He kissed her lips. "I love you, Carla."

"Love you too."

She watched him leave and quickly rushed back into her home. Her parents were out at work, and she didn't have a lot to pack anyway.

Her diary lay on her bed, and she picked it up.

"You're going to stay here." Going into her

closet, she put it in the secret compartment before starting to pack.

After thirty minutes, she was ready just as her cell phone buzzed.

Easton: **Meet me at my place.**

She frowned but shrugged. He knew what he was doing, and she trusted him.

Moving past her mirror she stopped as pictures of her and Taylor caught her eye.

"I'm sorry, Taylor."

Putting her fingers against her friend's face, she smiled. She knew her friend would be happy for her, just so long as she was there.

Leaving her home, she didn't have a car, so she walked toward Easton's home. She smiled and waved at some of the neighbors, nerves eating away at her as she stood outside of Easton's home.

She never felt great being here.

Easton had told her many times that his family were snobs. That they had a plan for each of their sons, which she found sad.

Making her way up to his home, she knocked, and the door slid open.

"Easton," she said.

She didn't see anyone.

Walking down the long corridor, she came to a stop as someone told her to come inside.

Entering an office, she saw two older men. One of them was Easton's father, the other Axton's.

There was no sign of Easton.

"I'm so sorry. I didn't mean to interrupt," she said. "I was just looking for Easton."

"Easton is a little busy right now. Come, sit, talk with us."

She didn't like this. "I would really rather…"

"If you walk out of this house I will make sure that your parents never work again. I will take their home and put on the street where they will beg for scraps like the pieces of shit they are," Nial Long said.

Turning around, she stared at him, feeling sick to her stomach.

"Well, she's not as pretty as I imagined she'd be," Axton's father said. She didn't remember his name.

"No, but he seems to think she's 'the one.' Stupid boy. I'm getting tired of cleaning up his mistakes." Nial threw some money at her feet. "Get rid of the kid and stay away from my son."

"I don't want your money."

"My son is not leaving this town with you, understand? He will never be the father of your baby. You will get rid of it."

She shook her head. "No."

She cried out as he stormed over to her, grabbing her arms.

"You seem to think I'm asking you for this. I'm not fucking asking. I'm not. You're nothing, little girl. Nothing to him, and that baby will be nothing. I am the one in control here. I tell my son what to do. You don't see him now, do you? You don't see him coming to your rescue. That's because he's a good boy, and you are nothing but a fucking slut."

She cried out as he shoved her hard. Falling to the floor she hit her head, and gasped.

"Don't make a mess on your rug. It's a nightmare to get clean."

"Leave me alone. I'm … I'm telling. I'm going to tell the cops on you. I'm pregnant with your grandchild."

She cried out as pain slammed into her cheek as he punched her. She tried to fight him as he straddled her and then his hands were around her neck.

Eyes open wide, she tried to claw at his hands, but they wouldn't stop. He was choking her to death, and she tried to stop him.

Easton!

Help!

No one came, and everything went black as he choked her to death.

****

The hand holding the gun was shaking, and Axton saw Taylor was having a really hard time keeping that thing fucking steady.

"Your dad killed her at your place?" she asked.

Tears kept falling, and even though she'd fucking betrayed him, he wanted to go and comfort her.

"Yes."

"How did she end up at the lake?" she asked.

"He drove her," Paul said.

This made her gasp as she looked at her friend.

"How do—"

"I saw her and him. I saw him … dump her. I watched as he cut her wrists, but as she was already dead…"

"Oh, my God, after all this time. You knew. You fucking knew the truth!"

"Taylor."

"Stay away from me!" She yelled the words. "Oh, my … you all protect him. A rapist and murdering bastard. You protect him. You fucking make sure he can live in peace." She stepped back, and Axton saw her shaking her head.

"Taylor," Paul said.

"No! After all this time, you knew."

"I didn't know everything. I didn't know … Easton."

"You said you loved her. Why didn't you tell me any of this? Is this why you didn't want me to go through with it?"

"I loved Carla. I still do. I wanted to know the truth. To know who got her pregnant. I didn't know everything, and even so, you wouldn't have been happy with me, Taylor. Not after everything that had happened."

She shook her head. "No. That's not love. You would have told someone or you would have done something." She laughed. "Wow, all this time, after everything I went through. You saw, Paul. You knew. I can't do this anymore. I've got to go."

"Taylor."

"Who took care of her, huh? All you ever fucking cared about was yourself. All of you. Your fucking family. Your reputations. No one cared about Carla in all of this. You all let her be lost. How many women have been lost because of them? You may not have killed her, but you all are all responsible in some way. You all knew the truth of what those bastards were capable of, and you let it happen."

"Taylor," Axton said.

"No, I don't want to know right now. I don't even care what you have to say."

"We fucked without protection," he said.

She gasped, and he saw her pale.

"Dude, she's holding a fucking gun. Do you really want to talk about this right now?"

She stared at him, and he saw how lost she was.

"I paid an escort to help me fuck just to find out the truth."

Right before his eyes he saw Taylor come back. The old one. The one that wasn't intent on finding out the truth but the girl he saw through high school. The one with the quick smile and dimples, who was always joking around with her friend. The one he looked at from afar but knew he could never have.

"Stay away from me," she said.

He didn't run toward her as she climbed into his car or even stop her as she pulled away from the lake.

Axton watched her go.

Staring at Paul, he didn't like that fucker all that much in that moment.

"We've got to stop her," Easton said. "She's going to let everything out."

Axton turned back to the lake, replaying that night again. Holding her in his arms, keeping her back. She didn't even know that he'd been the one holding her.

"Maybe it's time," Axton said.

"Are you serious right now?"

"I don't know when will be the right time, but I'm sick and tired of keeping those bastards away from it all and picking up the pieces of what they do."

In the process of getting Taylor out of the car, he'd pulled out the file on Carla. His father, the son of a bitch, had always made sure to have every little detail on paper. It was something his own father had done before him. Keep your friends close and enemies closer. His father didn't believe in friends, just enemies and power. This kept Nial in place. Just another piece of evidence that cemented the four kings for good. He, Easton, Karson, and Romeo had all been different. They were nothing like their parents. They had formed a bond of friendship that couldn't be taken from them, or abused. They were stronger together. Bending down, Axton picked it up, and there was a picture of Taylor and Carla together.

"She's never going to forgive me," Paul said.

"She will."

It wasn't in Taylor's makeup to stay mad at her friend. Paul had hurt her with his revelations, but that didn't for a second mean she would hate him. Closing the file, Axton stared back at the lake. It was time for people to know the truth of what happened that night.

Chapter Fourteen

One month later

Axton entered his office and stared over at Taylor's empty desk. They had yet to find a replacement PA, but for now that was fine. He didn't like the thought of anyone else sitting in her desk. That seat was still and would always be for Taylor.

The truth for the most part was out, or it would be in the next couple of days for media coverage. Since the day at the lake, a lot had changed. First off, he didn't go straight to the police but home. He went through the files with Romeo, Karson, Easton, and Paul.

Piece by piece they pulled together the information they needed, and after that, he brought in his PI to help him.

When they had all finally given the evidence and they'd been questioned, all four of them had made it appear they were frightened of what would happen. That years of violence and threats kept them from letting the police know what their parents did. No one couldn't prove they were lying. Axton worked closely with the detective involved to make sure the truth about Carla was finally put right but also the truth about the cover-ups his own father had been part of was also brought to light.

"Someone left something in your office," Romeo said, coming out of his office.

"They did?"

"Yes."

Axton made his way into his office and paused as he saw the file she'd managed to get, along with a shoe box and a rose. Right on top was a letter with his name on it.

He recognized Taylor's handwriting so clearly.

So many secrets had come out in the last few hours of them being together.

Dear Axton,

It feels so strange to be the one writing to you, but ... I don't know if I could do this in person so this is the best way I know how. I know if you're reading this then I've gone back home to King's Ridge. I'm tired of running. Of pretending to be something I'm not. I've been fighting this for so long I didn't even realize what I'd become. Everything I've done was because of that night. That night I saw Carla in the lake and pulled her out, something changed in me. I knew my friend. I knew she wouldn't do something like that. Carla wasn't ... she'd never do something like that. I got Paul to find out the truth and knew in some way you were connected. The four kings, which I guess is actually five. I don't know. I also knew one of you was with Carla, had gotten her pregnant. Her diary is here. Along with all the information I took. I didn't share any of it, nor did I post it. I wanted to, but I didn't think it was right anymore. I knew the truth, and none of this was your fault or Karson, or Romeo, or even Easton. I hope he's doing okay.

I know you think I broke your trust, and you're right, I did. There is no excuse for that. I came to you for one reason and one reason alone. I went out of my way to bring you and the Four Kings' Empire down. I intended to publish all of this, to watch you all disappear. I felt that Carla needed justice. That the truth of what you were all about had to come out for others to know. I was tired of everyone pacifying you, of leaving you alone. Most importantly, I was doing this to find out the truth about Carla. I now leave it all with you. It's yours anyway. I never should have stolen this or tried to. I'm so sorry for all the deceit and lies.

Through your anger and hatred, which you are right to feel, I want you to understand something. You were protecting your father, your best friends. Keeping Easton safe and everything. Everyone was looking out for each other, but through it all, no one looked after Carla. I know it wasn't anyone's job to take care of her, but she needed someone and she only had me.

She was like a sister to me.

I was taking care of her.

Her parents had the right to know the truth.

She didn't die of suicide. Easton's father killed her because she wouldn't get an abortion. She refused to be pushed aside like trash, and because she stood up for the love she felt, he killed her.

Do with this as you wish. I am sorry for my part in trying to bring that monster to justice. No matter who you are, or your bank balance, or what you do, you break the law, you should pay. But I blamed you. I believed you should have done something. I was wrong. You were like me, a teenager. There was nothing you could have done, and I know and understand that in a way, you did do something. You made sure they lost their power. I am so sorry for the pain I've brought your way. For the blame I laid at your feet. That is my fault, not yours. This was all on me. Not you.

Also … I'm not saying this because of the baby, but I love you. I think you're the best man I have ever known. I wish more than anything that I'd have saved my first time for you. That we'd not come together because of my plan. I wish that I'd seen you put those letters and the roses in my locker. I love you, Axton, more than anything in the world.

I hope one day you can forgive me. I understand if you cannot. Please tell Paul I'm sorry. He's a good friend.

All my love,
Your Taylor

Beneath the letter was the box and rose. He saw the files she'd taken, which the box rested on. The files were from his personal collection. The deals his father had blackmailed and manipulated. Stuff that was supposed to stay secret. They were all there, and none of them had been made public.

The Four Kings' Empire would have struggled, but he didn't for a second believe they wouldn't have survived.

Opening up the box, he was still for a moment.

They were all the letters he'd put in her locker. It hadn't been hard to find out her combination. She used her birthday or Carla's for everything. Lifting them up, he saw his writing. Each piece a part of him that he'd given to her. He'd not wanted to pull her into his world, knowing his father wouldn't allow it. She wasn't the woman he wanted his son to marry. Not rich enough nor with the right contacts.

She'd been a nothing.

A no one.

Useless.

He'd wanted her because she was everything to him. From that day all those years ago in kindergarten when she'd been playing on the swings. He'd watched her climb high as if she was flying, her laughter capturing his attention. His mother demanded he be a good boy. To not play with anyone else other than Karson, Romeo, and Easton. He'd done what he'd been told. When Taylor had fallen over, grazing her knee, he'd wanted to help her. He'd watched as Carla had gone to her. The two had become such good friends, and he'd been jealous.

From afar he watched her growing up. Wanting

her, craving her, and knowing that if he showed any interest, his father would find a way to ruin her.

So, he held back, saving her, protecting her, loving her.

Making the sacrifice to let her go.

"She didn't do it?" Easton asked, startling him.

He looked up to see Easton's bruised face. "No. It's all here."

"And something more. She finally figured out you were the one that sent those roses. It was kind of cool to be there for her revelation."

"It's not like I had much of a choice at the time." He'd seen her love of roses, and he'd made a point of finding the most beautiful during high school to give her. He handed Easton the letter, and he waited as Easton read through it.

"She's right. People need to know the truth. Carla's parents have a right to know their daughter didn't kill herself," Easton said.

"Your father—"

"I know what he did," Easton said. "And he's hidden from his deeds long enough. I want the bastard to pay for what he did. We're doing the right thing. The question is, Axton, will you do the right thing?" He waved the letter. "She's having a baby."

He'd caught sight of that in her note.

"She is."

"What are you going to do about it?" Easton asked.

He shrugged. "Not a lot I can do."

"Man, we're not our dads," Karson said. "You've been wanting to be with her for a hell of a long time. Seems kind of pointless to be doing all this shit if you're not going to get the girl."

He stared at the files. "She lied."

"So. She thought she was doing right by her friend. We've done a lot of shit over the years. Carla was her best friend, man. You knew deep down something wasn't right with her. Wouldn't you have done the same for one of us?" Romeo asked.

"You're taking her side?" Axton asked.

Romeo snorted. "I want to throttle the fucking bitch. She lied and cheated, and … you love her, man. Life is not perfect. You've wanted her a long time. You held yourself back. Shit went down, and … we can't be like our parents. You can hold this against her, or you can try and start fresh." Romeo shrugged. "This is your decision."

"You've loved her for a long time. A lot longer than I ever did Carla. Come on, Axton. It's time you put yourself first for a change. Go and get the girl you've been drooling after since kindergarten. Neither of you had this chance before. You're not perfect, she's not perfect, but together, maybe you could make something perfect." Easton slapped him on the arm.

Axton looked at his friends. "You know, you're all really good friends."

"We all know, and we're not going to kiss and hug. That shit is not us," Karson said.

"I'm going to be heading out of town for a few days. Clear my head while all this blows up," Easton said.

"You need one of us with you?" Axton asked.

"Nah, I'm good. Just going to get drunk, fuck, and pretend the last ten years didn't happen." Easton pulled him into a hug. "I don't give a fuck what Karson says. You're all my brothers, and I'm damn happy to have you fuckers at my back. Mean it."

Hugging his friend, he slapped him on the back, and they pulled apart.

"I better go and get the girl," Axton said.

He was going to be a fucking dad. It seemed almost too surreal.

****

Bent over the rose bushes, Taylor began to pull at the weeds and make sure the bed was perfect. She hated anything getting in the way of her beautiful roses. The house she was renting was just a small two-bedroom with a tiny garden, but it was more than enough for her.

Her savings were getting her by while she looked for work close to home. She hadn't ventured into town as yet and had been living out of her freezer and pantry for food. She'd have to go to town soon, but she was kind of nervous about being there.

She hadn't done what she set out to do.

All of the secrets of the Four Kings' Empire remained with them, and she was happy about that. She didn't want to deal with that kind of aftermath and pain. Not only that, she was pregnant.

Not too far along, but she'd taken a test, then gone to the doctor, who confirmed it. She had a baby growing inside her.

Placing a hand on her stomach, she leaned back on her knees and just shook her head. It seemed so surreal.

Falling for Axton wasn't part of the plan. Being with him wasn't either. She had fucked up in a big, big way.

"This seems more you than that apartment back in the city," Axton said.

Twisting around, she saw him standing just inside her back yard. He had a large bag over his shoulder, and he wasn't dressed like she was used to.

She got to her feet, her heart starting to pound as she looked at him. "You're not wearing a suit."

"I decided to take a few days. Relax. Get my head together."

"Oh."

"I got your letter," he said. He reached into his bag, which was one of those massive sports bags that opened at the top. "You should have these."

He held the box where she had kept all of his letters. Staring at him, aware of her how she must look, covered in dirt, she couldn't think of a single thing to say.

"You know, I first saw you in kindergarten. It was our first day, and you were on the swings. Going higher and higher. You had the most amazing giggle. I couldn't look away from you, not that I wanted to. You were so beautiful. So different. The other kids were trying to copy their parents. You weren't standing around copying your parents. You were real. You wore a pair of dungaree shorts, and as you fell off, you scraped your knee. There was a little blood, and you were crying."

"Carla came over to me."

"And she helped you. I wanted to be the one to help you."

"You never said anything."

"I couldn't. I was to be a good boy. To do as I was supposed to do. I wasn't allowed to have what I wanted. So, I spent the entire time watching you. You never knew that I was always there, waiting to see you. That I'd arrive at school, hang out in my car just to see you arrive, and watch you walk into school. I loved walking behind you. You always tried to hide it, but you had a fucking great ass. You have no idea the number of times I wanted to take you for myself. No one else deserved you."

"I never knew."

"I know. I didn't want you to know."

"All this time."

"You have no idea what it felt like to see you walk toward me that day. Coming for a job," he said.

She saw him grit his teeth, and tears filled her eyes.

"I don't do feelings, Taylor. I don't. Life is a lot fucking easier without them. My dad made sure of that."

She wiped away the tears that kept on falling. Her heart was breaking for him.

"When it comes to you though, I can't seem to stop. You make me want to forget everything, and I don't care about anyone else, just you. Just us. So, I'm telling now, Taylor. Not because of the baby, or anything else. I love you more than anyone else in this world, and I have loved you from afar for a really long time. You are my everything. I will give up the Four Kings' Empire, I will do whatever it is you ask of me, so long as you're mine."

She sniffled. "But I lied to you. I did what I did. I was an awful person. You shouldn't forgive me. I was going to ruin you."

"I don't care." He dropped the bag and placed the box on the ground. Within seconds he was holding her face, tilting her head back. "I don't care about any of that. I get it, okay? I do. I forgive you. I was even going to tell you everything. From the past to now. I love you. I even … I forgot the condom on purpose just so that I would have a reason for you to be mine. That's how fucking much I want you, Taylor. I'm through with all the bullshit. All I want now, is you and me, and no one else." He stroked his thumb across her bottom lip.

"You would give up everything to be mine."

"Yes."

Before her eyes, she watched the mask he put in place for the world fall. He stared at her, and she saw the love that he spoke of. The passion, the need. It was there, burning in his eyes, shocking her to the core.

Cupping his shoulders, she went onto her tiptoes and kissed him. "I love you too, Axton. So much that it scares me. It's why I couldn't go through with it. Not after I knew. I couldn't do that to you. You've already paid so much. Thank you ... for not ... prosecuting me for everything I did. For stealing and lying."

"If I could go back and stop it, I would. For you. I would never want you to go through what you did. You ... you're the strongest person I know. I would never hurt you, nor would I dream of letting anyone take you away."

"I fucked up," she said. "I ... ten years I wasted becoming this person. You love that person?"

"No, I don't. I love you, Taylor. I knew you were there all along. The bullshit was just, it doesn't matter. We're here now, and we're together. The way it's supposed to be. It's you I love. Nothing else." He pushed some of her hair off her face. "And I don't know if you know this, but they arrested Nial Long for Carla's murder."

"What?"

"I'm done paying for others' mistakes. The Four Kings' Empire will continue, but it will be on our terms. We're also in the process of merging with Paul. To put it back the way it was supposed to be."

"Five kings?"

"Pretty much, but our name won't change. We're merging, and Paul will oversee our technology division. I also reinstated his father as a CEO as well at Paul's request. Out of everyone, he had a right to the company, and I won't see him brought down any further."

She couldn't believe it. "I ... I don't want you to stop being you. I love you, Axton Farris. Suit or not." She ran her hands down his chest.

"I'm going to spend the rest of my life making this up to you, Taylor."

"No, Axton, you owe me nothing. This is me. *I* will make it up to *you*. I'll be the woman you deserve."

"How about we just agree to start fresh, to never hold anything back?"

"For the rest of our lives?"

"Yes." He pulled a velvet box out of his pocket. "So long as you'll have me."

"You're proposing?"

"Yes. I want us to get married before the baby is born."

She chuckled. "This is really fast."

"I know, it's the way I like to work. I'm not going to give anyone the chance to steal you away from me. Also, you and David are not allowed in the same room together alone."

"You do not need to be like that."

"You're my woman now, and I don't like the way he looks at you."

"Fine. The same goes for all women," she said.

"That's more than fine with me." He gripped her ass and pulled her in close as she slid the ring he'd purchased for her on her finger.

She tilted her head back, and as his lips brushed hers, she closed her eyes. Not holding back, she wrapped her arms around his neck, kissing him with a passion where she gave him everything. She gave him her all, and in doing so, she felt his love even in his kiss.

There's no way she could have ever seen this coming.

"Now, tell me how to get my hands dirty."

"You want to garden?"

"I want to fill this garden with roses for you."

He gripped the back of her neck, and she smiled

up at him. She could certainly handle the next fifty years of him.

Epilogue

Five years later

"But Daddy, I want to hear your and Mommy's story again," Carla said. "It's so magical."

Axton smiled. Lying down on his daughter's bed, he smiled over at his wife, heavily pregnant with their second child. The last five years had been a blast, and when he thought about the time they'd missed together, he knew he wouldn't take any moment for granted.

"You're not bored of this story?"

"No, Daddy, I love how you fell in love with Mommy, and wouldn't tell her, and that it took ages for you to get together."

"Okay, let's start this. It was a hot day in kindergarten, and I had to go to school even though I didn't want to…" He told the story with Taylor laughing along with him at certain points.

He skipped the part of the lake like he always did and moved on to when they saw each other again.

"When I looked at her, I knew she was the most beautiful woman I'd ever seen." He took her hand and kissed her knuckles.

He didn't need to finish the story as their little girl was fast asleep.

They both eased out of the bed and left the nightlight on. Carla was a heavy sleeper, and they wouldn't hear from her until the morning.

Gripping his wife's waist, he pressed her against the wall.

"I want to fuck you again."

"We did that in the shower."

"You think once is enough?"

"Look at my king, can't get enough."

He grabbed her arms and pinned them above her head. "I can never get enough of you, not that I'd want to, Taylor. You are fucking perfect."

With one hand holding both of hers above her head, he claimed her lips, sliding his tongue into her mouth, tasting her.

Gripping her neck, he used his thumb to tilt her head back. "I can have you whenever I want, that's the agreement."

He saw her eyes flash with desire.

This was why he knew they were perfect for each other. No matter what, their hunger rivaled everything. In the past five years, he'd taken the Four Kings' Empire to a new level, one that didn't involve the scandal and pain of the past with his father lurking over him. That time of his life was over, without fear of repercussions. His father was rotting behind bars for blackmail and extortion while Nial Long served his own time for killing Carla.

Against all odds, he had defeated them, with Taylor's help. Without her coming back into his life, he'd have never made his father face the charges that he should have.

Now, he also got his happily ever after. What he'd been dreaming of having since the first day he saw her.

He'd vowed that day she would be his.

Now he had her, and there was no way he was letting her go.

The End

www.samcrescent.com

EVERNIGHT PUBLISHING ®

www.evernightpublishing.com

30311012R00174

Printed in Poland
by Amazon Fulfillment
Poland Sp. z o.o., Wrocław